ANCHOR OF GOLD

HOLLY MANNO

Edited by
SARAH BENELLI

ATLANTA

The President's Reception was in full swing as I stood at the center of the Georgia Aquarium. The scene was set with dim lighting while neon bursts of color flitted against the walls and ceiling. The theater-sized screen behind me projected live images from a surveillance camera situated near one of the large aquariums. The fish swam easily, unaware of our ogling from afar. As I stood there, I could relate.

Sponsored by the world's largest security organization, for one week every year Security Summit International drew thought leaders and representatives from every major company. The conference encompassed four days of events that wouldn't be complete without over-the-top entertainment the participants had come to expect. The $100 billion electronic security industry was a cash cow that grew regardless of economic challenges, and if it didn't, the finance guys would play their paper and shell games to make it look like it did.

"Madeline Craig, meet Sheldon Bright." My new boss, Robert Grain, made the introduction as I accepted Sheldon's fleshy hand to shake.

I could see a look of amusement cross his face as he studied my dress. He had trouble maintaining eye contact; instead, his blue eyes swept up and down my body. "The lady in red. Good evening, Madeline, and may I say, you look beautiful tonight."

"A pleasure to meet you, Sheldon." I plastered a salary worthy smile on my face as I greeted the fair-skinned, middle-aged man.

Who was I kidding? At nearly 41, I was also middle-aged but for some reason, I didn't see myself that way. Maybe it was because I couldn't identify with many of the men that surrounded me each day, and tonight's guest list proved no exception. Sheldon had yet to relinquish my hand.

Robert may have sensed his lingering, since he asked, "Do you guys want to get a drink?"

"Yes," I agreed, and moved toward him.

As Sheldon replied, his eyes bore into mine. "I can think of nothing better than to get to know the newest member of your team, Robert."

There comes a time when a situation presents itself and you have to find something positive or you'll be the one to suffer. It wouldn't kill me to ignore his overtures, even laugh at them a little. It could make the evening easier and who knew, maybe it would bring us some business. As lowering as it was, I must try to look at him as a benefactor. It was sales, after all, and I could do that. "Well, Sheldon, as they say, no good story ever began with a salad, let's head to the bar."

He and Robert shared a chuckle as I passed them. I led the way, knowing full well Sheldon was staring at my ass and Robert would do nothing to discourage it.

We began with a round of shots and others joined our circle to chat. Many I knew from previous events or dealings.

I needed to be there but my thoughts were diffused. There were other matters that pushed into my mind. I excused myself and after a stop at the ladies, I took some air on one of the empty decks surrounding the building. I gave myself a minute, or more, to face the horrors of the past few days.

IT'S SERIOUS, MOM

"Hey," I called to Nathan, my live-in finance, "I got a message from Peter. He's coming over for dinner tonight."

He walked into the kitchen, opened the fridge and grabbed a beer. After taking a deep sip, his dark eyes peered toward me. "Would have been nice if he could have found the time to visit while Blane was here last week."

Blane was Nathan's fourteen-year old daughter and Peter was less than enamored with the idea of a blended family. Nathan's taunt sped my heart-rate. "You know he was working last weekend. Can we get through one meal without some kind of pissing match between you guys?"

"I'll be on my best behavior." His voice dripped with sarcasm.

"Can't you please be the adult? Be civil, for me."

"Yeah, I will." The lifeless tone in his voice was like a slap. "I'm going to the store. Is there anything we need?"

A little breather might be good for us. "Yes, actually, can you pick up some more cheddar cheese? I used the last of it."

"Sure." He set the opened beer back in the refrigerator

and collected his keys from the counter. "I'll see you in a few." With that statement, he left.

As I rinsed the lettuce for the salad, I looked out the window and said a silent prayer. For once, could Nathan and Peter find civility? The persistent action of birds flitting by gave me hope. Their busy beaks grabbed a few final seeds before their nightly slumber.

I thought back on when Nathan and I first started out. Peter was only sixteen years old and Blane just eight. The kids were different but they both came from divorced parents and were only children. Peter was at the opposite end of the spectrum of being interested in a sibling, but had always hoped for one as a boy. At first, he embraced it, even liked spending time with Blane, and she adored him.

Once Nathan gave his ex, Lela the green-light to move hundreds of miles away, everything changed. Peter recoiled like a young snake, striking everything in his path until all of his venom was spent. He was disgusted by Nathan's decision and ability to, as he put it, "let his daughter go." His anger came from the abandonment he felt because of his own father's absence. The past has a sickening way of rearing its head, keeping you in a perpetual state of remembrance.

Beeping sounds at the front door indicated that Peter had arrived and was letting himself in. Tossing aside the towel, I left the kitchen to greet him.

"Hey, baby." I walked over and hugged my only child with the kind of brevity he now demanded.

"Hi, Mom." His tone was calm and his blue eyes looked dark underneath. Not the most alarming observation given his age of only 21. No doubt he'd had a long night after work the previous evening.

"How are you doing, baby? Looks like you may have had a little too much fun last night?"

His silence wasn't unusual and I had to check myself. Walking on eggshells was something I'd never get used to. My once sweet and friendly son had grown into a surly adult. At times I felt my mere breathing annoyed him. Every friend I discussed this with seemed to feel it was normal, reassuring me it was a phase and by 25, he'd come around. I doubted it, but allowed myself to be comforted by their assurances.

I remembered how close we were when he was small, when we both were in a sense. Peter was born when I was nineteen. The two of us took on the world together. Though life was hard for a young mother, my overwhelming love for the boy overshadowed the many rough spots.

Peter asked, "Is Nathan home?"

"No, he went to the store. He'll be back in a few."

"Good. I need to talk to you." His tone was as flat as his tired, blue eyes.

As I followed him through the hallway and into the living room, a tingle of concern ran down my spine. He sat on the couch, folded his hands and stared down at the coffee table.

Sitting beside him, I spoke first. "What is it, honey? What's bothering you?"

Peter looked up, his knee touched mine, and his eyes welled with tears. He hadn't cried in front of me in over a decade. "Mom, I have cancer."

Of all the things I expected to hear, this was nowhere on the list. The blood rushed from my head and my ears began to ring. I must have misheard him. "What do you mean?"

"I have cancer, testicular cancer."

Panicked, my mind was racing. Oh my god, the world is a cruel place. He's only a child, my only child, how could these words be spoken? "What?"

Peter went silent for a beat. He had little patience for his mother on a good day, today was definitely not a good day. "I have a lump. They need to remove it and when they do, they'll test it and see what else they has to be done."

Too many questions were in my mind, colliding against one another. I was unable to articulate a single one. Finally, logic took over. "When?"

"On Thursday. I'll have the surgery, and after that it'll take a week to get the results."

My brain was finally catching up and so were the questions. "How large is the lump?"

"It's small and on one side. They don't think it is in my testicle yet, but they won't know for sure until they test my lymph node."

The panic must have been evident on my face. It did nothing but piss Peter off. "Would you let me go with you to the procedure? I could drive you and help after."

"Absolutely not. Sarah is going to help me. I can't deal with your looks and seeing the worry all over your face. I need to take care of this myself." His tone was harsh with the undercurrent of fear. My little boy was afraid and that was the real reason for the hollow under his eyes. No doubt he hadn't slept since he learned the news.

The world could be a devastating place. The heartbreak of our distance, his revelation, and the fact that I could do nothing to protect him made me feel like screaming. I knew I needed to stay composed or he'd run and there would be no additional information. His badge of honor and the wall between us was reinforced by reminding me of his adulthood. There was a tidbit I could inquire about that might defuse the matter. "Sarah?"

"Yeah, we're dating. I don't know if it's serious yet, but we are getting close. She's the one who found it."

I silently thanked Sarah for giving my son pleasure and

finding the weapon of destruction in his ball sack. "I'm glad you have a friend. What is she like?"

"I don't know, Mom. She's different. It's hard to explain."

No smile came to his face and I wondered what that meant. Was he that worried or not into the girl? "Can I ask what else the doctor said?"

Peter stood and walked toward the window. His lanky frame was highlighted by the oversized clothes he wore, a trend he hadn't gotten over since high school. His response was stoic. "He said I may not be able to have kids. He said I may lose my balls and that I should think about sperm banking depending on what they find out. He said I may not be able to have sex anymore."

Oh hell. That was way too much information for a young man of only 21 to face. I couldn't panic, at least not in front of him. Time to put on the brave face I'd carried with me for so many years when he was small. I walked to his side, put my hand on his shoulder and said, "It's going to be all right. This world is a confusing place and so many things happen that we can't explain, but remember what I always say . . ."

"I know, Mom, everything happens for a reason. That shit doesn't affect me anymore. I'm not a little kid. I know it's all lies, and I didn't come here to get the same old crap from you."

Knowing what egged his anger didn't take the sting out of his words. Time to change the subject. Stress wouldn't help and until we had more answers, maybe it was best to set it down. "Do you want a beer?"

"No. I can't drink anymore. It makes me sick. Apparently, that's one of the signs of cancer. I'm going to take off."

"What? I thought you were staying for dinner."

"I'm not hungry; besides, I can't go through this conversation again with Nathan. He's not my dad and I don't want to hear his opinion." He leaned over and kissed my cheek before walking out the door.

I squelched a horrific sense of panic as the door closed behind him. My baby was sick.

NATHAN RETURNED AND I WAS IMMOBILE. AS IF MY WILL TO move had been exorcised from my body, I sat, stoic and unable to face the next conversation I must have.

He called out, "Hello. I'm home." After depositing the bag of groceries in the kitchen, he rounded the corner and entered the living room. "Hey, what's going on?"

Somehow, I would have to reenter my body. Somehow, I would have to utter the words aloud. He kneeled on the ground in front of me. His expression was worried and I hadn't even told him yet. "What happened? I just saw Peter drive away."

Panic boiled within the confines of my flesh. I had to speak, but to give life to that terrifying truth, how could I? The words exiting my mouth sounded distant, as if spoken by another. "Peter was upset."

Nathan's eyebrows rose, creating deep creases in his forehead. "Why was he upset?" Placing his hands on my knees, his gaze was unwavering.

"He's sick," I managed.

A flicker of annoyance crossed his face and he stood. He went to the kitchen and began unpacking the groceries. "He came all the way here first, then told you he was sick? You don't have to lie to me. I know the kid can't stand me."

Like a guitar string stretched too far, I could feel the extraordinary tension tearing at my center. Their adversarial relationship frequently pulled me beyond my limits. Now was not the time for their childish feud. I stood and made my way into the kitchen. Nathan didn't look up when I entered. I knew as soon as I said those words aloud, all time would stop. Upon hearing the shocking news, for once, he would be the man I needed him to be, wouldn't he? "He's really sick."

The refrigerator door slammed and Nathan's face appeared. He studied me intently before he replied. My fear must have been obvious; his soft tone belied the truth in my eyes. "What's wrong?"

A mother should never have to say these words aloud. "He has cancer."

IT SNAPPED

And, if that wasn't enough, Nathan insisted we still go on a group beach trip we'd agreed to back before all of this happened. I was reluctant. But his logic that it would be good for me after the shock of Peter's diagnosis and as a pre-cursor to the conference next week made sense. I agreed to keep our plans. What a thing that turned out to be.

AS I CAME TO THE BOTTOM OF THE STAIRS, BAG IN HAND, Nathan greeted me at the landing. He reached for the duffel and asked, "Is this it? Are you ready to get on the road?"

"Yep. I'm set," I said, and followed him out the front door.

After we settled into our seats, Nathan asked, "Do you have the address?"

I opened the information on my phone and read it aloud, "340 First Street, Cannon Beach."

Nathan input the data into the navigation system and we started off. The drive to Cannon Beach would take about two hours and I wasn't thrilled to be doing it. Months ago, I agreed to join several business acquaintances for a weekend at the beach. They had rented a house and several couples were getting together. It could be a fun group, but there were always some interesting dynamics and the person I knew best, Morgan Jones, was intensely nosey. She had a tendency of pressing boundaries by asking personal questions framed in the context of, "I'm your friend." Unfortunately, her commitment to friendship was short lived. Like a carrier pigeon, she would disburse and expound upon intimate conversations to anyone who would listen. Gossip was her commodity and she was rich with it.

I hoped the weekend would be fun. I was worried about Peter and frankly, I didn't feel like going at all. As if reading my thoughts all wrong, Nathan cleared his throat and asked, "Are you looking forward to catching up with Morgan this weekend?"

He knew I had mixed feelings about her. On one hand, her pie in the sky approach and unwavering self-confidence was appealing, yet to be the subject of her scrutiny was another matter.

"I'm excited to spend the weekend at the beach."

His tone was neutral and he said, "Does that mean you're not feeling very congenial?"

I looked out the window, considering his question. The trees flew by in a green blur and the road began to ribbon as we entered the forest. My thoughts were too diffused. If I told him how surreal the moment seemed, that feelings of fear and anxiety warred within me, that would end the weekend before it even began.

Instead, I said, "I'm tired. It's been a long week. I hope this getaway is somewhat restful."

He chuckled. "If you wanted rest, hanging out with the

Joneses was the last thing you should have agreed to. They love to party. You know that."

He was right of course, but it was too late to cancel now. "Maybe we can take some time away from the group?"

He looked over for a second, then back at the road, before responding, "Sure, ok."

Nathan always had an aloofness about him. Outside of greetings and sex, he was rarely affectionate. It was something I'd never gotten used to. Today, his distance didn't bother me.

With so much weighing on me, I was in no shape to keep a conversation going. I succumbed to exhaustion and closed my eyes.

THE SOUND OF THE CAR DOOR CHIME ROUSED ME FROM MY nap. Nathan stood at the doorway and said, "Hey, didn't mean to wake you. I wanted to stop at the liquor store to get some supplies. Do you want to come in?"

I ran my hands over my face and stretched. "No, I'll wait for you."

"Okay, be right back."

I surveyed our surroundings. We were about thirty minutes from the coast. Reaching for my phone, I wanted to make sure there were no customers to get back to. It was still before five o'clock on a Friday and that could be the witching hour when it came to security. I scanned my phone for missed calls and urgent emails, but found none.

It wasn't long before Nathan returned and stashed a bag in the back seat of the car before settling in behind the wheel. "Hey, sleepy head. Everything okay?"

"Sure. Why do you ask?"

"Just wondering if everything was good with work."

"Yep, I wanted to make sure and the good news is there are no fires to put out. I am free of work for the weekend."

"Good deal. Well, I picked up some of those bubbles you like and a couple of bottles of booze for the group."

Time with the Joneses usually meant a liver workout. From the sound of his grocery list, this weekend would be no exception. "Thanks for the bubbles. I know Morgan will be happy too."

Once we were back on the road, Nathan asked, "So, are yo looking forward to Atlanta? What's your new boss and team like?" I'd just started with at the firm. The conference was my first event with them.

I replied, "My new boss is fine. If I had to describe him I'd say he's an odd combination of task manager and Tomcat. On one hand, he has a mind that won't forget any business detail or follow-up item. On the other hand, he likes to drink and has a penchant for women with round bottoms. Let's just say, he's not shy about his sex life."

Nathan seemed a little miffed as he replied, "You just met the guy and you already know this about him?"

"He's not very private. The good news is, my butt's scrawny so it's of no interest to him."

Nathan sniffed before saying, "I hardly think a guy with a big sex drive is looking past you, Maddie." His tone was sarcastic. "Sounds like it will be an eventful conference."

"I guess." I paused and redirected the conversation. "Some good opportunity should come out of it though. I need to book a trip to San Diego next week to see the TransTruck site. We're meeting at the event and that could turn into a lucrative account."

"San Diego, huh? I thought your territory was the northwest."

"It is, but they have a large facility down south and it doesn't make sense to have another rep work on the project when they're headquartered in my area."

He paused before saying, "Sounds like the travel is going to be more than they told you."

"Why are you acting surprised? I told you there would be travel before I accepted the job."

"Yeah, but it's okay to put your foot down now so they don't always expect you to be on the road ."

With tenure of ten days in position, Nathan was well aware I had no bargaining chips. He was being an ass. "You know I can't do that. Can we please drop the subject?"

He was terse. "Sure, whatever you say."

In an instant, his jibe inflamed my already raw emotions. Not to mention the fact that he rarely did whatever I said. I responded before calming myself. "Hey, Nathan, please don't forget why I took this job."

He fired, "Really, are you going there again?"

I was about to say something clever and cutting, when the navigation system interrupted. It came to life, announcing our next turn. Thankful for the distraction, I stared out the window as Nathan made the final maneuvers. Within minutes we were at the driveway of a large white home, overlooking the sea. It had a spectacular view of Haystack Rock and I only hoped we'd find some way to enjoy it together.

Before we made a complete stop, the front door flung wide and a barefoot Morgan came bounding out. Her long red hair was pulled into a high ponytail and she was wearing a black off-the-shoulder dress. Her moves were reminiscent of a Labrador puppy, causing her large breasts to set out on a rhythm all their own.

Ambling behind was her petit husband Sean. His elven face was upturned as he came our way.

Sean's round cheeks appeared to hold his beady blue eyes in place; both were emphasized by his shiny bald head. I got out of the car to greet them.

"Hi, Madeline. Good to see you," Sean said somewhat formally, and gave me a timid hug.

Morgan greeted Nathan, her fluttery hug matched to her pitch. "Hey, stranger. Nice to see you again."

"You too, Morgan," he agreed.

She came to me. "Hey, hey, you made it!" Morgan cheered the words and pulled me into a hug that settled my face above her bosom.

Pulling back as quickly as possible, I said, "Don't you look great!" Morgan was meticulously coifed as usual. "I love your makeup."

"You know me sweets, brows and boobs. The rest is a blur. I bet you're ready for some libations," she said as we walked toward the house.

Until that moment, I hadn't been, but if I was going to get anywhere near her level it would require liquid enhancement. "I am definitely ready."

We walked into the house and what I saw stole my breath away. The home overlooked the water, giving us the most amazing ocean view. The living room and kitchen were open and designed to unfold toward the glorious Pacific. The space was done in a modern, minimalistic style with ashen wood floors, white walls and furnishings. The architecture and interior design all conspired to frame the shimmering blue sea. To my side was a sliding door to a large patio. The rest of the group were already there, settled at the table or relaxing on lounge chairs. The long, wide beach seemed to surround us and I couldn't wait to put my feet in the sand.

Morgan directed Sean, "Honey, go show Nathan where

they're staying so he can drop those bags, and then join us for a drink."

Easygoing and ready to host, Sean waved Nathan on. "Come downstairs. You have the whole place to yourselves."

Morgan wasted no time in providing a drink as she made her way to my side. Two glasses of pink liquid in hand, she handed me one and said, "It's a shot really delicious and you're going to love it. Ready?"

I wasn't, but screw it. "Yep. I'm ready."

She started, "One, two, three."

I swallowed before she could finish the last number and instantly wondered what it was. Might have been good to ask her first. The drink tasted bitter, with a hint of citrus and a chemical finish. "Yuck." I couldn't hold it back.

"You didn't like it?" She actually seemed surprised.

"Not really," I said. Why lie?

"Well, the good news is you won't be tired for long. Time to get the party started."

I asked, "What do you mean? What was in that?"

"Oh, just one of those new energy drinks, with vodka, absinth, and a couple of other surprise ingredients."

Holy shit. "Morgan, I don't do well on those energy drinks. They make me feel very strange. I think I'm allergic to them or something."

She chuckled. "Well, too late now. Why don't we go outside and say hi to everybody?"

There was no sense dwelling on the drink, hopefully it would be fine. Instead, I said, "Sure, let's go."

I followed Morgan's swinging ponytail as we made our way through the door. She cheered to the group, "Everybody, Madeline is here."

Lucinda Fick came to us first and pulled me into a fierce hug. Her rope-like arms flexed and once again, my head was nestled in cleavage. Perfumed brown curls tickled my nose. I looked up and said, "Nice to see you, Lucinda. Where's Ken?"

She smiled crookedly and said, "Business trip. He's stuck in Asia for another few days." She giggled a little and I wondered how much she'd had to drink. Obviously, she and Morgan got an early start. Her husband, traveled frequently for work, but made up for it with lavish gifts. The last time I saw her, he was also absent but a diamond tennis bracelet was there as a stand-in.

"Well, it's good to see *you*," I said.

Sean and Nathan came outside and we said hello to the other couple, Terry and Lynn. Once the greetings were complete, Morgan announced, "I'm going to mix up a pitcher of yum so we can get this party started. Madeline, will you help?"

"Sure," I said. I followed her back into the house.

We made our way toward the kitchen and I watched as she pulled a pitcher from the cupboard and added ice. "So, Maddie, you headed to the SSI conference this year?" Morgan's line of work touched on mine and she was always interested in talking business.

"I am. It's my first month at the new company so I'll be meeting the customers, learning the product, and getting to know my new team."

"Yeah, I can imagine. I heard the President's Reception is incredible. Will you go?"

"Yes. The venue will be great. It's at the aquarium."

"Nice. I hope you get some opportunity from it."

"I should. I've got to get down south soon to meet with TransTruck and take a look at a few of their sites."

"Wow, TransTruck is huge."

"Yeah, we'll see how it goes at the conference. What about you? What have you been up to?"

"Girl, you know me, always charging. I just finished a big specification that I helped a tech company put together. Once it goes out to bid, I'll be their supplier of electrical components for the next five years. Cha-ching!"

"That's great. Congratulations!"

Morgan was relentless. She worked and partied with equal vigor. I watched as she mixed another deadly concoction and thought about her intensity. She and Sean made a conscious decision not to have kids. Instead, they worked, and when they weren't grinding, they were living it up.

Giving the pitcher one last stir, Morgan looked pleased. She poured the mix into shot glasses and asked, "How's it been going with you and Nathan? Are things a little better now than the last time we spoke?" She leaned in.

I put my game face on and said, "Everything is going fine with us. Thanks. What about you and Sean? Are you guys doing well?"

She practically purred. "We are doing great. He's the best and with me as his wife, what could he possibly complain about?"

I joked along, "So true. You guys are the ideal pair. You're very lucky to have found one another."

For a moment, she studied me. The flash of a question showed on her face, but she didn't press. Instead, she picked up the serving tray full of glasses and said, "Let's get this party started."

I walked ahead and held the door as Morgan passed and made her way to the table outside. After setting the tray down, she distributed the small glasses to the group before handing one to me. Taking hers in hand, she raised it in toast, "Here's to a weekend we'll never forget. Cheers everybody!"

I swallowed the overpowering elixir in one gulp. From my throat to my gut, I felt the stinging fluid emblazon its way through me. The fact that I'd barely eaten and was behind on sleep sped the effects. I stood, watching as the rest of the group finished their drinks. One by one glasses were set aside and the party was in full swing. To the side, I saw Nathan talking to Sean and Lucinda. I noticed Terry and Lynn found a table closer to the beach and I waved. We hadn't seen one another in some time and I enjoyed their banter. Lynn could be so feisty with him, but Terry gave as well as he received. It was adorable to watch them spar.

Walking over to their side of the deck, I ventured, "Hey, you two. Happy Friday."

Terry's nasal voice chimed in response, "Hi, yourself."

Lynn stood and gave me a hug. When she pulled back she said, "Good to see you, skinny." She mocked disgust.

I teased in reply, "You too, Lynn. I love the highlights." Her hair transitioned from ash brown to glorious streaks of grey and the color of raw cotton. She had dancing blue eyes and a sparkle to her that wasn't obvious at first.

She gave me a cheeky smile and said, "Thanks, I just got it done. Of course, my husband here didn't notice."

Terry raised his hands in surrender.

Taking her side, I said, "I join her team, Terry. You are a blind man."

"Jeez," he squeaked, "you too? You have to understand, to me she is always perfect, head to toe."

I chuckled, but actually felt bad for the guy who no doubt had his fill hearing about his oversight. "That's a pretty good line. I buy it."

Lynn looked flushed at his comment, but postured. "Took you a while to come up with that one didn't it? Go fetch us a bottle of bubbles. Hurry," she commanded.

His face was defeated, but his body rose to obey. He made his way toward the house, leaving Lynn and me on our own. After the door closed behind him, she laughed and said, "What have you and Nathan been up to, Maddie?"

I responded generically, "The usual. He's been working a lot and I just started a new job so we've been pretty busy with that. What about you guys? How have you been?"

"We're getting a divorce," she blurted.

I had no way to prepare for those words and my expression surely registered shock. What could I say to such a startling revelation, especially after she stated it without preface? Fortunately, I didn't have to.

"Hey," Lynn poked my arm and jutted her chin, a sign I should follow her gaze, "looks like Lucinda is making herself friendly with Nathan this time around."

I turned to find Lucinda standing nay towering close to Nathan's side. Her strong hip bumped his and her hand rested on his shoulder. Their backs were to us since they faced Sean. As I watched, a rush of jealousy slapped me and my breathing hitched. I didn't like the way she was leaning into him, but more, I hated the way Nathan was looking at her. He never looked at me that way.

Turning back towards Lynn, I vowed to put myself in check and returned to her outlandish comment about getting divorced. I said, "They're just talking Lucinda language. She doesn't know how to communicate without clinging and she likes the attention." I changed the subject. "Nice bait and switch by the way. Let's rewind to your earlier comment."

Lynn leaned back in the chaise, looked me straight in the eye and said, "We're getting divorced. We're just starting to work through the details."

I was shocked; from my recollection, the two had been married over twenty years. I always thought they were a great couple. Real and flawed, but in it for the long run. "Wow, Lynn. That's a lot. Are you guys sure about this?"

She looked toward the door. I followed her gaze to find Terry had just walked back outside. On his way, he stopped to say hello to the looming Lucinda, Nathan, and Sean trio. I turned to face Lynn and she said, "We're not sure about anything, but it's been hard for so long and we're both tired. We need to go to our separate corners. You know how it is."

I felt deflated as I agreed, "Unfortunately, yes. I do know how it is." At that moment, Terry arrived with the bottle of bubbles and glasses in hand.

"What do you say, ladies? Let's get your drinks filled." He turned the cork until it popped and froth oozed from the neck of the bottle. Terry filled three glasses, handing one to Lynn, and then me, before taking one for himself.

His high-pitched voice chimed, "Cheers."

Lynn and I joined in. "Cheers."

Like a couple of bloodhounds on a champagne trail, Morgan and Lucinda appeared at our table. Lucinda spoke for the both of them, "Did I hear the sound of fun over here?"

Terry feigned ignorance as he took the bottle and hid it behind his back. "I have no idea what you are talking about, Luce."

She lunged playfully, as he tried in vain to avert her grab. Unfortunately, his reflexes were no match for hers and she nabbed the bottle with ease. Feigning surrender, Terry joked, "I want you to know, I let you have it."

Putting on her most flirtatious pout, Lucinda sent an air kiss in his direction then took Morgan's cup and dumped the contents into a nearby bush. She did the same with her own before emptying the rest of the bottle into their glasses. Morgan raised her drink and in her most gregarious voice said, "Cheers, everybody."

It was then that Nathan and Sean joined us at the table. A look passed between Lucinda and Nathan which I tried to ignore. It had been a while since we'd seen the group and I now remembered that they always had a little connection. I tried to put it in context, but the drinks were catching up with me. I needed to keep my bearings since I knew it would be a long weekend. As the group chatted, I half listened, but my attention was elsewhere.

I felt spacey and out of place. "I'll be right back," I said and went inside to use the restroom. A few minutes alone was what I needed to compose myself. While I washed my hands, I studied my reflection in the mirror and noticed that my eyes were dilated. I felt and looked a little flushed. The mixer Morgan used was affecting me. I splashed cool water on my face before heading back out. As I walked through the living room, I stopped to watch the group through the glass. Nathan was once again saddled up near Lucinda. Everyone was laughing and having a good time. I was preparing myself to reenter the party.

Perhaps he felt my attention, since that was when Nathan started toward the house. I waited for him to come inside so we could have a minute to talk. The door opened and he said, "Hey, there you are. What are you doing in here?"

I answered, "I needed a minute. What do you say we take advantage of the beach? Want to take a walk on the sand with me?"

His expression was pained when he said, "Actually, I was coming to tell you we are all thinking about going to the casino. What do you say?"

The last thing I wanted to do was go to a smoke-filled casino. All I wanted was to feel the sand beneath my feet and to walk along the vast beach with Nathan, but the group was driving and I was a passenger. I was disappointed, but rationalized; we did have the whole weekend and maybe it would be better to save the walk for a more relaxed time. I agreed, "Okay, if that's what you want to do, I'm in."

"Great." He smiled and passed me on his way to the kitchen. He took a bottle of Fireball from the counter and tugged my elbow as he made his way back to the door. I followed him outside and to the table.

I stood by Morgan. She looked down at me and asked, "Hey, sweets, are you ready to gamble?"

Not much of a gambler, I put my game face on. "I'm ready when you guys are."

"Yes!" she chanted. "But first, shots!"

Great, I thought, tomorrow is going to suck. I watched Nathan and Sean pour and distribute shots of the inescapable cinnamon sludge to everybody. I shuddered as Sean handed me a glass.

Once everyone had a drink, it was Nathan's turn to toast. "Bottoms up, everybody." Lucinda sent him a seductive look before downing her shot.

I was getting pissed, but stopped myself when I thought about how pathetic she was acting. Lucinda was married and her flirtations were so overt. She must be overcompensating for her husband being, once again, MIA. I drank the sweet syrup and made a silent pact to ignore her and have fun.

Phone in hand, Morgan announced, "Okay everyone, the Uber is fifteen minutes away. Grab your stuff. Let's get going."

THE VAN ROLLED TO A STOP IN FRONT OF A GARISHLY LIT casino entry. Spotlights shone against the black exterior, highlighting carved glass statues and leafy green vegetation. It was a strange combination of glitz meets theme park.

When it was our turn to exit the van, Nathan went first and turned to offer me his hand. We stepped aside and waited for the rest of the crew. Sean came to stand by Nathan and Terry quickly joined. Clearing his throat, Terry spoke loud enough for us all to hear. "I think now would be a good time to separate from the ladies. The boys need to venture out on our own for a while. Don't you agree?" He looked hopefully from Sean to Nathan.

Nathan met my eyes. I shrugged and said, "Go for it."

Morgan was nearby and countered Terry with her own plan. "Come on, ladies. Let's go and see who has more fun and money at the end of this night."

She turned and started toward the double doors. I watched as her round bottom seemed to thrust in reverse and her legs faltered on four-inch heels. She righted herself and walked inside. Lucinda followed, her short black dress flounced as she spun around and it barely covered her well-toned ass. I felt ridiculous in the fitted white dress, but after seeing Lucinda and Morgan's effort, I couldn't stay in my travel clothes. Lynn also changed into a ruffled blouse and pencil skirt. How she fit in with these two was a mystery. She glanced at me and we silently agreed to join them.

Once inside, we were assaulted by even brighter lighting. The gagging scent of cigarette smoke and pandemonium of the casino caused me a momentary panic attack. I'd already had too much to drink, almost nothing to eat, and was coming off a stressful week. This was the last thing I had in mind, but I had to realign. If tonight was going to be different than I expected, why not make the best of it? Following the group, I concentrated on evening out my breath.

Eventually, we arrived by the roulette table and Morgan

stopped. We stood watching, as hands moved frantically, placing colorful plastic coins on numbers and sections of the table. The white ball jumped and skipped along the wooden wheel. When it finally stopped, the group burst into a myriad of conflicting sounds. Winners were ecstatic, but the losers, they'd had enough. Four players vacated the table, leaving an opening for us to sit.

Lucinda strode ahead, claiming a chair beside a rowdy group of thirty-something men. The guys looked over in time to watch her settle her sparsely covered bottom in the chair. I thought the shiny black heels and cheerleader-style dress put her in a vampy Barbie category, but the guys were lapping it up. Lynn hesitated forward and took the seat beside her. I sat next and finally, Morgan.

We exchanged cash for chips and I studied the LCD display for any patterns. From the readout, I could see that black hit quite a few times in a row and there were a lot of odd numbers over the past eight spins. I took $20 in chips and placed two on red and the other two on the even box at the center. The rest of the players were frantically moving coins until the dealer waved her hand, signifying all bets were final.

The ball rolled back and forth along the wheel as we waited anxiously for it to stop. When it did, the roar from the group drew the interest of people at other tables. It hit on red and the number 18. I won both of my bets. As the dealer made her rounds, adding chips to some, taking stacks from others, I watched Lynn and Morgan's pile double while Lucinda's coins were swept away. She seemed unconcerned. The blow of her loss was softened by the attention of the chatty men at her side.

Now that the table was clear, it was time to place a new bet or vacate my seat. I decided to stay for one more deal.

Pocketing $20 in chips, this time I would gamble with the casino's money. I placed one coin on the line between the green 0 / 00 and the black number 2, and the remaining three on black.

The dealer gave the wheel a powerful wind and we were in play. Hasty, last-minute bets were made until the wave of her hand signaled time. The table went silent except for the soft tumble of the white ball as it raced smoothly along on the spinning wheel. It popped up and down until finally, landed on number 2. The table erupted as the dealer made her rounds, adding and reducing chips along the way.

She left me, the big winner, for last. "Congratulations, honey," she rasped.

"Thank you," I said. I watched as she stacked coins next to my bets. I'd won $141 this round and $20 on the first.

"Woo hoo!" Lynn stood and jabbed my shoulder. "You won, girl!"

I laughed and stood too. "Yes I did. Better quit while I'm ahead."

Lynn agreed, "I'm with you. After that round, I'm even. These days, I'll take it."

I wondered if her comment had deeper meaning. I said, "Come on, drinks are on me."

Morgan chimed in, "Don't leave me behind. I know better than to turn down a free drink."

I didn't remember offering one to her, but what did I care? It was found money and she brought me to the source. "Fair's, fair," I said. "Lead the way."

She stood and we all looked toward Lucinda, who was occupied with the gentlemen at her side. Since she was batting her eyelashes and placing bets, we surmised she was staying put. Morgan turned and we followed her through the casino toward a sweeping set of stairs. When we were at the base, she said, "Drinks and dancing, here we come."

I hadn't been to this casino before and wasn't sure what to make of her comment, but I followed her up the stairs. When we got to the top, there was a doorway surrounded by curtains. In front of it, a large, bald bouncer sat precariously on a high stool. He eyed us and nodded without saying a word, a sure sign we were too old for the place. Morgan strode past him as Lynn and I trailed.

Behind the curtain, the club was filtered by dingy pink light and the vague essence of nicotine mist. To the side a pink neon sign flashed "Open."

"That's us," Morgan pointed.

Seventies dance music boomed and the disco ball's colorful beams dappled the room with light. A few daring couples had broken the ice and were on the dance floor. When we got to the bar, I asked, "What do you want to drink, girlies?"

Morgan was decisive, "I'll have a manhattan."

Lynn looked unsure, then said, "What the hell? margarita!"

"Be right back," I said, and covered the few remaining steps to the bar. I waited a moment until the bartender arrived.

"What can I get you, young lady?" he solicited.

"Thanks," I said, "I need one margarita, a manhattan, and a vodka soda, please."

"Okay." I watched as he found the ingredients to make our drinks. Reflected through the mirror and various liquor bottles, I saw Lynn and Morgan. Behind them, the room was filling up. Their drinks were ready, so I ran them over.

When the bartender finished making mine, he said, "That'll be twenty-four dollars. Do you want to open a tab?"

"No, thanks." Pulling the cash from my purse, I said, "Keep the change."

His long lashes framed his cheerful dark eyes and he said, "Thank you, young lady."

"You're welcome," I said. I turned to face the girls.

Lynn held her glass up and said, "Here's to good luck."

Morgan and I raised our glasses and chimed, "To luck."

We took a sip and Lynn ordered us, "Come on. I see an open table by the dance floor."

Morgan and I followed Lynn until we arrived at a large booth at the front of the room. Settling into the black velvet bench, we could see the entire club. Our entertainment was a couple that looked to be professional dancers. We watched them twirl and twist around the floor.

Morgan leaned in and signaled for us to tip our heads closer. Lynn and I did and she said, "Did you guys see the way Lucinda was flirting with those guys at our table?"

I almost snorted the cocktail out my nose, but coughed instead.

Lynn laughed and said, "There's nothing new about that. She's always got her designs on someone. Wonder what goes on between her and Ken behind closed doors."

Morgan sneered. "He goes away on long trips and she gets nice things. That's their thing. Did you know he bought her a new sports car, some fancy BMW model?"

Curious, though I wasn't all that comfortable with the source, I asked, "Do you think he's compensating for something, Morgan?"

She sat upright. Pressing deep into the back of her seat, she scanned the room before leaning back in, even closer this time. "He's got an awful lot of business in Asia, you know."

Lynn was the next to push. "It's for his job, right? Are you saying he's having an affair?"

Morgan bristled and put her hand to her heart. "No, I'm not the one saying he's cheating." She paused for dramatic effect. "Lucinda thinks he is. She told me a while ago. I shouldn't have said anything, but I thought it might help you understand why she's a little . . ."

"Slutty?" Lynn accused.

Morgan looked down, then back up at Lynn. "I guess so, yeah, slutty."

I said nothing, but thought, no—Lucinda is now and always was an attention whore. She acts the way she does to get what she wants. Better to keep my observations to myself. I sipped my drink.

Lynn wasn't ready to drop the subject. "Well, if she doesn't like the idea of Ken cheating, then why does she insist on flirting with the husbands of her friends?"

Morgan feigned shock. "Who has she been flirting with?"

Lynn wasn't about to skirt around the subject and said, "Cut the crap, Morgan. You saw as well as I did, she was glued to Nathan all evening. Before they arrived, she was prancing around in her bikini in front of Terry and Sean."

Always the first to start gossip, in the end she circled around until she became the defender. "No, you misunderstand Lucinda. She's just comfortable with her body and very friendly. She doesn't mean any harm."

As the words exited Morgan's mouth, I looked up in time to see Lucinda and Nathan walk arm and arm into the club. From across the room, I noticed his effort to stand a little straighter, since in her heels, she was taller than him. In that moment, he looked like a stranger. It was as if I had exited my body and instead was observing the scene from the rafters. I watched as they made their way to the bar. Their elbows rested on the counter and their shoulders touched as they waited. She nudged him playfully and he smirked. I felt sick as a voyeur. Finally, the bartender arrived and interrupted their cuddle session.

Lynn touched my shoulder and asked, "Are you okay, Madeline?"

I looked to my right and her face said it all. She felt sorry for me. I had no words.

Morgan piped up, "What? They're ordering drinks. I'll invite them to join us." Not pausing for a reply, she scurried off leaving Lynn and me alone.

When she left, Lynn said, "I know how it feels when your man is the object of Lucinda's attention. I'm sorry you're the victim tonight."

I was suddenly overwhelmed. After the week I'd had, the tension between Nathan and me, and those strange cocktails, things weren't sitting right. It was awkward watching him and Lucinda together and worse that Morgan knew my discomfort.

I wanted to make light of it, but everything was catching up on me and I meanly said, "Lucinda is the one to feel sorry for. She's kind of pathetic, with her showy outfits and loud over-confidence. Why do you think Ken travels so much?"

Just as I finished my sentence, Nathan came toward the table. Lynn rushed to stand and said as she passed him, "Hey, Nathan. The ladies' room is calling." She turned and left us.

Nathan sat next to me on the bench and asked, "How's your night been so far?"

He wanted to have a normal conversation after the way he was just up against Lucinda? I tried to keep the chatter superficial and said, "I won a nice round of roulette. Made a hundred and forty-one dollars."

His eyes didn't sparkle as he looked over at me. "Really? That's great."

I asked, "What about you? What was the big boys adventure about?"

"Nothing really. We played a few rounds of poker. Terry wanted some bro time."

A second later, Morgan and Lucinda showed up. Morgan said, "Hey kids. What's happening?" and they scooted into the booth.

Right behind them, Lynn and Terry approached. Terry danced the few remaining steps before sitting in the booth and pulled Lynn down by his side. She looked annoyed but rolled with it. Terry turned to the group and said, "What's up?"

Nathan responded, "Just got here, and where is our friend Sean?"

Terry replied coolly, which was out of character for him, "He's at the bar, getting drinks."

Moments later, Sean arrived with a tray of cream-colored shots in hand. "Hello, everybody. These are duck farts, compliments of the Joneses." He passed the tray around until each person took one, then said, "Salute."

The table mimicked his cheer and everyone, except me, shot the creamy liquor. Already my heart was racing and I was flushed. The discomfort I felt was no doubt a result of the chumminess I'd just witnessed between Lucinda and Nathan. With all I'd already had to drink, the last think I needed was more. When the last glass hit the table, Lucinda demanded, "Okay, everyone. It's time to dance. Get moving."

The bench came alive at her command. Terry egged Lynn off the side, followed by Lucinda and Morgan. Nathan and I were still sitting when Morgan said, "Come on you two. No chickening out."

Nathan looked over at me. I implored with my eyes, hoping he'd understand that we needed a minute alone. He read my expression and called over his shoulder, "Right behind you." He turned back and asked, "Is something wrong?"

His question was so vague, yet altogether ludicrous, it inflamed my already raw nerves. I scathed, "Of course not. What could be wrong? Other than you clinging to the side of Lucinda Barbie all night long."

My childish comment must have been well aimed, for Nathan fired back, "Me clinging to Lucinda? Are you crazy?"

I hissed, "We watched you walk in together. Morgan and Lynn were with me. We all saw the way you were looking at each other."

"Maddie, what you saw was me being nice to your friend who is drunk. I left the poker table and was on my way to find *you* when I saw her having a hard time with some guys at the roulette table."

"What do you mean, a hard time?" I asked.

"I don't know. She was trying to extract herself and I stepped in and acted like she was my girlfriend for a minute. You know, called her honey and stuff. It was no big deal, but we carried on the charade in case they were watching us walk through the casino."

I was floored and said, "Are you kidding me?"

"Why would I kid you about that?"

I didn't know how to feel at the moment. On one hand, I knew Lucinda was in no need of rescue, but was she low enough to feign neediness to get Nathan's sympathy? It was possible. In a snap, I chose to throw my heart into the moment, to forget the pettiness and try to have fun. I pushed against Nathan's leg under the table and said, "Get out. I want to dance with you."

He nodded and with a smug look on his face, said, "Yes, my lady. At your service."

He took my hand in his and we raced to the dance floor. Bright lights and people swirled around as we danced to the funk sound of Kool and the Gang. For the briefest moment, it was there between us. He finally made eye contact and when he did, the air around us was alive with possibility. My heart sped, and for the first time in a long time, it felt like I had his attention. The sensation was heady and it made me want him.

I leaned in and was about to kiss him when I felt a tap at my shoulder. It was Sean. Morgan pushed him forward and said, "Girls room." This left Sean standing between Nathan and me. A second later, Lucinda strolled up and tapped Nathan's shoulder. He turned to find her there.

Our stillness was odd so we all began moving again. This time more stiffly as we tried to find a groove in this new dynamic. We stood in a square until Sean took my hand and gave me a twirl. I moved with him while keeping a chaste distance. It was impossible to ignore that Nathan and Lucinda were beside us and paired up. They danced tentatively and didn't touch at first. Lucinda swung her hips and her skirt rose with the effort. No matter her alcohol consumption, she moved seductively on her ankle-breaking heels. She hardly seemed like a woman who needed saving.

The song ended and it was now time to slow things down. The DJ selected "Hello" by Lionel Richie. Sean and I looked at one another and were saved by the return of Morgan. She announced, "I'm here to claim a slow dance with my hubby."

I smiled and stepped aside before turning to find the restroom myself. After a quick pee, I saw my reflection in the mirror and a fresh application of lipstick was in order. I opened the tube and smoothed some on as the door opened. It was Lynn.

She said, "Hey, are you okay?"

Reading her concern after Nathan and Lucinda's entrance,

I reassured her, "I'm fine. It was a misunderstanding before. A funny story that I'll share, but later, okay?"

She looked puzzled, and said, "Okay. Anytime you want to talk, I'm ready."

Her concern confused me, but I thought she might be sensitive, given her situation with Terry. I asked, "Is everything okay with you?"

She said, "Our status hasn't changed, but I do have to say, you are incredible."

Confused, I asked, "What are you talking about?"

She said, "How are you handling the fact that Nathan and Lucinda kissed? You're so cool about it."

The ground beneath my feet shook and I had to grip the sink before denying her words. "They didn't kiss. He put his arm around her and called her honey to get those guys from the table off her back."

Lynn's face said it all. She was the bearer of bad news and found no pleasure in it. She said simply, "I'm sorry, Madeline."

After putting the lipstick tube back in my purse, I looked up at Lynn and said, "Thanks for letting me know." My voice sounded foreign. The normalcy I'd forced was a thin cover, hiding my true feelings, which were chaotic. I continued before exiting, "I'll see you back out there." I didn't give her time to reply before I turned to leave.

The door opened and I was immediately assaulted by a tune from KC and the Sunshine Band. As I surveyed the club, it looked exactly as it had moments ago, before I learned that Nathan lied, and before I knew he had kissed Lucinda. I felt queasy.

I looked toward the booth where we had been sitting and Sean and Morgan were there with Terry. Nathan and Lucinda weren't so I scanned the dance floor. Sure enough, there they were, dancing and chatting in each other's ears. She touched his shoulder and he leaned in close to talk.

As I watched them, I tried to rationalize their actions. Maybe they were just sharing friendly banter. Was I being overly sensitive? It felt like Nathan wanted to hurt me, and what was Lucinda's problem? Was she so desperate for attention she needed to go after Nathan? Weren't the guys at the roulette table interesting enough for her, or was she competing with me? There were too many questions swimming in my head. I had no idea how to walk back to the table without feeling like a complete ass.

I decided to get some air. Making my way back through the curtain and down the stairs, I exited the casino. When I got outside, I could see a vacant bench. I walked to it and sat. The ocean breeze swirled invisibly, pushing my hair back. Strobe lights moved along the walls and sky above, urging passersby to stop, but for the moment I was alone.

I sat there trying to understand what was happening. I knew Nathan and Lucinda had chemistry. She was so flagrant with her sexuality, and he couldn't pull himself away, but to kiss? I saw the guys at the table, they were no risk to her. Not only was a kiss unjustified, but his reaction to rescue her with his lips seemed a little too Freudian. People don't do things, joke or not, that hasn't entered their minds. The awful truth was that Nathan wanted to kiss Lucinda and I wanted to kiss Nathan.

My thoughts were interrupted by Morgan's arrival. "There you are."

I watched as she approached and when she sat, I said, "Hey."

For a beat, she was quiet, until she finally said, "I heard about Lucinda and Nathan. She told me. It was innocent, but I imagine you don't feel the same way about it."

I felt the blood rush to my cheeks, a combination of fury and sadness swept over me. I said, "There is nothing innocent about kissing your friend's man. You and I both know there was no risk with those guys at the table."

Morgan was silent for a minute then ventured, "Is everything okay between you and Nathan?"

Her question seemed asinine, given the recent developments. I snapped, but remembered who I was talking to. "Everything is great."

Morgan's fake lashes were distracting as she questioned me. "Are you sure, Maddie? You know you can talk to me."

I did know I could talk to her, and that next week she would have no problem telling the world my deepest confidence. I chose my next words with that in mind. "We're fine. I'm just exhausted after the work week. You know how it is."

This fluffed her ego, since she loved being the resident expert. She said, "Yes, of course I understand. Why don't we rally the group to head back to the house? We brought the Karaoke machine. I know Sean would love to hear your rendition of Desperado. What do you say?"

Going back to the house with the group—now knowing that Nathan kissed Lucinda—was anything but appealing. But I couldn't sit on the bench all night and I was definitely over the casino scene. "Sure, I'm game."

"Okay, sweets. I'll go and round everyone up."

❧

THE ROOM EXPLODED IN HOOTS AND CLAPS AS TERRY'S squeaky rendition of Rhianna's "Stay" came to an end. Nathan's buzzed voice was much louder than necessary in the confines of the room, and he said, "I'm next. Where's the book? I'm going to sing, 'Just a Gigolo.'" After the evening's revelations, his song choice was fitting. I watched as he handled the book, fumbling through the pages until he found the right page.

I tried in vain to stifle a yawn and Morgan noticed. She and the group had continued to drink even after we got back to the house. I knew enough to stop after watching Nathan and Lucinda together.

Morgan's firm dialect, like a mother admonishing her child, sliced through the room. "Madeline!" I snapped to and faced her from my place on the couch. "You're tired. You need to go to bed."

Her tone got the attention of Terry and even Lucinda, who both looked toward me and back at Morgan. Terry defended, "Leave her alone. She's just sitting there."

Lucinda joined in, "Yeah, she's not tired. She hasn't sung yet."

Morgan's piercing stare was relentless. She was moody when she drank. Her personalities ranged from sloppy, to doting, sometimes motivational, and even snappy. The latter personality confronted me.

Nathan heard the exchange, but ignored it to focus on his song. He gave Sean the number and he entered it into the console. Seconds later, the room vibrated with Nathan's voice and Van Halen as the backdrop. I looked on as he squished his face and poured everything he had into the song, belting the words without inhibition. I felt invisible and more to the point, unwelcome. Morgan's directive that I go to bed gave away her position. She thought I was overwrought and that was the reason I was bothered by Lucinda and Nathan's kiss. She and Lucinda had been best friends for years so I knew where her loyalties were. I looked over to find Terry's attention on me. His expression was sympathetic and it embarrassed me more. My thoughts were interrupted by Nathan's highest note as he concluded the song. The room lit up with applause and howls.

Lucinda, who had been sitting next to Morgan, jumped to her feet and ran to hug Nathan. She begged, "I want to do a duet with you. Will you sing My Endless Love with me?"

Nathan laughed and said, "How could I say no to that?"

We all watched as Lucinda took the book and searched for the song. When she found the one she was looking for, she announced the number to DJ Sean. He input the code and the music began. She and Nathan took the mics and acted out one of the silliest songs of all time. They smiled and stared into each other's eyes and I thought I might scream.

Something took over. I don't know how to explain it, but as I sat in that room, where I felt so out of place, I knew what I needed to do. Standing, I made my way around the couch and to the bedroom where we were sleeping. I stood in the doorway, trying to calm myself, but it wasn't working. I didn't want to be there any longer. If I stayed, I knew I would spend the weekend on pins and needles, watching Lucinda and Nathan stare into each other's eyes.

A heady rush came over me and I decided to leave. I walked to my bag, tossed in the few items I'd removed, and zipped it up. Taking it in hand, I walked down the hall and up the flight of stairs. As I did, I could hear Nathan and Lucinda, chiming away. This time they were singing "Wild Horses." Another great choice from the duet. If I had any lingering doubt, hearing them sing together pushed it aside. I opened the front door and walked outside.

From my vantage point at the trunk, the living room was alight. For a moment I paused, watching Lucinda and Nathan finish their song. I could hear the applause from the group as they linked hands and took an over-the-top bow. I'd seen enough. As crazy as it was, I got into the driver's seat, turned on the ignition, and made my way out of the driveway.

◈

As I entered the main highway, the road was dark and desolate. It was after midnight and the area between the coast and Portland was not very populated. I traveled along the one-lane country road, deep in thought. Was I acting insane? There was only one answer to that question. I was. I'd left the house in the night without saying a word to anyone. The ramifications of my actions hadn't fully sunk in. One thing was certain—next week Morgan would share this tantalizing bit of drama as widely as possible.

A rush of tears burst from my eyes and a sad cry escaped me. The harsh truth settled and I knew—Nathan didn't love me. With our relationship in such a delicate state, if he wanted to make it right he'd have chosen walk on the beach with me. He would have wanted to dance with, sing with, and kiss *me* tonight, but he didn't. The road ahead wound in unimaginable twists as I tried to see things clearly through the shiny bubble of my own tears. For the first time in five years, I was ready to give up. Our relationship had become my anxiety, and his actions showed me I had nothing left to fight for.

After what seemed an eternity, I pulled up to the house. It was almost 3 AM and I was beyond exhausted. Just house after leaving later my world felt different. When I got inside, I unlocked the screen to my phone. The icon showed that I had several messages.

The first was from Morgan at 2:30. It read: *Call me. I want to know you're ok.*

The next was from Terry at 2:32. *If you ever need to talk, Lynn and I are here for you.*

The final message was from Nathan at 2:33. He wrote: *I can't believe you left. Text me and let me know you're ok.*

Rather than reply to him directly, I sent a group text. There was no way to minimize the insanity of my decision to leave in the night, but I tried.

At 2:58, I wrote: *Sorry I didn't say anything before I left, but I didn't want to ruin the night for everyone. I am exhausted and need to prepare for the conference. I made it home. Please don't worry and have a great weekend. Until next time . . .*

After hitting send, I turned the phone to silent and went to the bedroom. Crossing to the window, I closed the curtains and pulled back the blankets before collapsing into the bed. Once my head hit the pillow, a fresh wave of tears ripped through me and I understood the enormity of my choice to leave.

❧

Sun light spilled through the windows and bore into my swollen eyes. I stirred. For the briefest moment I'd forgotten the events of the previous evening, then a sickening jolt of reality hit. What had I done? Why didn't I go to sleep instead of driving away into the night? The why was simple, if I were honest with myself. It wasn't that Nathan kissed Lucinda, as shitty as that was, or even because he lied about it. I left because I didn't want to be ignored anymore.

Doing the only thing I knew how, I put one foot in front of the other and got out of bed. The dreaded situation must be faced. I crossed the room and with a shaky hand, took my phone from the charger. I felt faint as I unlocked the screen. There were messages from Morgan and Nathan.

I read hers first. 8:10 AM *Maddie, are you ok? Nathan is*

worried about you. He may get a ride back with Lucinda this morning.

As her words pummeled, I couldn't convince myself to be numb. If he rode back with Lucinda, after the cruelty of their kiss, that would be too much. I felt like a child, experiencing her first devastation. Though I was dizzy with emotion, I couldn't stop myself. I had to read what Nathan wrote.

Going to get a ride back this morning. I'll let you know the plan.

There it was, in the missing text. The detail that Morgan shared, as Lynn had the night before, but Nathan omitted. He didn't say how he was getting back. Fury intermixed with a guttural sadness and I lost my breath.

He hadn't messaged back, so I didn't know if he was on his way yet. I looked at the clock and saw it was nearly nine. The drive would take them a couple of hours, which gave me at least one hour before Nathan could possibly return. I knew I needed to compose myself, to prepare for what was coming, but I couldn't do it alone.

I opened the contacts icon on my phone and scrolled until I found my best friend Shawna's number. She and I had known each other for over twenty years, after meeting in college in Los Angeles. Shawna married our classmate, Chris Parr, a few years later and they now lived in a fairy tale home overlooking the ocean in San Diego. As I listened to the phone ring, I only hoped she would pick up.

"Hello?" Her sweet voice was a welcome sound.

"Hi there," I croaked, hoarsely.

"How are you doing, Maddie?"

Her innocent question pushed me to the edge of tears and I had to pause before saying, "Not great."

She pressed, "What's going on? Tell me what I can do?"

Gulping for air, I steadied my voice and said, "I think we're done, Nathan and I."

After a brief silence, she asked, "What happened? Why do you say that?"

I didn't have the energy or time to go into everything that had happened. "It's too much."

Shawna replied softly, "How can I help?"

My wheels were spinning and I said, "I need to be in San Diego next week. What if I come before the weekend and spend a little time with you guys?"

Shawna responded, "Oh no. You're kidding. Chris and I are leaving on Tuesday and we'll be gone for ten days. He has a work trip to Germany scheduled and I'm joining him."

I was heartbroken, but couldn't let Shawna know how disappointed I was. She would only feel bad and worry. "That sounds a lot better than entertaining me."

"Hey, I have an idea." Shawna's excited speech got my attention. "Stay here while we are away. I was going to have a pet sitter come anyway. You'd save me the money and it would give you some time to think things through."

Her offer couldn't have come at a better time. I had no idea how to look at Nathan after the way the weekend unfolded and I did have to be down south for work anyway. I made a quick decision and spoke before I changed my mind. "You've got a deal. I'll make the arrangements today and send you the details."

Shawna said, "I'm sorry I won't be here with you, but I hope it's what you need. I love you, girl."

Tears welled in my eyes and one slipped down my cheek. I worked to keep my voice steady as I replied, "I love you too, Shawna. Thank you so much. Bye."

❧

From the window in my second-story bedroom, I heard a car engine and peered out in time to watch Nathan exit Lucinda's car. The nerves that had been simmering all morning exploded into a steady boil and coursed through my entire being. He actually rode back with her. There was no mistaking that action or the meaning behind it. Sliding my hands down my pant legs, I wiped away the perspiration and stood.

The front door opened and closed. I listened to his footsteps against the wooden floors as Nathan found his way into the living room. Steeling myself for what was about to happen, I took a breath and went downstairs to find him. When I got to the living room, he turned to face me. Our eyes met and I felt like a crazy person. Looking into his sad brown eyes, I was devastated to know his somber expression had less to do with leaving me than the life upset we were facing. For long enough I had been in denial, excusing Nathan's actions and lack of desire. After the events of the previous evening and his choice to ride into town with Lucinda, denial was no longer a viable crutch. Nathan wanted out.

He broke the silence first and asked, "Can we talk?"

I nodded in agreement and watched as he made his way to the oversized leather chair he preferred. Taking a seat at the couch, I waited for him to break the ice. He sighed deeply and stared at the ground beneath his feet before saying, "It's fair to say this is no longer working."

The words "fair" and "working" didn't correlate for me. It would be fruitless to dig into the matter. I could tell he didn't want to talk, and though we both had things to apologize for, me leaving in the night seemed a small thing given his kiss and long drive back with Lucinda. I replied generically, "No, I guess not."

Without a hint of hesitation, he said, "Maybe it's time I find my own place."

Although I'd known where our conversation would lead, the panic that settled at my heart and sucked the air out of my lungs couldn't be stopped. Our life together was ending. Five years of memories and effort were being cut, like superfluous words in a manuscript. My tears were unstoppable.

Before I could compose myself and respond, Nathan continued, "I hate seeing you like this. Look, I know I haven't made you happy. We've had so much to deal with and I don't know what else to do. I mean, we can't even go for a fun weekend without all the fireworks."

My heartbreak turned to fury as did my retort. I sneered, "Seems to me you were looking for fireworks, just not with me."

Unapologetic, Nathan defended, "Madeline, you're too sensitive. That thing meant nothing. Everyone else knew it was a joke. Why are you being so insecure?"

His words pelted me like bullets and if I weren't sitting, I would have hit the ground. I could scream and argue, but he didn't care. If he did, the morning would have turned out differently. For one, he would have found another way home and once he arrived, he would have been apologetic, not indignant.

Rather than justify him with a fiery response, I said, "Since I'm leaving tomorrow morning and I'll be gone all week, maybe that will give you enough time to find a place."

He huffed and said, "A week isn't very long, but I'll do what I can. You know we don't have to rush. We can choose to be civilized."

My self-control was waning. I imagined picking up the candlestick from the table and hefting it at him. Instead, I stood and said, "Please find something as soon as you can. I'm going upstairs to finish packing."

Before I left the room, Nathan called, "Maddie."

I turned and waited for his next words. His eyes bore into mine and he said, "I'm sorry it's come to this."

His words were perfunctory and irrelevant. A fresh wave of tears came as I replied, "Yeah, me too."

IT'S DANGEROUS TO GO ALONE

I shook my head and snapped myself out of my indulgent pity-party break. The deck was quiet but I wasn't flown in to ruminate about my unsteady family life. I returned to the mixer with a straight spine and a smile.

Several drinks and a dozen introductions later, we were finally on our way out of the reception. As I shuffled along the sidewalk, humidity weighed heavily, making each step an effort. The three-inch heels I wore didn't help matters. Sheldon accompanied Robert and me back to the hotel, since he was staying there as well. I wondered how he was managing the sweltering heat in that elegant suit and tie. The revolving door spun and we stepped into the lobby. Greeted by a cool rush of air and the glass elevator rising ahead, I could finally breathe. To the left, I noticed the lobby bar was packed. More suits enjoying libations as a kickoff to the event.

"What do you guys think, nightcap?" Robert suggested.

Thanks to the alcohol, I was feeling more congenial. I could see no harm in it. I wasn't scheduled to work at the booth until the afternoon. Plus, it would be less time tossing and turning. "Sure, why not?" I agreed.

To my surprise, Sheldon declined. "I see some people I want to say hello to. Why don't I catch you both at the cocktail party tomorrow night?"

"Of course. Sheldon, it was a pleasure to meet you. We'll see you tomorrow evening."

Robert took his hand for one last hearty shake and said, "It was great seeing you. Have a good night." Sheldon made his way toward the bar and was swallowed up by the sea of bodies.

Robert turned to me. "Are you game?"

I studied his face. Until this evening we'd only met a couple of times during my interview process. He was handsome in a masculine way. His wide hands, square jaw, and large brown eyes somehow made up for the lack of hair. I needed to get to know my new boss, and in the security industry, drinks were the chosen path to relationship building. "I'm game. I usually have a hard time sleeping in a hotel on the first night. Let's go."

Robert let me pass and I led the way toward the mass of people. My practiced forward focus was intact so as not to embarrass anyone who may be looking a little too intently at me. Ahead, I saw a few people I knew from the previous company. The excessively "close" industry made frenemies a real thing. It was important never to burn a bridge, not knowing how it could affect your opportunities down the line. I willed a smile and straightened my shoulders as we drew near to the table of $2,000 suits.

The very boisterous Abbot Williams stood and took a few steps in my direction. "Well, aren't you a sight?" His round cheeks smooshed his eyes closed as he smiled.

He pulled me into a hug as if we were old friends who

missed each other. I could feel his round stomach against my own. When we released, I looked up at him and said, "So good to see you, Abbot."

The table was focused on our exchange. A few of the others wanted to say hello, but were conflicted. After all, I was the traitor who resigned. How could I consider leaving them? In this world, egos had a way of puffing up expensively clad chests.

"How are you?" I asked. "It's been a while. I see the gang is all here."

"They are." He smiled down at me and pointed over my shoulder. "Carly and Kim are over there," he pointed.

I turned and saw the two ladies who were my former colleagues. Before addressing them, I remembered that Robert was standing beside me. "Abbot, let me introduce you to Robert Grain. He's my new boss so don't tell him anything too scary," I joked. They chuckled and shook hands.

"Excuse me a second. I'll go and say hello to Kim and Carly."

Turning toward the ladies who looked anything but excited to see me, I took the last few paces to their table. Big smiles were met with insincere greetings as we exchanged our hellos. From my peripheral, I could see there was a man at their table. Kim was the first to remember her manners. Gesturing with her hand, she said, "Madeline Craig, meet Travis Baker."

Time stopped. The world went silent except for the distant crash of the ocean. Muted waves fell all around me, like the sound you hear when you put your ear next to a conch shell. Piercing grey eyes met my blue ones as his large hand took mine, and it felt like home.

Never before had I experienced this reaction when meeting someone for the first time. People write about it, sing about it and talk about it, yet the mystery and power remains. What happens when your eyes lock with another's not every time but those crucial occasions when your eyes meet and some deep connection, the undercurrent of knowledge holds you, confirming all you cannot see, touch or feel? Like air, the power is there but you can't grasp it. What does this moment mean and how will it affect your life? For you know it will.

Then I noticed it. He was wearing a wedding ring. He was off limits and that was that. I said, "It's a pleasure to meet you, Travis. What brings you to the SSI conference?"

He rose from his chair and slowly released his hand. When he reached his full height, he must have been six foot four. His dirty-blond hair and sideburns were on the long side. The look suited him.

When he spoke, his bass-filled voice matched with his exterior. "The pleasure is all mine. I'm a customer of Kim's and we came to meet with a few new technology vendors. How do you know Kim and Carly?"

I replied, "We used to work together. I left SI about a year ago."

Though his hand released mine, his eyes never broke, and for an instant it was as though we were the only two people in the room. Something clicked and I had a funny feeling, like we already knew each other.

I sensed a presence at my side, that snapped me out of the momentary trance. It was Robert. Time to make another introduction. "Robert Grain, meet Travis Baker. Travis, meet Robert, my boss."

They shook heartily and Robert was the first to speak. "Good to meet you. How do you know Madeline?"

Travis looked at me; his gaze felt almost proprietary. "We've just met. Kim introduced us."

The ladies perked at their mention and Robert's arrival. Carly leaned closer. I noticed she was wearing cowboy boots and a denim skirt. On the other end of the spectrum was Kim, who chose an ill-fitting pair of calf-length pants and a flowery blouse.

I made the introductions. "Robert, meet Kim and Carly."

Carly was eyeing Robert like a piece of candy. They shook hands and she turned to Travis. Her imploring gaze and long, wavy hair spoke volumes as Kim shrunk by her side. "Are you ready to get your karaoke on?"

He smiled, but looked back at me before speaking. "What are you and Robert up to? Do you guys want to join us on a field trip?"

After my reaction to Travis, I knew this could be trouble, but before I could respond, Robert confirmed for the both of us. He was either interested in Carly or Travis, since he might turn out to be a customer. "Sure, we're in."

Carly lit up at Robert's comment. She must like the look of him. I knew her well enough to be sure she didn't care to share the limelight with other women. Kim was the only exception and I suspected it was because she chose to blend into her surroundings. Carly not only liked to stand out, but she wanted to be memorable at all costs. Foul language and suggestive comments were her trademark. My guess was that Kim reveled in watching Carly do all the things that she wasn't brazen enough to try.

Travis took command and said, "Well, let's head out and find a cab." He tapped the shoulder of a man who was sitting a table behind and the two exchanged words. The short, stocky man stood and we were introduced. "Charles Bradford, meet Robert and Madeline. They are going to be joining us for karaoke."

Charles smiled broadly, showing off his crooked lowers,

and proffered his hand. I greeted him, "Nice to meet you, Charles."

Robert was next and the two exchanged handshakes.

Charles smiled and looked toward Travis. "I thought you were ready to call it a night."

Travis adjusted in his size 12 shoes. "Well, the prospect of karaoke woke me up."

Charles coughed before speaking. "Sure, why not?"

With that, we made our way through the bar and out the revolving doors into the sultry Atlanta night. Travis whistled to a van for hire. The driver pulled up to the curb and we all jumped in. A short while later, we arrived at the front of a club. Red neon lights stood out against the faded green façade, calling all would-be entertainers to join in on the fun.

Travis paid the driver while Carly grabbed Kim's hand and led us all into the club. Once inside, we were overwhelmed by throngs of people and an off-key rendition of Olivia Newton John's "Let's Get Physical." Carly's voice rose over the rest as she directed us to the bar. She bellied up first and virtually hefted her enormous chest onto the counter. This got the bartender's attention and he made his way to our group. Carly decided for us all. "We'll have six shots of Fireball."

Marching orders intact, he turned and poured our drinks. Carly looked at me and winked. The men stood behind, grateful for her advantage at expediting the ordering process. Soon, the small glasses were filled to the brim and Carly distributed them. When everyone had a drink, she toasted, "Here's to a night we won't remember."

In unison, the group called, "Cheers!" and the overly sweet liquid was downed. Before we'd even set our glasses down, Carly commanded, "Wait here, everyone." We did as told and watched as, once again, she garnered the attention of our barkeep. "Another round please." She batted her long black lashes at him and he smiled. As a bartender, you'd think he'd be immune to flirtatious women, but her style seemed to work for him. In an instant, we were each holding another tiny glass of the cinnamon elixir. She raised her glass and said, "Karaoke!" We joined in the merriment and downed the shots. Tomorrow would be a rough one, but tonight the world was our oyster.

We replaced our glasses on the counter and Carly said, "That was a good start but not nearly enough, what is everyone drinking?"

At this comment, Robert stepped in. "Let me open a tab so everyone can order." The two stood side by side at the bar and it seemed like something was brewing. We gave them our order and Carly and Robert agreed to bring the drinks. Kim and I were told to find a suitable spot on which to post up.

We navigated through the crowds until we found an unoccupied cocktail table. With a view of the stage and dance—floor, it would be the best place to lean when our drinks kicked in. A few moments later Robert and Carly arrived, hands full with cocktails.

We picked up our respective drinks and this time Robert started the toast, "Here's to the unplanned."

Everyone raised their glasses and I noticed Travis looking my direction. I averted my eyes and sipped on one of the strongest vodka sodas. Having consumed several drinks at the reception, with the two shots already kicking in, I had a little chat with myself. *Keep it together Maddie.*

As the night wore on, the group mingled. I kept a good distance from Travis. Though I did, whenever I looked his way—which was too often—I noticed him looking at me. It felt like an invisible force was pulling us together. Thankfully, an interruption arrived in the form of Carly. She grabbed Kim and me and dragged us to the dance floor. We goofed and moved to the music of "Baby Got Back" as Carly proved the point.

Several songs and cocktails later, the long night, and the days leading to my trip were wearing on me. My new boss was dirty dancing with Carly and a beautiful black woman they'd just met. Kim was talking to Charles and Travis. I felt disconnected and suddenly so exhausted. It didn't appear as though they were interested in leaving anytime soon and I knew it was time for me to go. The liquor, with the high anxiety I had neatly contained all evening, was about to be my unraveling.

Without saying goodbye, I made my way to the front door and slipped out. As soon as the air hit my face, tears exploded from my eyes. I scanned the street for a cab and was devastated to find none. No matter, I couldn't go back inside. I made the irrational decision to walk to the hotel. Having never been to Atlanta before, and since we arrived at the club in a cab, I wasn't sure how to get back, but that wouldn't stop me. I walked as fast as I could up the hill. Tears flowed uncontrollably. My face was wet and I couldn't stop crying. Reality caved in on me and I allowed my thoughts to run rampant. My son's illness and the demise of my relationship assisted by copious amounts of alcohol shredded my composure. I forged ahead irrationally since I had no idea if I was going in the right direction. All I knew was that I needed to be away from people. Nothing would be worse than if they saw me like this.

Then I heard it. At first, I ignored the sound of my name. Putting one foot in front of the other I increased my pace, but he was gaining on me. Soon Travis was by my side. I wiped my cheeks with the back of my hand and averted my face from him. The embarrassment I felt was…beyond.

His deep, soothing voice asked, "Where are you going?"

I stopped walking and staring at the ground said, "The hotel. I didn't see a cab so I thought I'd walk."

The giant by my side admonished, "You can't walk alone at three in the morning. It's not safe."

I had no idea it was that late. I said lamely, "I just had to go." Another explosion of tears overtook me and I covered my face. "I'm so sorry."

"Hey, don't be. Why don't I walk back with you?"

What kind of man would willingly put himself at the side of a weeping woman? "I don't think that's a good idea. I'm not doing very well right now."

He reached for my face and the gentlest finger raised my chin while his thumb brushed aside my tears. "I can use the exercise."

When he removed his hand from my face, I was irrationally disappointed. The gesture of wiping away a stranger's tears was a kindness I had no way to expect. I watched as he pulled the phone from his pocket and typed on the screen. Siri chimed in and the navigation began. It was a sobering moment.

Not one to cry, I had no idea what to do to stem the insistent flow of my tears. Guilt swallowed me and my thoughts continued to run rampant. Halfway across the country, when my son needed me close, I was drunk and wandering the streets of Atlanta. Peter and I were bonded in a way that only a single mother and son could be. Ours was an imperfect connection, but it went deep. The thought of him facing something so serious on his own overwhelmed me. The status of my newly broken"engagement" with Nathan, weighed on me.

Travis placed his arm around my shoulder and gave me the slightest push forward as we started out. For a few minutes we moved in silence. Occasionally, I had to look over to the side so he wouldn't see each fresh burst of tears.

After a while, he broke the silence. "I don't want to be nosey, but do you want to tell me what's going on?" His gentle tone was too kind. I was threadbare, which caused another breakdown of waterworks.

When I could finally talk, the words took a supreme effort. "This is mortifying."

Travis was silent.

"It's my son. He's not doing well."

Nodding his head as if he understood, he asked, "What's the matter with him?"

Do you know the feeling when there is something so awful you're afraid to say it aloud, lest it could breathe life into the words? Like the *Harry Potter* stories, when they refuse to say "Voldemort" for fear he may manifest at the mere utterance of his name, I was in one of those moments. Of course, I knew I wouldn't change anything by speaking the words, but if I told him, it would become all the more real. Still, he was a stranger and had shown me kindness by walking me back. As awful as it would be to share, an explanation for my odd behavior was necessary. I would only talk about my son and not about my relationship. That was a line I wouldn't cross. "He has cancer and tomorrow they're doing surgery. I just started this job so I can't be there."

His expression mirrored the horror I felt. "I'm so sorry. How old is he?"

"He's only twenty-one."

Travis looked shocked. "You have a twenty-one-year-old?"

That wasn't the question I was expecting. It caused me to cheer slightly. "Yes, I do."

"Wow. You must have started very young."

"I did. He was born when I was nineteen."

"What type of cancer does he have? If you don't mind me asking."

"Testicular. They think it's contained and hasn't yet spread. They'll know for sure after the surgery tomorrow."

"Oh my. That sounds very scary. I can't imagine going through that at twenty-one or even now. How is he doing with it?"

I shook my head. "He's edgy, angry, and a little scared, I suppose. We've had a hard time lately and he's being extra independent, almost defiantly so, if that makes sense."

He chuckled. "Sounds like a twenty-one-year-old guy to me."

I was grateful for his simple words that diffused my high anxiety. "You think?"

"Absolutely. There's something about that age for guys, especially when it comes to the way we are with our mothers. He'll let you know when he really needs you. Until then, all you can do is offer to help."

His words were the comfort I needed. The sense of guilt I felt for taking the trip was temporarily assuaged. "He's my baby and the idea of him going through this, and what could happen next, it's hard to accept. You spend their whole life protecting them only to find you have no real power. I'm so sorry to bother you with this."

He turned to me and said, "Don't be."

For goodness' sake, a few hours prior the man was unknown to me and he could be a potential customer. I needed to lighten things up. "Bet you wished you'd stayed with the rest of them in the bar. Much better than being stuck with the stereotypical drunk and crying female."

He laughed then. The sound was deep and sincere. It filled the air and made everything okay. "I'm the lucky one.

How often have you been to these events, met lots of people, but get to know no one? This is what it's all about and what better reason to cry than about our kids?"

Suddenly, a figure came from the shadow of a doorway. He stopped and put an arm in front of me to halt our progress. A pregnant woman approached. Her skin was dark and the whites of her eyes seemed to glow from her face. I looked toward the doorway where she'd been sitting and saw a blanket and a package of Oreo cookies. Her speech was hurried and as that southern accent pitched us, I had the chance to learn more about my walking companion.

She pleaded, "Do you all have something to spare for a pregnant lady?"

Travis asked her, "What can we help you with?"

The tale began. "All I have is these Oreos and I need to get some food. You see, I'm pregnant." To emphasize her point, the woman raised her shirt and showed us her swollen stomach.

Obviously, she wasn't doing well.

Travis got her talking. He said, "Only Oreos, that's not enough; but I have to admit, I do love them."

The woman laughed, much louder than necessary since we were standing feet from her. Transforming from hilarity to flirt in seconds, she drawled suggestively, "You funny, Big Pappa."

He chuckled and reached for his wallet. Pulling out some bills, he handed them to the woman. "Get you and that baby something good to eat."

"I will, Big Pappa. Don't you worry, I will." With that, she left us and went back to her shelter in the doorway.

Travis placed a hand around my back and began walking. After a few minutes, he said, "Good thing I came after you. If

I hadn't, you may have been attacked by the pregnant, Oreo-eating woman."

Though the situation wasn't funny, sometimes you had to make light of reality. "My savior," I chided.

"And don't you forget it," he joked. "You know she had to be pretty tough, poor woman, living in the doorway, eating Oreos and not even the double-stuffed kind."

For the first time in days—who was I kidding, for the first time in years—I laughed. The situation was no better, in fact, that sad interaction should have made things worse. Somehow, this man, simply by walking next to me, made everything feel lighter. That was the moment I understood the song, "You Can't Always Get What You Want." I needed his companionship tonight and I was grateful for his presence.

"So, what about you? Do you have kids?"

"I sure do. Three of them actually. Cody is fourteen, Elizabeth is twelve, and our littlest guy, Baxter, is turning seven next week."

"How lucky for you. It must be fun having a pod of them."

His face lit up as he told me stories about each of his children. Clearly, he was a loving father and devoted family man. The reality of his familial status kept me in check. I'd never gotten involved with a married man in the past, nor did I have any intention of doing so. Still, there was no denying the chemistry between us. He was not only easy to talk to, but he'd seen me blubbering and didn't run. Instead, he wiped the tears away in the most natural way possible. This was an important evening. I didn't yet understand what it meant, but that was life. Some things are bottomless.

Time slipped by and soon we found ourselves in front of my hotel. Travis spoke first, and said, "I'm staying down the way so I'll leave you here, but I want your number. I'm going to text you to make sure you got into your room okay."

It had been so long since anyone had taken care of me, making his gesture all the more special. "Thank you for walking me back and for listening. You've been so kind."

He snickered. "I'm glad I saw you walk out the door. In all seriousness, walking around city streets at this time of night is a dangerous idea, especially when you're a shorty."

Feigning anger, I placed my hand on my hip and looked up at him. "Who are you calling shorty?"

"If the shoe fits, Cinderella." He chuckled and pulled me into a hug. The fragrance of his cologne made me want to linger. Thankfully, he released me quickly. As he walked away, he called over his shoulder, "I'll text you in a few. Go get settled."

I wanted to follow his orders. The funny thing was, I was looking forward to that text. As I entered the lobby, it was desolate. I rode the glass elevator to my floor and found the room. After tossing my dress aside, I climbed into bed. I was about to doze off when the phone buzzed.

Travis wrote: *It was great to meet you Madeline. I hope you're settled in.*

I was tired but wanted to let him know that I was fine so I sent a reply. *Thank you again Travis. I'm in my room safe and sound. Good night.*

His reply, seconds later, flashed across the display. *Sweet dreams, but only double-stuffed Oreos will do.*

I smiled and fell asleep.

NO REMEDY

Blinding yellow light, redirected from the mirror and shot beams into my swollen eyes. The evil sliver of daylight from a haphazardly closed curtain was to blame. As I tried for movement, my ears were ringing and my jaw felt like I took a punch the night before. Nothing compared to the excruciating sting above my right eye, until you took survey of my intestinal tract. Alcohol was once again my enemy.

Reaching for the phone by the bed, I squinted and found the button for room service. Somehow, I found the strength to speak. "Hello, I'm in room 317. Would you please bring me a pot of coffee, hot milk, and the rancher breakfast? Thirty minutes? Okay, thank you."

Replacing the handset, I contemplated going back to sleep until room service arrived. I opened a wary eye and saw it was almost nine. I didn't need to be downstairs for two hours, but there wasn't enough time to sleep, eat, and get ready. Duty called. As I worked to get out of bed, my queasy stomach rolled in remembrance of last night's overindul-gence. There was a half-full bottle of water sitting at the bedside table. I opened the lid and chugged it down as if my life depended on it. It would either help or it would make me throw up. As I made my way to standing, it felt like the ground was rushing up at me. Breathe, I told myself. Stumbling all the way, it was time for a shower.

As the hot water ran down my back, I thought about last night. In the light of day, I was even more embarrassed that I cried in front of Travis. He was so nice, and those soft hands, how he wiped away my tears, it was unbelievable. He must be a great dad. What a strange and intense night it turned out to be. Maybe it was what I needed. After all, when was the last time I had a real conversation? Lately, Nathan and I seemed to spend most of our time bickering. Even in the beginning, we didn't have the kind of openness I'd experienced last night. It must be true what they say, sometimes it is easier to talk to a stranger.

Turning the knobs to off, I took one towel and wound it around my long blonde hair. I'd recently had it trimmed and added bangs so it was easier to manage. Finding a second towel, I dried myself and put on a white robe. There was a knock at the door. Thank goodness, breakfast had arrived. Tightening the sash, I went to answer.

"Good morning, Ms. Craig. Where would you like the tray?"

I gestured toward the sofa and coffee table and looked on as the man set the table for me. Turning, he handed me the bill. I quickly added a tip and signed. "Thank you so much."

"Of course. Have a great day."

As soon as the door was closed, I practically ran for the coffee. The only thing stopping me was the ever-present pain in my head. It actually felt like my brain was moving around in there. Settling into the sofa, I poured the warm milk and coffee into a cup. One sip…two… three…okay, now the world was making sense.

I realized I hadn't spoken to Nathan since I left the morning before. I wondered if there were any messages from him. I went for the phone and as I did, I saw a notification but it was from Travis. I re-read the last message he sent the night before. It made me laugh. He was funny and sweet. Looking at the call log, there were no missed calls from Nathan, but it was only 6:45 a.m. on the west coast. Since he worked from home and had no commute, he was probably still asleep.

⁂

THE MASSIVE SHOWROOM FLOOR WAS BUSY. A FEW VENDORS were putting the last touches on their booth installations. The doors would open in less than an hour.

As I stood with my new work group, I studied our setup. Video cameras of all shapes and sizes were installed on faux walls and covered every square inch of the space. Walls of monitors proudly displayed the images, ensuring no move would go unobserved.

While we waited for our VP of Sales to arrive, people joked and shook hands. Some hadn't seen one another since the last conference, giving them a lot to catch up on. The team was comprised of twelve, me being the only female.

Robert arrived and made his way over. "Hey there." He spoke slowly, as if still recovering from his evening of debauchery.

"Good morning, Robert. How was the rest of your night, or dare I ask?"

He smiled and looked away. I'd been around long enough to get his drift. "What about you? You took off with Travis?"

I'd expected the inquiry and knew the answer would sound fishy, even though it was innocent. "Yeah, I was a little wrecked and I had to go. When there were no cabs outside, for some reason I thought I could just walk back to the hotel. Thankfully, Travis saw me leave and walked me back."

Our VP, Lori Haines, arrived which saved me from his follow-up questions. Lori's long legs and four-inch heels silenced the group. A few guys were ogling which should have shocked me, since she was their boss's boss, but it didn't. For the first time in my career, the organization I worked for employed a woman in an important leadership position. Although a woman was at the helm, aside from me there were no other females in the sales division.

Approaching us, her cool blue eyes peered down at me. "Good morning, Madeline."

"Good morning, Lori," I replied.

"Robert let me know that you introduced him to Kim and Carly from SI yesterday. We've been trying to open a door with them for a while. Do you think you could work on getting their group to test our products? They are one of the largest northwest-based integrators and having them on our side would be a win for us all."

"I'm happy to give it a try. Kim and Carly are great, but we'd do better to work through Tom Manning. If we get his stamp of approval, we're golden."

"Perfect. Will you get them to our party tonight?"

No pressure, I thought. "Let me see what I can do."

She didn't stop there. "Did you also meet with Travis Baker and Charles Bradford from Swift?"

Was there nothing the woman didn't know? "We did. A group of us went for drinks after the President's Reception."

"Terrific, get them there as well. I'm counting on you." With that, she and her sleek brown bun turned and walked to the front of the group. Let the kickoff begin.

As she addressed the team, I wondered how challenging it

would be to accommodate her request. Then I remembered that Robert had a certain amount of pull. He could take care of getting Carly, Kim, and Tom to the party and I would see about Travis. The least I could do after his knight-like escort was to invite him to the hippest event of the week. Hopefully, he didn't already have plans. I felt a pang of excitement at the prospect of seeing him again, followed by an instant sense of remorse. Time to tune back into the present. They were paying me to do a job.

Lori's final comments kicked me into gear. "All right team, this is an important week for us. I need everyone to bring their 'A' game to the table. Pay attention to your schedule, meet prospects, and above all, show our customers a great time. Hands in the center."

The team closed in around Lori, stacking hands as she led us in a final cheer, "Go WVI."

The group mimicked in unison, "Go WVI."

Since I wasn't scheduled to work booth detail until 1 p.m., I thought it a good idea to get some fresh air and a bite beforehand. The breakfast I'd ordered was premature. Since my stomach was still rolling when it arrived, I only managed a piece of bacon for fear it might come back up. Now that I was feeling a little better, I was getting hungry.

Making my way to the exit and the streets outside, I crossed the intersection in search of a quiet place to sit. Already many of the restaurants were filled with suits and even a skirt or two, all waiting for the official bell signifying the start of SSI 2018. I ventured a little further from the venue. As I walked, I pulled out my phone. Tomorrow Peter would be having surgery. I wanted him to know I was thinking of him so I sent a text, certain he'd ignore my call if I phoned.

Good morning son. I'm thinking of you and sending posi-

tive thoughts. I know everything will be okay and I hope you do too. I love you. Call if you need anything.

I didn't expect a reply. In fact, I'd be alarmed if he texted back since it would be so out of character. All I could do was hope for the best while giving him the assurance that his mother was there for him, even if she was 2,000 miles away.

THE SECURITY SUMMIT INTERNATIONAL WAS IN FULL SWING. As I entered the venue, one of the officers verified my badge allowing me to scan through the turnstile. Each year the SSI conference attracted over 20,000 security professionals. Vendors displayed their latest technology and software developments while customers perused the isles.

Some came strictly to observe the hired "booth babes," most of whom were adult entertainers, daylighting for some extra cash. It was easy to pick out the hired help. There were few females in attendance, and the ones who were "models" dressed in costume-like business attire. They bought their skin-tight dresses from Forever 21, paired them with glass heels and last night's makeup. It was a look that spoke to the majority of the crowd, making it harder for the real women in security to retain credibility. I didn't blame the women; in a way, I admired them. Theirs was an honest existence. They earned money playing into the yearnings of men. When someone propositioned them, they didn't have to delicately tap dance around ego. Instead, they either accepted or declined the interested party's advances, doing so without the veil of professionalism clouding the way. They were there to earn money and no one seemed to mind.

I wove my way through the conference floor until I found

our booth. Robert was already in place. I approached him. "Hey there," I said.

"Madeline. You missed Travis. He stopped by to see how you were."

Robert's tone was suggestive and I knew I needed to put things in check before the rumor mill went rampant. Men could go to these conferences, hook up with "entertainers," and have all the folly imaginable, but if a woman did anything, it would be exaggerated and follow her throughout the incestuous industry. "Great, did you ask him to the cocktail party tonight?"

"I did. Even gave him the ticket."

"Thank you. I was going to reach out to him when I got here but that solves that."

Robert said in a teasing manner, "He was disappointed that he missed you."

"I'm sure he was being nice. We had a good talk last night. From what I gleaned, he's a very devoted family man and caring person."

Robert sputtered a little. "I'm sure he is."

The vestiges of my hangover were still clinging and I wasn't in the mood. "Anyway, I have a client coming soon. I'd better drop my bag and get organized."

"Okay. Do you want any help with the customer?"

"Thanks, but Brock and I have known each other for years. We have a few things to catch up on. If he has questions I can't answer, I'll get one of the engineers to join. For certain I'll introduce you at the party. He's the head of security for FutureShape."

Hearing this caused Robert's eyes to light up. "Really? They're the world's largest computer company."

He stated this as if it were news to me. "Yes, they are. I'm going to give him an overview of the products that best fit with their infrastructure. If he gives me the green-light, I'll ask them to test some of our cameras in their facilities."

He spewed, "That could be enormous. Do you know they have over two hundred US facilities, not to mention their global footprint?" His speech was excited and doled out rapid-fire style.

"I do. Let's take one step at a time. Excuse me, Robert. I'm going to prepare."

Opening the door to the coat closet, I stepped inside. It was quiet in the cramped space and it gave me a moment to check my phone one last time before the meeting. I saw a text notification from Travis. *Hello Madeline. I stopped by to check on you and spoke to Robert. He invited me to your event tonight. I can make it.*

An unstoppable smile crossed my lips as I replied, *Sorry I missed you and thank you for checking on me. I can't begin to tell you how grateful I am you put up with me last night. It's embarrassing what a mess I was. I'll see you around 6?*

Before I could place my phone back into the bag, it buzzed. I opened the message and read it. *I enjoyed every minute of our walk. Looking forward to seeing you tonight. I'll be the guy holding a package of double-stuffed Oreos.*

ONLY WISHING

Dusk fell, blanketing the top of the buildings in a faint pink hue. The evening was still and the temperature had dropped to under eighty degrees, making the scene as ideal as any movie set. The cocktail party had just begun and already the rooftop deck was alive with the sound of voices. Servers were lighting Tiki torches and tabletop candles, for in no time, it would be dark. I looked toward the bar and noticed the bulk of my teammates, bellied up and flirting with the pretty bartenders.

I half listened to the VP of Security of TransTruck Co. share with Lori his need to update the cameras at one of their distribution facilities, and wondered again how I fell into this world. When I wasn't working, I forgot all this knowledge. Just as Etch a Sketch tracings vanish with the slightest of shakes, real life cleared my brain of details like ingress points, lens settings, and ambient lighting. When it was show time, I transitioned to the expert everyone expected. The concept that I—usually the smallest person in every room— could devise a plan to protect some of the world's largest companies assets and critical facilities, was still foreign to me. I wasn't a fraud. I'd spent years learning the technology, applying it to building design, comparing my solutions against stringent security standards. I helped create the illusion of safety. For anything a person could devise, another could circumvent, but that didn't stop the investment. People needed a little smoke and mirrors.

"Well, what do you think, Madeline?" Lori addressed me. "Are you ready to head to San Diego to take a look at Harvey's site down there?"

Harvey Ross smiled kindly. His faded blue eyes and unruly brows danced at the prospect of showing me around the facility.

"I'd be happy to. I'll give you a call next week to finalize the plans. Thank you for giving us the opportunity." I smiled graciously and it was time to extricate myself. Kim and Carly had arrived with Tom in tow. "Would you please excuse me? I need to greet a few people." I shook Harvey's hand before leaving, "It was a pleasure to meet you. Until next week?"

His handshake was firm. "Madeline, I'll speak with you then."

Making my way toward my guests, I took in their appearance. Today Carly was wearing a colorful Kaftan dress, which looked cool and comfortable. Her liquid green eyes were enhanced by its ornate pattern. Kim had chosen a simple black day to evening dress. Tom stood out against the two, for he was at least six foot five and all business. His straight blonde hair fell into a part down the middle, emphasizing an oversized nose.

As I arrived, Kim was in friendly mode. She hugged me tightly, as if we were long lost sisters, then Carly took her turn. "Don't you two look beautiful tonight?" I said. Turning toward Tom, I shook his hand and said, "Thank you for making it, Tom. I know Lori is looking forward to seeing all of you."

As soon as I finished my statement, Robert arrived on the scene. He and Carly exchanged an awkward look before greeting one another with a demure hug. Since he had just met the ladies the previous evening, I was certain he and Tom were not yet acquainted. "Tom Manning, meet Robert Grain. Tom is the technology director at SI and Robert is my new boss." The men shook hands.

A moment later, Lori joined us. After making the introductions, I stood aside as she homed in on Tom. She seemed intrigued by him.

Then it happened. Behind the group, I saw Travis arrive and my night was made. The real-life incarnation of my protector was proof that something interesting could occur. I left the group and walked toward him. As I approached, our eyes locked. The undercurrent of our silent communication drew me. It was impossible to ignore the weight of our magnetism. Before I knew it, I stood at his feet.

He spoke first. "Hey there, Shorty."

"Good evening, Travis." I smiled calmly though I could feel my heart rate flutter at his nearness and the nickname. A reminder of our hug came, as the faintest hint of lemon and spice from his cologne occupied the space between us.

His eyes looked boldly into mine and he said, "You look beautiful."

Self-consciously, I looked down at myself. The fitted black dress I wore was new. I chose it for its sheer back and the way the fabric draped around my hips. When I looked up, I thought it funny

"Thank you, and may I say you look handsome as well." He wore an untucked white shirt and tailored jeans. "Would you like a drink?"

His gaze lingered. I knew I should mind, but after our walk and the unexpected intimacy of the previous evening, I was undaunted. A part of me wanted him to see me, like very few people ever had. He finally broke the silence and said, "Sure, lead the way."

On our path to the bar, we passed the very interested Kim-and-Carly duo, and raised the eyebrows of my fellow coworkers who were still crowding the counter. I wondered what the boss thought of them. Instead of mingling with customers, the guys were playing drinking games and flirting with the staff. Maybe their actions spoke loudly to me because of my own predicament. Though I did have a valid business reason for socializing with Travis, that wasn't why I had butterflies dancing around my belly. To redirect my nerves, I asked, "Do you know what you'd like to drink?"

He stooped down and said softly, "Thanks. I'll have a Jack and Coke please."

The men stopped their play as we approached. Manners intact, I took the time to introduce him to a number of my new teammates. Leaving them to chat, I bellied up to the bar to place our drink order. As the bartender approached, it was all the clarity necessary to understand why the men were immobile. The woman was striking. Her silky tanned skin and pale blue eyes were complimented by a short afro. She greeted me with a smooth smile and asked, "What can I get you?"

"I'll take a double Jack and Coke and a vodka soda with lime, please."

She smiled and poured the cocktails. "Here you go, hon."

I thanked her and made my way back toward the guys. When I reached Travis, I held out his drink. "Thank you, Madeline." He lifted his glass toward mine and toasted, "Here's to Oreos and Atlanta."

A small chuckle came before my glass joined his. "Cheers."

Her networking timing down to a science, Lori approached and I made the introductions. "Lori Haines, meet Travis Baker. Travis, Lori is our VP."

"Good to meet you, Lori." I noticed Travis voice was even deeper as he said hello.

"And you, Travis." Lori spoke firmly and her eyes smiled. "Would you like to have a seat?"

"Sounds great," he confirmed. "After all day at the conference, my feet could use a break."

Lori cut a path through the crowd. Along the way people vied for her attention, but a laser focus kept her moving forward. We found a small cocktail table near the railing. The view of the setting sun and surrounding buildings were an impressive backdrop, paving the way for the kind of meaningful conversation that leads to large sales. As the pleasantries began, I saw Robert. He motioned for me to join him. Sheldon had arrived. I stood and addressed Travis and Lori. "Would you excuse me? I need to greet Sheldon Bright."

Lori's eyes narrowed and she said, "Say hello for me. Let him know I'll stop over in a while."

Travis looked up and smiled sympathetically. He understood it was my job to mingle. As the night wore on I did my duty, chatting with most of the clients in attendance. By the end of the evening, I had plenty of business to follow up on. Things were finally winding down.

Throughout the night I checked on Travis. Each time I looked his way, his attention was on me. No matter where I stood, I had the sense he was keeping an eye on me. I liked the feeling, which wasn't good.

Finally, the event was coming to an end. I found my way back to him. He was the lone participant at the table. Seeing him there, I knew he was waiting for me and it felt like my night was just beginning. That was when Kim and Carly arrived with Robert in tow.

Travis stood. "Hey, everyone."

Robert gathered chairs so there'd be enough for us all to sit. When everyone was settled, Carly's animated questioning began. "I understand you were saved last night."

"Saved?" I asked.

Kim chimed in, her normally meek voice was raised, "Yes, of all people, you should know how dangerous it is to walk alone in the middle of the night and in a strange city. What were you thinking?"

Shit, this was embarrassing. Obviously, my departure was not missed by the group. It would be tough to explain my mental status without going into a lot of very personal detail.

The tinge of a sneer evident in her tone, Carly continued, "Thankfully this big, strong man came to your rescue."

Before I could say anything to save face, Travis diffused the situation. "It worked out since I was ready to call it a night."

Still, Carly's attention never left me. I knew I needed to say something to redirect the accusation. "If someone hadn't been such a pusher and forced us all to drink shots, maybe I could have hung in a little longer."

They all laughed, including Carly. Kim said, "Yeah, thanks to that same 'someone,' I had the worst hangover in the world this morning."

Carly reveled in being the instigator of our long night out. "What if we do it all over again tonight!"

Robert chimed in first, a devilish smile played on his lips, "I'm game."

Kim answered next, "Okay, count me in."

Suddenly, my coworkers who'd spent the evening

hovering around the bar arrived at our table. Robert made the introductions. Now that the party had grown from five to twelve, no plans could be made; instead a night of spontaneity lay ahead. The staff were busy extinguishing candles and carrying chairs inside. It was time for us to go.

Carly rallied the troops. Walking at the front of the crowd, she said, "Okay, everyone, let's go to our next spot."

The group followed as if she were the Pied Piper. We filed down the corridor and somehow fit into one elevator. The air was perfumed by alcohol, sweat, and the occasional reprieve as I got a whiff of Travis' cologne. Soon the doors opened and we flooded the lobby, spilling forward and onto the city streets.

Carly marched ahead. Her determined cork heels lit the way to better places and we were off. Travis and I brought up the rear. I couldn't help but wonder where Carly and the night would lead us. Ahead was a red phone booth; Carly stopped in front of it. She yelled at the group, silencing everyone. We watched as she opened the door and went inside. I found it strange that we were waiting for her to make a phone call and why didn't she use her cell? After replacing the receiver, she addressed the group. "Okay, we're in, but there's one problem. Only ten of us can enter. The other two have to wait until a couple of people leave." It was a speakeasy and they were near capacity.

There it was, the moment that changed everything. A fork in the road was placed in front of us. I felt a tap on my back and looked up to see Travis' eyes meet mine. Knowing what he wanted, I took the cue and walked to the front of the group. When I made it to Carly's side, I said, "You guys go ahead. Travis and I will pass for now."

Carly smiled cynically before turning and disappearing through the hidden door. Kim was next to pass. As I watched the others squish through the narrow entry, I knew that tomorrow would bring strongly suggested rumors about us. No matter how innocent the situation, it was already assumed that something was going on between Travis and me.

After the last of them entered, only he and I remained. For a moment, we stood awkwardly. He broke the silence first, "Are you hungry?"

Who could eat at a time like this? My words betrayed me. "I am, actually."

"Me too. Do you like burgers?"

"Nope. I love burgers."

He taunted, "Oh yeah, then why don't you marry them?"

His playground joke was made to disarm the tension between us, but that was impossible. I wanted to repeat the connection we'd had the previous evening and I knew that was wrong. Travis belonged to someone else. I was out of line for wanting even a small part of him. Still, I rationalized, his family wasn't here tonight and if we handled ourselves, he and I could be friends.

Keeping the banter light, I said, "Wow, you really went there."

He chuckled and a deep, comforting sound filled the air. "Touché. Come on, Shorty. I know just the place."

We walked the few blocks in silence, lost in our own thoughts. It should have been odd but it wasn't. From the instant I set eyes on Travis, I had the overwhelming sense I already knew him. Though we were strangers to one another, there seemed to be an unspoken knowledge between us.

We arrived at a 24-hour diner; red neon lights flashed OPEN. "This is us. I hope you're hungry." He held the door for me.

We were greeted by a very cheerful young woman, wearing a red and white striped dress and joker's hat.

Surveying the space, I saw an arcade area and the kind of booths that families settled into while munching on banana splits. It was a nice switch from the stuffy establishments I usually dined at while traveling. We followed the hostess to a table by the window and settled in opposite each other. Accepting the oversized menus, we heard about the specials. "Today's soup is beer cheese and the cocktail is the Hawaiian Punch. Don't let the name fool you. It's no kids drink. Your server will be right over."

Travis grinned and said, "She's not kidding about the Hawaiian Punch. I haven't been here in quite some time yet I still remember that cocktail. They picked the right name for sure."

Not only was I still reeling from my alcohol intake the previous evening, I knew it was prudent to keep my bearings. Never before had I found myself in a situation like this. Over the years I'd worked with many people, most of them married men, yet none had ever compelled me the way he did. It was time to set us both up for success so I said, "That's a little scary. I'll stick with water."

Before Travis could respond, our server arrived. "Hi, you two. I'm Rachel. How are you tonight?"

Travis joked, "Grateful, for your air-conditioning."

She laughed and batted her eyelashes before responding, "It is a hot night. Do you all know what you'd like to drink?"

He spoke up and said, "One punch and a couple of glasses of water, please."

Her cornflower blue eyes danced with excitement. "Great choice. You're in for a fun time. What about the food? Have you decided?"

He asked, "Could you give us a few minutes, please?"

"I'll get your drink order in and check back on you." With that, Rachel was on her way.

"Daring move, sir," I kidded him.

He replied, "I took a risk and hopefully it'll pay off. You see, I can't possibly finish that drink on my own. Will you be my partner in crime?"

The double entendre, intentional or not, weighed on me. I had a quick mental conversation with myself. I was more than capable of doing the right thing. I'd made it over forty years on the planet, and in all that time I'd never crossed the moral line of getting involved with a married man one drink would not change that. I vocalized my intentions, "You may be out on that limb all by yourself."

A flash of disappointment crossed Travis' face and I wondered if we were dancing too closely to the fire. Time to lighten things up. I commented, "This menu is enormous. Since you've been here before, what do you suggest?"

He smiled wide. Apparently, he was passionate about his burgers. "The jungle is my go-to. It has just about everything you could imagine on a burger and some stuff you've never even thought of. Will you share it with me?"

As I read the description, it became clear that I would need a fork and knife to tackle even half of that feast. "How are we going to share a burger with beef, fried chicken, bacon, egg, and all of that other stuff? This is going to be messy."

He grinned from ear to ear. "Good thing you're wearing black."

Just then Rachel returned with our drinks. My puny glass of water paled in comparison to the yard-high, bright red, pineapple-garnished monstrosity he'd selected. I didn't miss that there were two metal straws in the glass. "Have you decided on some food?"

I pointed to Travis who relished in ordering. "We are

going to share the jungle. Would you please bring extra ranch and hot sauce?"

"No problem," she said, and left.

I said, "We're going to be crawling out of here."

Travis pursed his lips as if contemplating something important. "You haven't lived until you've tried their Hawaiian Punch."

What could it hurt? I reached for a straw and as I leaned forward, he stopped me. "Wait." He took a hold of his own straw. "On the count of three, start drinking. The person who stops first loses."

This could turn into trouble quickly. "Wait a minute. I didn't order this concoction. I was only going to give it a try." The warning bells were a distant whisper. I convinced myself that it would be a fun drinking game and maybe it would lead to another real conversation.

"Okay then. Don't play if you're too chicken." He shrugged one shoulder as he teased.

That did it. Tightening my grip on the straw, I met his eyes with determination. "Start counting."

"One . . . two . . . three!"

I drank and it did taste exactly like Hawaiian Punch. The alcohol content was either very low or the drink was so well blended that it was undetectable. I was also thirsty, which helped me continue guzzling, but how could I compete with a man more than twice my size in a drinking contest? My stomach ached and a cool, dull bubble complained to my throat, *Stop, we're filling up too quickly.* Rather than cough red liquid from my nose, I resigned to the fact that I would lose the game. A second before I stopped slurping, Travis pulled back and gasped for air. We took our time catching our breath and I studied our progress with the drink. It was gone.

When he spoke, I could see his tongue had turned deep red. "You won."

I didn't feel like a winner and wondered if he let me win but I owned it anyway. "Ha! I did and you were so sure of yourself."

"Not at all. You just seem like a person who doesn't back down from a challenge. I got you to do what I wanted. Do you really think I needed that whole drink?" He smirked as he patted his stomach.

The impulse to smack his arm was unstoppable. I did it, then remembered myself. "Oh, sorry." I said it, but did I mean it?

"Can't say I blame you. I kind of left myself open for that one." He chuckled. "Were you okay this morning? I mean, that was a pretty late night. How were you feeling?"

A shiver ran up my spine in recollection. "It was rough for a while but I'm feeling much better now. I wonder what tomorrow will bring?" I laughed. "Hey, was there alcohol in that?" I gestured toward the empty glass.

A sly smile played on his full lips. "A little."

"Great," I said. "Well, the good news is, I do remember how to get back to the hotel from here."

He tilted his head as if considering, then said, "That depends on your perspective."

Confused, I asked, "What does?"

He looked serious for a moment. "I'm not sure if it's good news that you know how to get back to the hotel on your own. If it weren't for your quandary last night, I wouldn't have had the chance to get to know you."

Were we tap dancing around something? "I don't know what I would have done if you hadn't shown up. I was a mess."

"I'm glad it worked out the way that it did." His tone

became serious. "Things could have turned out very differently had I not seen you leave."

Maybe he was nice. "I have to tell you, I'm not usually prone to tears. You caught me in rare form."

He reassured me, "You had every reason to be upset. If one of my kids were sick, I can't imagine how I would handle that."

Curiosity, and the strange comfort I felt as I sat across from him, egged me on. "Now that you've seen me at my worst, and you know some very personal details about my life, it's only fair that I learn a little something about you."

I couldn't read his expression, but his downcast glance told me he may have some sadness of his own. "What can I tell you about my life? It isn't all that interesting. We live in the suburbs of Chicago and I've been there since high school. I met my wife after college. Mutual friends introduced us. We hit it off and the timing seemed right so we married within the year. Sixteen years, three kids, and a mortgage later, life is different. When I'm not working, life revolves around the kids. They're active in sports and academics so it is a full-time job getting them places, not to mention watching them in action."

His face lit up when he spoke of his children. I couldn't stop myself so I asked, "And your wife, what does she do?"

"She hasn't worked since the kids came along. Her life is about them, shopping, and her family. They're all close by so she sees them a lot."

Had I crossed the line with that question? His face was stoic. Thankfully, Rachel arrived at the table carrying a skyscraper-sized burger.

"Here you go, kids." She slid a second plate from beneath the tower and placed it in front of me. "Do you need anything else at the moment?"

My eyes were about to roll out of my head. Travis replied, "No, thank you."

"Good luck with it." She smiled and left us to dismantle the beast.

With the ease of a surgeon, Travis carved through the sandwich. As I looked on, I couldn't help but admire his sure hands. He smoothly navigated the process and before I knew it, my plate was heaping with layers of the artery-clogging food. His grey eyes danced. "The trick is, you have to taste everything at once. Let me help."

He cut a wedge and filled the fork to the brim before foisting the utensil toward me. I opened as wide as possible and my mouth was as full as a squirrel hoarding nuts. Another humbling moment as my new friend watched me struggle to chew the enormous bite. Finally, I could talk. "That was really good. Thank you."

He smiled and devoured a forkful himself. His cheeks were filled to capacity and I had to admire the gusto with which he tackled the giant burger. We ate silently for a few minutes until Rachel reappeared. "How are you two doing? Should I bring over another Hawaiian Punch?"

I shook my head, eyes pleading with Travis. Another of those and I would be out. He smiled and replied, "I don't think the lady can handle it. We're good for now, thanks."

After she left Travis addressed me and I had no way to anticipate what was coming. "You're probably wondering why I'm here with you."

Trying to rebound, I replied to his unexpected candor in kind. "You're probably right. Why are you?"

He took a sip of water and looked me dead in the eye. "I wasn't planning to be out last night. In fact, I was already in my room when Charles called and said the girls wanted to go to Karaoke. Most of the time when I travel, I spend the evenings working from my hotel. If I hadn't come out, you and I probably wouldn't have met."

I thought about what he said. "Same here. I had just finished at the President's Reception. Robert and I were with a customer when he suggested the night cap. It was definitely a coincidence that we met."

His next words pinned me. "I couldn't wait to meet you."

The brief silence seemed eternal. "What do you mean?"

"I noticed you the minute you walked into the bar. Mostly because the girls pointed you out and started talking about you."

I wasn't surprised to hear that and I wondered what they said, but decided against asking. After tonight, the rumors about Travis and me would be rampant. In the security industry, anything involving a woman need not be true nor proven to be written in stone. If I would pay the price, at least let me get something interesting out of it. "What did you notice?"

He hesitated before saying, "I don't want to give you the wrong impression. I'm not the guy who goes to conferences and uses that as a way to have fun while I'm away from home."

My silence gave him the room to continue.

"You looked," he paused as if considering his words carefully, "out of place and at the same time, completely at home. Clearly, you know a lot of people and those who don't know you, want to. You walked with the kind of confidence that turned heads, yet something told me you were actually uncomfortable. To be honest, I was mesmerized by you."

I didn't know how to react to his observations. Once again, I was embarrassed by his purview. How did he have such insights? I had to diffuse the situation and said, "You are so out of practice." I laughed at him. "What kind of pick-up line is that? Don't you know you're supposed to act like a jerk before asking if I'm *really* going to finish my burger?"

His intense gaze rested on me. "You look like you could use the meal."

I had so many questions. I knew our circumstances were such that I had no right to ask. Instead, I stuck with the safety of the burger and forked a mound into my mouth. As I swallowed the bite, I tested, "I bet you had a different perspective about me after our walk back."

He raised his eyebrows. "You're right. I did."

He wasn't making it easy on me. "And?"

"And what?" he mocked.

"What did you think about me after our walk?"

He took in a breath before speaking. "I hope this doesn't scare you or somehow sound sexist." I was braced for anything now. "I think you are incredibly special and that you're the kind of person who takes care of everyone else. It made me wonder who takes care of you."

I was instantly saddened and it wasn't his fault. He had no way of knowing my life or the circumstances that happened before I arrived. As far back as I could remember, I felt a duty to take care of everyone and everything around me. Anytime I shared problems with friends or family, the same comments were made. "You're a strong person. You'll get through this." If I told him the truth, would our dynamic change? What dynamic? We'd just met the day before.

"I'm kind of independent, I guess." If I didn't mention my recently ended relationship now it would be odd, so I brought it forward. "I live with someone."

His eyes narrowed and I prepared myself for his next question. "What's that like?"

I contemplated his question and the best way to answer. "It's not all that easy. We're pretty different and there's a lot of tension between him and my son. We've been together, on and off, for five years now. He's moving out as we speak."

He looked at the table then back at me, "I have an idea."

I wondered aloud, "Oh yeah?"

"I know we're strangers and there are a lot of reasons why we shouldn't change that."

I had to agree. "True."

He said, "Let's change that."

Was he propositioning me? His tone and demeanor didn't seem lustful, yet I had to wonder where he was going with that statement. "How so?"

He looked flustered and replied, "Wow, I just realized how that sounded. I am not trying to be forward. It's just . . ."

I wanted to put him at ease. I also wanted to know what he was getting at. "It's what?"

He was silent for a moment. It seemed like he was working something out. "I wasn't meant to be at that bar last night and neither were you. You left the place not knowing where you were going. You didn't even say goodbye. I don't think it was just a coincidence that I saw you leave or that we found ourselves together in the first place."

I could agree with that. "Okay, I see your point."

"This might sound dumb, but I believe that everything happens for a reason."

I used to think that way, though current circumstances caused me to question pretty much everything. Still, I wanted to hear his theory. "What are you thinking?"

"I'm thinking that we were meant to meet and even though you are strong, someone needs to keep an eye on you. I know that it isn't my place, but I'd still like to be your friend."

If we were to be friends, he would need to know the real me. My directness might scare him away and if it did, that would be fine. "What would your wife think about us being friends?"

His eyes didn't falter. "She wouldn't like it."

"Then why do it?" I had to know.

"Because we've never had the kind of open conversation you and I did last night. When I get home from a trip, it doesn't even register for her. Half the time she has her nose buried in her phone, even when we're driving places. Sometimes I feel like I could leave, and as long as the bills were paid, she wouldn't even notice."

I looked at him and tried to decipher if he was being honest or simply making the same excuse you always hear married men tell the soon-to-be side chick. Still, he painted a convincing image. He was kind enough to listen to my sob story, so the least I could do was show him the same courtesy. "You don't really feel that way, do you?"

His face was crestfallen. "I do. We've had a lot of conversations about it. She even admits she's not the same person she was before we were married. We tried counseling, but that didn't go very far."

I was curious about his experience since Nathan and I had also gone to counseling. It was an interesting waste of time. Before each session, he and I would negotiate the things we would and would not discuss, leaving the toughest issues for our own private rumination. "My ex and I tried counseling too. How was it for you?"

He sniffed. "It was good for a while. I was able to share my frustrations and I learned some of hers. After a few sessions, things seemed to be moving in a better direction so we stopped going."

"Can I ask, did you ever agree to leave certain issues out of your talks?"

He chuckled cynically. "We did. The stuff we really

should have opened up about, somehow got swept under the rug. I was happy for the little bit of appreciation she began showing me after the sessions. For a while, it felt like we were making headway. What about you?"

"Same here. We got a lot of good advice about communication, but shortly after we stopped going, things went back to the way they were."

"And what does that mean?" he asked.

I grappled with the situation. If I told him about my relationship, if I let him in, was that wrong? Then I realized he understood. I convinced myself that he may have some great insight, a tidbit of perspective that could even help me see things differently.

I shared with him our latest and final argument. As I did, I wondered why I was telling this personal story to a stranger and one whose intentions I did not know. When I was finished, to my surprise, he didn't offer an opinion. Instead, he said, "I'm sorry you were treated that way and after what you're already going through with your boy."

He paused for a beat, then inquired, "What about Peter's father? Is he in the picture?"

After all of these years, the question of Peter's biological father still caused me angst. Reasoning it was better to get it over with, I said, "No, he's not."

"Sore subject?" he asked.

"You could say that."

He ventured, "Can I ask what happened?"

"Oh, you can." It was my turn to stare out the window. I wrestled for a time until the floodgate lifted and the words spilled out of me. "I met Parker during my freshman year in college. He and I were in the same sociology class. At first, he was so crazy about me and he showed it. For a while there, we were inseparable."

As I flashed back to the time, I was no longer angry. "Parker was Mr. I Love You. He couldn't say it enough and talked all the time about how he couldn't wait to start our life together. I can still remember the way he looked at me, like I was the only person in the world. We'd only been dating for a few months when I found out I was pregnant. When I told him, he said he was happy. The only proof that he wasn't came in the form of the letter he left me before dropping out of school and leaving town. After that, I never saw him again."

Travis' jaw clenched and his eyes narrowed. When he finally spoke, I could hear his thinly veiled rage. "What kind of man leaves a woman on her own at a time like that? Not to mention his unborn child . . ."

I wouldn't come to his defense, but I used the same line on Travis that I'd told Peter all those years, "The kind of man who is only a boy. The type of person who can't take care of himself, let alone a family; at least that's what I've always told Peter."

Travis' expression was unreadable as he processed the information I shared. He said, "The guy just walked out on you?"

It was a rhetorical question and I remained silent.

He raked his hands through his hair and continued. "How any man could walk out on a woman in that position is beyond me, let alone when that woman is you. Even more confusing is the grace you give him. I'm sure it would have been easier to let anger influence you. Clearly you took the high road."

A sardonic smile crossed my lips and I said, "It's better than telling your child that he is the offspring of a blue-eyed, ginger-haired sociopath."

My joke missed the mark, for Travis' expression remained serious. "I suppose." He paused. "You never looked for him?"

"No," I replied. "To me, if he could walk out like that, I wouldn't force him to be a part of our lives. I only hoped my love for Peter would somehow be enough to make up for his father's absence."

I realized that once again, I'd bared my soul to this man, who only yesterday was unknown. Aside from my closest friends, most people considered me to be a private person. With Travis, the words seemed to flow. "I seem to be doing all of the talking. What about you?"

"What about me?" He paused in consideration. "I'm lucky in so many ways and I have Jenny to thank for it. She gave me three beautiful children. Every day I am amazed by them." He stared out the window as if recalling the time. "We'd been dating less than a year when we got married. Needless to say, we didn't know each other very well, let alone ourselves. Before you get married everyone is always telling you how hard it is, but you never understand until it's your turn. Life has a way of taking over and pretty soon, the small spaces between you become wide gaps. I guess that's where we are today."

What a beautiful and sad summation, I thought. I appreciated his words, but experience caused me to question his motives. Was he for real or had he missed his casting call? I needed to say something pertinent. "It's kind of normal to get lost in life once you start a family. Maybe when your kids are grown, you guys will rekindle the spark that brought you together. She must be pretty special if you were married within a year of dating."

The smile didn't reach his eyes. In fact, he looked sad. "We were young and having fun. It was the kind of next step that made sense at the time."

That was a strong admission. I wondered what it was like to take care of a family yet feel like an outsider in your own life. Then I realized I didn't need to ponder that question. I already knew the answer. We had more in common than I expected.

Rachel arrived just in time to lighten the mood. She surveyed the nearly empty plates and asked, "Should I clear these or are you guys still working?"

I held my hands up and Travis replied for the two of us. "Would you? I'll take the check as well. Thank you."

Once she departed, Travis leaned in and asked, "Are you ready for our next adventure?"

I had no idea what he had in mind but I didn't care. It had been years since I'd felt this kind of openness with anyone. Maybe it wasn't ideal to make friends with a married man but I was only human. We'd shared some deeply personal information about our lives and I sensed he needed the company as much as I did. Why couldn't we be friends?

"I will be, after a visit to the ladies' room. Seems I'm floating after a certain somebody challenged me to a drinking contest."

"Sorry about that," he said with a laugh. "I'll meet you out front when you're ready."

☙❧

THE BRIGHT FLUORESCENT LIGHTS CAST SHADOWS ON MY FACE and there was no place to hide. As I washed my hands, I studied myself in the bathroom mirror. Alone with my thoughts, I had to be honest. The conversation Travis and I were having could be dangerous. Although I didn't know his intentions, I could at least empathize with the way he felt. I knew what it was to be in a relationship without intimacy. I also knew there were two sides to every situation and his wife may have a different perspective on things.

Was I being selfish by spending time with him? I was. He was married, with a family, yet I wanted to find comfort and some deeper meaning in our acquaintance. For now, it was a lovely escape from reality. Who could blame me? Tomorrow, my only son would undergo surgery and someone named Sarah would be there to take care of him. My fiancé was no more. Selfish or not, I was human and I needed to get through this period of time. Talking to Travis didn't need to turn into anything more than it already was. We could be friends. Over the years I'd worked with mainly men, a number of whom I called friends, and I'd never concerned myself with their marital status.

Tossing the damp towel in the bin, I opened the door and made my way out front. When I walked outside I saw him looking at his phone. He turned in my direction as I approached. He was good-looking, but not in the obvious sort of way. A giant to me, his large frame was complimented by manly features. I loved the way his nose looked as if it could take a punch and probably had. He may not be the guy that made ladies do a double take, but once you got to know him, heard his bass-filled voice, and saw the way his eyes lit up as he spoke of his kids, that was his big appeal. He was a real person.

He asked, "Well, are you ready for our next stop?"

Not sure what he had in store, I was a little reluctant, but knew I had the power to stop the evening at any time. "What did you have in mind?"

His playful expression matched his words. "You'll see. We don't have far to go and you'll still know the way back to the hotel once we get there."

Teasing, I said, "How reassuring."

"Come on," he said with a smile, "This way."

For a few minutes, we walked quietly. Then he asked, "Were you able to talk with your son today?"

Unfortunately, I hadn't, nor was I particularly surprised by his lack of a response to my text. "No. I sent him a message but he didn't get back to me. The surgery is scheduled for nine tomorrow morning. Hopefully, I'll be able to talk to him before he goes in."

Travis was quiet for a few minutes. I wondered what he was thinking about and how he perceived the distance between my son and me. From what he shared about his children, it sounded like they were close.

Suddenly, he stopped walking and pointed ahead. "There it is, our next stop."

I followed his gaze and was horrified at what I saw. It was a Ferris wheel and I was deathly afraid of them. Frozen, I stared. The silence must have been longer than I realized.

Travis said, "Earth to Madeline."

We'd shared some honest truths with one another, what was one more? "I can't do that."

He was obviously confused. "What do you mean?"

I felt like such an idiot. "I am totally afraid of heights, and Ferris wheels in particular."

He chuckled, placed a hand on my shoulder, and gently shoved me forward. "Don't worry. I'll protect you," he said.

I was panicking. "No, you don't understand, I've actually been removed from Ferris wheels in the past. There's something about the moving car and no seat belts that scares the hell out of me. It's been a thing, all my life."

His expression was a mixture of challenge and disbelief. "Is that all?"

My voice hitched. "What do you mean is that all? I'm

afraid of heights. Anyone who sits next to me will have a hellish experience."

He didn't stop walking and instead spoke as if I were a child. "We can play the wishing game."

"The what?" I asked.

"The wishing game. My daughter is also afraid of Ferris wheels, so we made up this game to help her get over it."

I had no idea what the game involved and I didn't care. My panic at the prospect of going on the Ferris wheel was already causing heart palpitations. "I don't think a game will work on me. In case you haven't noticed, I am a grown up."

"I can see that." He paused and waited until I made eye contact. "Here's how it works. On the way up, you keep your eyes open and look as far as your eyes can see. As you reach the top, close your eyes and make a silent wish. Wait until you feel ready, then open your eyes and do it all over again."

"How does that make the ride any less frightening? We will still be suspended, untethered, and rocking through the air."

"Yes, but it gives you something to look forward to each time you go around because you get to make a wish, or the same wish over and over. It naturally increases the odds of your wish coming true. It's the law of averages or something. And everybody knows that nothing bad happens while you're making a wish. It's a proven fact."

"I'm sure this works on your daughter, but I'm an adult and one who really doesn't like Ferris wheels. I know it is irrational and they almost never malfunction but . . ."

He wasn't taking no for an answer. "Now I understand your problem."

"Excuse me?" I was a little miffed. "What problem?"

"You stopped wishing on stars."

He had that right. "New tack? Nice try."

"If you really don't want to go, I understand but you're missing out. The view from up there is amazing and I promise, you'll like the wishing game. You could even make a wish for your son."

"Wow, that was below the belt. What if I freak out and you see another—even more embarrassing outburst from me?"

"Then at least you'll have tried and who knows, maybe your wish will come true."

What was I thinking? I'd been here before, several times actually, and each time it turned into a mortifying scene. "If I do this, you cannot tease me."

He raised his right hand and swore, "You have my solemn promise. I will not tease you."

"I'm serious, Travis, consider yourself warned. This is not going to be fun for you and you'd better save your laughter until you get back to your hotel. Got it?"

His expression was serious, except for the smile he struggled to suppress. "You have my word. I will not tease you."

My hands were sweating. "Okay. Let's get this over with."

As we walked toward the ticket booth, my heart was pounding. This wasn't my first attempt at getting over the fear of heights. I not only doubted his wishing game would work, I was certain it wouldn't. We reached the front of the line and Travis stepped forward to talk to the teller. Taking some deep breaths, I tried to relax. I knew I needed to get a grip so I wouldn't make a complete ass of myself, again. Ahead, people were lined up awaiting their turn on the giant wheel. I watched their excited faces and tried to convince myself this time it would be different. Too soon for my comfort, the transaction was complete and we were inching toward the entry. Travis touched my shoulder. "Come along, Shorty. Let's go."

We shuffled forward until only one couple was ahead of us. I was now hyperventilating and my palms were sweating as I watched the couple enter their car. The wheel rotated and the next car—our car—arrived. After the riders before us exited, we were guided to enter. It was a supreme effort for me to step inside. As I did, the cab rocked back and forth giving me a taste of what was in store once we ascended to the top. A feeling of panic overtook me as Travis joined and the door was secured behind us.

The reality that there was no escape caused sharp pricks of fear along my spine. His leg touched mine. I looked over and was met by his tender expression. The car lurched forward, swayed a little, then stopped again to allow another group to board. At this point we were only ten feet above the ground. That didn't matter since soon we would be rising higher and I knew there was no way to stop our momentum. Fear overtook sense and I thought I may scream.

His soothing voice brought me down a notch. "Remember, keep looking straight, as far as you can into the distance." He took my hand and I had a new reason to panic. His touch was so soothing, yet I knew this was crossing the line.

The movement resumed and he leaned close. "Get ready to make your wish, but don't say it out loud." His breath caressed my ear and pulled me in. Our hands were still intertwined as the wheel resumed its circle. Rather than scream, I affixed my gaze on the horizon. The wheel jerked to a stop at the top.

"Good job. You made it." His hand tightened around mine and he said, "You get to close your eyes now."

So afraid to budge even an inch, I couldn't respond. I had forgotten that part of his game. Desperate to flee the reality of my precarious surroundings, I scrunched my eyes closed and tried to breathe normally. The gentle rocking of the car freaked me out as I silently incanted, "Please let Peter be okay. Please let Peter be okay. Please let Peter be okay."

We fell backwards and the breeze pushed my hair into my face. Gentle fingers brushed the wayward strands back into place and I had to open my eyes. When I did, I saw we were only a short distance from the top of the wheel. Before I could stop myself, I looked down and the ground rushed up at me. Though my logical mind knew we wouldn't plummet to the earth, the fear was more powerful than the truth.

"Madeline"his voice was a gentle command"look at me."

I was frozen, afraid to move even my face in his direction. A moment later, he took my chin with his free hand and turned my face toward him. Our eyes met and I felt stupid. We were on a ride for goodness sake, not the face of a steep mountain. He soothed, "It's okay. You're doing great."

I didn't want to be this woman, but I couldn't put my fears to rest or ignore the awful way the car moved. I said, "I know this is stupid."

Just then, the wheel stopped spinning. The bar that held us from above made a terrible squeaking sound. My jaw was set and my teeth clenched and in one swift move, I released his hand to grip the bottom of the bench. I stared blindly forward and had no way to judge his reaction, nor any intention of moving so I could face him.

He spoke calmly. "Madeline. You're okay. These rides make noise like every other mechanical device. It's normal."

His voice brought me down a notch and my embarrassment turned into a matter of pride. I had to find some way to recover. Mentally chastising myself, I reached for a modicum of courage and allowed my eyes to meet the horizon. We were surrounded by the city. Bright lights twinkled in the backdrop, an old brick building anchored us, and somehow, the Ferris wheel blended in. It turned gingerly, but I still had the distinct sensation we were free-falling. My self-deprecating humor arrived and I joked without moving my face. "I thought maybe you had jumped out of the cab to escape my insanity."

His chuckle was soft and deep and he said, "What, and miss this? Not a chance." He moved, which caused the car to jiggle and my hands to white-knuckle the seat beneath me. "Hey, we're almost at the bottom. You're not playing the game right."

We nearly grazed the ground then started our slow ascent back up toward the moon. I tried to focus on the good parts of the experience. I felt the gentle caress of wind on my cheek, and watched the distant street lights change from green, to yellow, and red. His shoulder against mine brought weight to the moment. I was out of my comfort zone, but lately my comfort zone was becoming dysfunctional.

Squeak, squeak. The car stopped and once again, we were at the top of the world. Fear intact, I still fucking hated Ferris wheels.

I was near hysteria when his voice took control. "Close your eyes now. Don't worry, just make your wish."

I may as well have been naked in the street, for the humiliation I was experiencing couldn't have been worse. I did as he suggested. Shutting my eyes, I silently wished, "Let Peter be okay. Let Peter be okay. Let Peter be okay. Let Peter be okay."

After a while, as if he were addressing a child he said, "Great job. Time to look."

Obediently and only because it would be more foolish to keep my eyes screwed tight, I did. We turned slowly and within moments, were once again teetering on top of the world. As I looked on, having what can only be described as an out-of-body experience, our car appeared to float in the night sky. I peered down at the ground beneath the chainmail floor. We were dangling at least six stories high, taunting gravity and in the wrong company to boot. I not only doubted my wish would be granted, but I feared our missteps would bring us crashing to the earth.

As frightened as I was, I had to admit the view was incredible. If I could quiet the terrors for a moment, I might enjoy some part of the experience. I hadn't spoken aloud in some time. After a jerky shift backwards, I steadied my nerves and said, "Don't forget your promise, Travis. There is no teasing me about this, at least not to my face. Agreed?"

He reached for my hand and yanked, causing me to release my death grip on the chair. Keeping my hand in his, he repositioned my face with his free one and said, "You have my word. I'll not tease you, not even behind your back. You're doing amazing, actually. I was prepared for a whole lot worse. My daughter used to be pretty bad. Now she just likes to do the game for fun. It's been our thing for some time now."

His features softened as he talked about his little girl. I could question his motives, even his character, but I couldn't think badly of him when he'd shared such a lovely tradition with me.

"Well, thank you for sharing the game. I can't say I'm comfortable yet, but I will say—"

I had no time to finish my thought as our car made a sudden stop. The door swung open, a signal for us to exit. As I stood, I was amazed that for a moment, brief as it was, I'd forgotten to be afraid.

We walked a while before Travis said, "But you will say?"

This seemingly insignificant admission, wasn't. "But I will say, for a very short while at the end there, it was pretty spectacular." I chided, "Thanks for twisting my arm."

"I'd rather call it gentle persuasion." His cheeks puffed and the lines at the bridge of his nose scrunched as he grinned like a kid.

I suppressed the urge to sock him and decided on the silent treatment instead.

Travis picked up the conversation, "Thank you for doing this with me. I know it was a big deal for you. You were afraid, but you convinced yourself to do it anyway. It was kind of beautiful."

Was he for real? I had to wonder how the conversation was even happening. I wanted to be clever, to say something funny to deflect from the depth of his summation, but that would have been rude. Instead, I said, "Trust me, I'm not very brave."

He stopped short, and I turned to look ahead. We had arrived at my hotel. He bent to hug me and I gave myself permission to melt into it. I took a deep breath, inhaling his cologne. When we separated he said, "You're braver than you think, Madeline. Have yourself a good night."

He turned and walked the opposite direction, leaving me speechless.

NO HOMECOMING

As the driver pulled up to the house, I could see that Nathan's car was gone. I'd expected that, still it was a strange feeling to know he wasn't coming back. I got out of the car, collected my bag, and braced myself before taking the final few steps. The door swung wide into a silent entry.

After bringing my bag inside, I closed the door and walked toward the living room. The house was spotless and a bit sparse in light of Nathan's departure. I knew he would take his belongings. It didn't stop me from missing the glorious nude charcoals that once hung above the fireplace, or the oversized tuba that doubled as a quirky side table. The room looked as barren as it felt.

I walked past the dining room and into the kitchen. There was a folded piece of paper on the counter. Nathan had scrawled "Madeline" on one side. I unfolded the page and read.

MADDIE,

I hope your trip went well. I got everything moved out while you were gone. The mail should automatically forward.
Take care and call if anything comes up,
Nathan

HIS PRESCRIPTIVE MESSAGE SHOWED NO MERCY; INSTEAD, IT underlined what was valid all along. The note slipped from my hands. That hesitance I'd blamed my damaged self for—which he had pointed out as my flaw—was deserved. Today was a nightmare of truth. I sank to the floor. My sobs ripped through the silence of the house, its walls the sole witness to my sorrow. I was completely alone.

After a time, I got up and went to the bathroom. Reflected in the mirror, was a woman with matted hair and a mascara smeared face. I looked terrible. Running the tap until the water warmed, I scooped handfuls and splashed my eyes. I shut the faucet and dried myself with a towel.

The house phone rang—which rarely happened—reminding me I'd forgotten to take my cell out of Airplane Mode. I went to answer.

"Hello."

"Hey, you were supposed to call me when you got home." My best friend, Shawna's, accusatory voice squeaked through the connection. I'd texted her the cliff notes about Nathan and I while in Atlanta, leaving the encounter with Travis out.

"Sorry. I haven't been home that long," I said.

"Are you ok?" she asked.

"I will be. It's a little strange right now, but I'll get used to it."

"Maddie, are you sure?"

Resigned, I gave her the real picture. "Look, I'm trying not to freak out, but it's hard. I still can't believe he's gone. I've already had a good cry and that's it for tonight. I plan on falling asleep while watching some mindless TV. Don't worry."

Shawna replied, "Okay, I'll check on you tomorrow. Call if you need anything, no matter what time. I'll see you next week."

"Ok. Goodnight," I said.

"Goodnight."

❦

AFTER A DREAMLESS SLEEP, I AWOKE TO THE SOUND OF THE birds dive bombing the roof. Their screeching calls were proof that I'd made it through the night. I looked at the alarm clock and saw it was 6:40 a.m. Pulling the covers back, I swung my reluctant legs over the side and stood. Smoothing the bed back into shape, I put on a robe and went downstairs to get a cup of coffee. The sound of a branch crashing to the roof stopped me. If I wanted to have my coffee in peace, I'd need to feed the birds first. I tossed several handfuls of peanuts out the front door and resumed my path toward the kitchen.

The pot was full and waiting, a result of my own foresight and self-care. Nathan always brought me coffee in bed, and it was the best waking up to the aroma. It made facing the work day a little more tolerable. I knew I'd think of him this morning, and I wanted to redirect it to the coffee, not the missing component of his personal delivery. Today I poured my own cup.

After adding cream, I removed my phone from the charger on the counter and went to the dining table. I clicked the airplane icon to activate service and settled myself in to review the messages I'd received since yesterday. After a few moments, the notifications illuminated. Several texts, emails, and voice mails had come in while my phone was turned off.

I tackled the voice mails first. Two of the messages were from Shawna, which I deleted. The last one was from my boss, Robert. I listened to his message.

"Madeline. It's Robert, calling at five twenty Thursday evening. I need a detailed update on your efforts in California this week. I've sent you an email with the metrics and information I need. Please get it to me before eight o'clock tomorrow morning."

I looked at the clock and it was a few minutes before seven. I quickly opened my work email account and scrolled until I found Robert's message. As I looked it over, there was nothing alarming. I'd already given the detail to Lori yesterday when she called to get the update.

I compiled a response to his message and checked to make sure I'd answered everything. I also attached three summaries I'd put together for the major accounts. I added Robert's name to the address bar and CC'd Lori.

GOOD MORNING, ROBERT.

I'm sorry I missed your message yesterday. It came in while I was on my return flight. Below and attached, please find the information you requested regarding the accounts I met with in California. I've copied Lori on the update, per her request.

I'm at my home office until 11 AM if you need clarification on anything. Otherwise, I'll be free this afternoon when my meetings are over.

Thanks,
Madeline

. . .

A FEW MINUTES AFTER I SENT THE MESSAGE, MY PHONE RANG. The call was from a number I didn't recognize, but I answered anyway.

"Hello, this is Madeline."

The deep voice on the other end announced, "Good morning, Madeline. This is John West, Robert's supervisor; we met during the SSI conference."

I replied, "Of course, I remember. How are you, John?"

He said, "I'm well, thanks," and didn't hesitate before continuing. "Madeline, I understand you had some important meetings during the conference. Can you tell me about them?"

"Sure. Actually, I just sent an update to Robert and Lori this morning. Would you like me to forward it to you as well?"

John responded, "I've already got a copy, which is what prompted me to call. According to Robert, you and he didn't speak about your activities while you were away. He also said he was unable to reach you when he called."

His words instantly caused my heart rate to rise. I was confused by his statements. "I'm sorry if I did something wrong. Lori and I spoke multiple times while I was in Atlanta. Robert and I too. I met with all the prospects they requested requested and several of my own."

"I understand that," he said, "but why did you keep Robert out of the loop? Were you told to do that?"

His question caused pricks of nerves at my neck. "Oh, no. There must be a mistake. Robert and I exchanged messages and worked on a couple of items with customers in our territory, but we didn't discuss the accounts in California. He never asked for updates and I thought that was because it wasn't in his territory. Lori was involved with those conversations."

"Madeline" John's tone was overly patient, "Robert told me he tried to reach you, but you didn't answer his calls."

My mind was racing. There was obviously something going on. "It's true. When he called me last night my phone was off, but I was on a return flight home. As soon as I received his message and email, I sent him the information."

There was silence for a moment and John finally said, "Are you in front of your computer?"

"I am," I replied.

"Good, let's go over the notes together. I need to prepare for a leadership meeting in thirty minutes."

"Sure. I am ready whenever you are."

AFTER AN EVEN LONGER THAN EXPECTED DAY, I DROVE THE last few blocks to the restaurant wondering what I'd gotten myself into by joining this company. The accounts I met with today were in dire need. I had walked into the meetings planning to discuss our new line; instead, I was peppered with complaints about the product and lack of response to support inquiries. When I met with the California accounts, I heard a similar list of concerns. The negative customer feedback—and that strange morning call from John—put me on edge. I should have been grateful when I arrived at the valet, for I knew a stiff martini was in my immediate future, but there was still the unpleasant task of telling Peter that Nathan and I split.

"Hello," the clean-cut young man said when he opened my door.

"Hi there. The key is in the console," I said.

"Okay. Here's your ticket. Enjoy dinner."

"Thank you."

A large man in a suit opened the door for me and I walked into the dim entry. The hostess—a dewy brunette of maybe nineteen—greeted me as I approached. "Hello," she said. "Do you have a reservation this evening?"

"I don't think so. I'm meeting Peter, who works here. He's my son." My pride knew no bounds and I wanted to claim him.

She smiled broadly and said, "Oh, how nice to meet you. He didn't mention you were coming."

I took a deep breath and said, "I'm not surprised. Let's hope he didn't forget."

"Oh, I'm sure he didn't forget. Do you want to take a seat at the bar while you wait?"

"Absolutely." I left her to find a spot.

The bar was awash with muted light. Bottles of liquor perched against a leather wall and a smiley middle-aged bartender approached. "Good evening. Are you waiting for a table or are you here to keep me company?" he asked with a grin.

"I think we'll stay here, but I'm not sure what Peter has in mind. He works here and I'm meeting him."

The man's eyebrows rose and I knew I needed to clarify. "He's my son."

"Wow, he is?" His voice was incredulous.

"Yeah, Robbie. This is my mom." Peter's voice came from over my shoulder.

"Hey, you." I stood and gave him a hug.

"Hi, Mom." He sat in the stool next to mine.

I leaned close to him and studied his beautiful face. His color had returned and the dark circles were no longer apparent. "How are you, baby?" I asked.

"Good. It wasn't a bad night here. There's a show opening so it was busy. How was Atlanta?"

That was a tough one to answer, so I stuck to the facts. "It was a busy work week. I made a bunch of new contacts. I'll be going down to San Diego next week. I'm staying at Chris and Shawna's while their out of town. I'll be the dog sitter, running Harvey every morning."

"Mom, there is no way that tiny dog can run more than a block. You are so baked." He shook his head and shoved my shoulder. "Do you want a drink?"

"Yep," I said.

Robbie returned to our side and asked, "What will it be for you guys?"

Peter looked at me and I said, "I'll have a Belvedere Martini with three olives, please."

Robbie asked, "What about you Peter?"

He considered for a minute and said, "Let me have an IPA."

I was surprised to hear him order that after he mentioned beer made him sick. He quickly clarified, "Let's see if it still bothers me. I haven't had a beer since before the surgery."

Great, I thought, not only did I have to brace myself for the conversation I needed to have with him, but now I would be on pins and needles hoping that Peter wouldn't react to his beer. I asked him, "How are you feeling, honey?"

"Pretty good, actually. I had my follow-up and everything is healing. I need to go back in six months for another scan to make sure it's good and after that, they'll check every year."

Ronnie returned with our drinks and not a moment too soon. Peter took his glass and with gusto said, "Let's hope I don't get sick."

It was a strange toast, but one I could get on board with. I chimed, "Cheers."

With the first sip of liquid settling down my throat, I resigned to get the hard part of the evening behind me. I was about to start when Peter said, "Do you want to order? I'm kind of hungry and I have a date later."

That I was a line item on my son's Friday evening should have miffed me, but instead, it took the anxiety down. I said, "Sure, let's order."

Peter gestured to Robbie, who arrived within seconds. "Dinner time, kids?" he asked.

"Yep," Peter said and looked at me.

"I'll have the steak and fries with a house salad, please," I said.

Peter agreed, "Make that two, Robbie."

"Very good. I'll put the order in." He turned to input the items into his register.

I took another sip of my drink and prepared myself for what I'd come to tell Peter. I said, "I have something to tell you."

He looked over at me and asked, "What's up?"

I took a deep breath and said, "Nathan and I split up."

His expression was surprised. "What do you mean, split up?"

"He moved out while I was in Atlanta."

"You're just now telling me?" he demanded.

"I wanted to tell you in person, and there has been a lot going on with you. I didn't want to add anything else to your plate."

He was silent for a while, then took a deep drink from his beer, nearly draining the glass. Robbie arrived at our side and asked, "Another one, Peter?"

"Yeah, thanks," he confirmed.

Peter turned to face me and I was not prepared for the serious look on his face. "You've done this before. Is it for real this time?"

He was right, we had done it before. I replied, "It is. He's not coming back."

Peter studied his glass and asked, "Are you okay with it? I don't like the idea of you being alone."

This was definitely not the reaction I had expected. Five years of war, and he'd finally won. Where were the confetti and balloons? "I'll be fine on my own. Don't worry about that."

He looked sad as he said, "I do worry about you, Mom."

Peter was stingy with kind words. His reaction underlined the facts of my independence. He was worried because there was no one to take care of me. He hated Nathan, or so it seemed, but a man who wasn't good enough was still better than no man at all. As much as he pushed Nathan and me apart, the continuity of us together was something to be missed. For even a dysfunctional constant was a constant.

I put a smile on my face and said, "That's what families do. They worry about each other, but don't worry too much. Okay?"

Peter's response was blighted by the arrival of our medium-rare steaks atop mounds of French fries. Ronnie spoke cheerfully as he set our plates down. "Bon Appetite, you two."

FLY SOUTH

From my seat at the window, I looked at the shimmering bay and myriad of high-rise buildings that comprised downtown San Diego. The cheerful flight attendant finished her rounds, verifying that seats and trays were in their upright positions. We made our final decent, flying so close to the structures that the wings appeared to narrowly miss them. The plane grumbled from its belly as the wheels extended and locked into place. We touched down, bouncing once, and taxied until we reached the gate.

I took the phone from my bag and sent a text to Shawna, who was picking me up. Collecting my barely legal carry-on, I shuffled down the aisle and through the congested airport. When I made it outside, I was assaulted by the bright sun and warmth that defined San Diego.

My phone rang and I answered, "Hey, girl."

"Welcome back to Cali," Shawna's happy voice rang in my ear. "I see you. I'll pull up. Look for the grey SUV."

I glanced around until I saw a face through tinted glass. It was Shawna and she was driving a brand-new, charcoal-colored Tesla Model X. I walked toward the car as she jumped out to greet me. We fell into a hug and for a moment, held tight. It had been over six months since we'd last seen one another and I'd missed her.

When we pulled back I said, "Look at you, Mrs. Baller. Nice ride."

Shawna smiled. Her white teeth gleamed against her full lips and tanned skin. She took my bag with ease, showing off her firm biceps, and placed it in the trunk. "You like?" she teased. "It's an early anniversary present from my hubby. Come on," she said, tossing her long dark hair, "Let's go."

We got into the car and I watched as she navigated from the curb and onto the main road. Within moments, we were facing the Pacific Ocean, and the rows of touristy restaurants that flanked the water. Runners and cyclists intermixed with pedestrians and the walkway was alive. The moored boats bobbed gently in the water, and the sun reflected against the mirrored glass buildings. It was an exceptional city and it felt good to be here.

Shawna asked, "Are you on the clock today or can we goof off a bit?"

"Today is my travel day and since Labor Day is a holiday, I technically get tomorrow as a compensation day too."

Shawna looked over, and a shadow of doubt showed on her face before she said, "Really? Nice gig you landed."

I could see her point, but she didn't know I was at a conference last week, leaving early Sunday morning, or that I didn't return until late Thursday night. "So far it's good. The VP is a woman, which is a first."

She said absently, "That's cool."

As she made a left, she said, "Since you're off the clock, I'm making a stop at Mr. A's."

I couldn't agree more. "Fancy. Okay, let's go."

WE STOOD WAITING AT THE PODIUM, AS THE OVERLY handsome maître d' took two menus in hand and commanded, "This way please."

We followed in the wake of his slightly excessive cologne and tried not to ogle his well sculpted backside. Shawna brought out the teenager in me and I jumped as she pinched my arm. Neither of us missed the beauty of our escort.

He stopped at a table against the glass wall that edged the sky-high patio. I struggled past a moment of vertigo as I peered through the glass that separated us from a twelve-story drop and the city below. Once we were seated, he handed us menus and said, "Michele will be with you momentarily."

I had to suppress a giggle as I noticed Shawna's inability to speak. I said, "Thank you."

We watched him saunter toward the doors and disappear into the building. Once he was out of sight, the ether wore off. Shawna looked at her Fitbit and proclaimed, "It's after noon, and you know what that means, right?"

I chided, "I have a vague idea."

As I said it, we were happy to meet another extraordinary example of the male species in the form of our waiter. His accent was elegant and added to the aura of mystery. His golden-brown hair and translucent brown eyes glowed under the strong sun.

"Good afternoon, ladies. I am Michele and it will be my pleasure to serve you today."

Childish together, we couldn't hide our admiration, something Michele was accustomed to. "Can I bring any libations while you study the menu?"

Shawna spoke confidently, "Yes, please, we'll have a bottle of the Brute Rosé."

Michele said, "Very good, Miss. I'll return shortly."

When he left us, I joked, "Wow, you're feeling swanky today."

She smiled as she touched my hand. "Every day with you is a celebration. Seriously, six months is too long between visits."

"I know. It's true. The funny thing is, planes do go both north *and* south. You could come my way sometime too."

She agreed, "You're right, and now that Kaylee has launched, I have a lot more time on my hands. Why don't I come up next month?"

It was so good to be with my best friend that I teared up at the suggestion of a visit. "I would love that."

Before I could get too soppy, hot Michele returned with a steward in tow. The young man placed two flutes in front of us, and an ice bucket, before uncorking the wine without spilling a drop.

Michele took over and poured the first taste of bubbles into Shawna's glass. "My lady," he flirted, "would you like to taste?"

The soft crinkle at the corner of his eyes and his teasing lips were distracting. I had to kick Shawna under the table to bring her to life.

She smiled foolishly before picking up the glass. After a sip she said, "It's delicious."

"Excellent," Michele said as he filled my glass and then Shawna's. "Would you like anything else at the moment or should I give you time?"

I spoke for the both of us. "Thank you, Michele. We do need more time. Is there an appetizer you'd recommend while we sip the wine?"

He tested, "Perhaps you'd like the cheese board?"

I nodded in agreement. "Thank you."

He left and I cleared my throat to refocus Shawna. "Ahem. Mrs. Parr, is there a problem we need to talk about? Is this an episode of *Californication* or something?"

She grinned and said, "Sorry. I haven't been out in a while. Lately everything has been about senior year, and getting Kaylee ready for college, not to mention what happens when Jordan comes home. You remember how busy my house gets. I need a little adult time to act like a kid."

"Please," I said, "I had no idea how desperate you were. Don't let *me* stop you from sexually harassing the staff."

"Fuck off," she said defiantly, in a soft, calling tone.

I couldn't help but laugh at her predictable behavior. My friend had not changed in over twenty years and it was one of the things I loved about her. "You look great by the way." She wore a turquoise satin dress that stood out against her ageless skin.

This made her smile, but her words contradicted. She confessed, "I'm losing it a little."

"Losing what?" I asked.

"You know. I'm climbing the walls."

"Empty nest got you spinning?"

"Yes," she blurted. "I hate it. Kaylee left on Thursday and already I'm going nuts. I keep crying and visiting her bedroom as if she's going to appear. The dog follows me and that makes me feel worse. Hopefully I'm not scaring him."

I tried to console her. "Woah, girl, calm down. The dog is fine. He knows they're gone and that you need him."

"He loves Kaylee and Jordan too. I'm glad you're going to be with him while we're gone."

Michele arrived with the cheese plate and placed it between us. "Enjoy, ladies. I'll check back in a while."

Shawna said, "Thank you."

When he left, she turned serious again and asked, "Maddie, no one needs me anymore. What am I going to do with myself?"

I thought I had all the problems, only to discover that my well-kept friend was struggling with her identity, now that her last baby was off to college. I reached for her hand and soothed, "You are going to do most of what you already did. Keep doing your charity work, supporting the WWF, and add something you've always wanted to try. Why not take that writing class you've talked about?"

Shawna looked away, her face was alight by the afternoon sun and sparkling bay below. Returning her gaze to meet mine, she said, "It went so fast."

Having experienced this a few years back, I could relate. I said, "Remember when you first found out you were pregnant with Jordan?"

She smiled in recollection. "I do."

I continued, "So do I. We were at my house. Peter was only a few months old and he was so colicky. The look on your face when you told me you were pregnant, the panic you were trying to hide, well here it is again."

Shawna raised her eyebrows and tilted her head before asking, "What are you saying?"

"I'm saying, this too shall pass. I know you are in unchartered territory, but as your life changed for the better when Jordan arrived, believe this change will also be great. You have incredible kids and they are striking out on their own. I know it's scary, but this is your chance to do some of the things you worried about giving up all those years ago."

She shrugged and pursed her full lips. "Those things I gave up were nothing compared to being Jordan and Kaylee's mom. I don't even remember what it was I thought I was giving up."

I couldn't have understood her sentiments more, but platitudes would sound hollow given the huge moment she was facing. Levity was in order, so I said, "Now we're at the root of the problem. You're experiencing the early stages of Alzheimer's."

Shawna snorted, but said nothing.

"Listen, you're going to be fine. If you weren't a little weirded out by this change, then I'd worry. You've got Chris and a beautiful life. Before you know it, the kids will be back for Thanksgiving and Christmas."

Shawna studied me over the rim of her flute, and said, "Enough about my story. Let's talk about you. I know how you are. It'll take some time for you to talk about Nathan, so let's start with your new job and the trip to Atlanta."

I puzzled, where would I begin? "Okay, the new job is fine so far. They're paying me well and it seems I have latitude, at least for the moment. When I talked to our VP about coming down, and told her I had a place to stay, she asked if I would spend a couple of weeks in the territory. They're looking for someone to cover the market after the last guy left. It seems like they are willing to do what it takes to support customers. I like that."

Shawna asked, "Is the VP your boss then?"

"Actually, no. I report to a manager in Seattle. He's interesting."

Ready for gossip, Shawna leaned in, asking suggestively, "And?"

I knew where her mind was going. "No, he's not interesting in that way, at least not to me, and that's good because I am not his type. The last girl he dated was a stripper if that gives you an idea of what catches his eye. From a work perspective, he's a little intense with frequent reminders about tasks. Hopefully he'll chill out once he realizes I'm on it."

Shawna commiserated with me. "That's kind of crazy. Of

all the people I know, you are the last person who needs reminders. Do you like him at all? I mean, is he a good guy?"

I said hopefully, "I think we'll get along. I was a little concerned about his reaction when the VP assigned this account to me, but he didn't seem phased. Maybe they'd already discussed it or he doesn't have an ego. That would be nice for a change."

"And Atlanta, how was that?" she asked.

As I sat across from my best friend, I wondered how much I would say about that trip. I covered the highlights. "It was productive for the most part. I connected with some new customers and got to learn about the company and meet my counterparts."

Shawna was sniffing me out and we both knew it. "And Peter, how are you guys doing?"

I exhaled. The resolute air expelled from my lungs and into the world, like the hope I still had for Peter and me to reconnect. "We're doing okay. Thankfully, he made it through the surgery and the end result turned out much better than it could have. I'm so grateful for that."

Shawna waited the appropriate time before pressing, "What else?"

The moment had come to unpack my heavy bag. "You mean me and Nathan?"

Her silence was all the confirmation I needed.

For the first time since we sat, I looked out at the view. A lonely bird flew by and settled to perch on a neighboring building. His chest puffed up as he surveyed his terrain. I knew the silence was lingering and I finally said, "It's over. He's moved out for the last time."

Shawna's dark eyes bore into mine and she asked, "Are you sure about this? I know things have been rocky for a while, but something big must have happened for you to reach this point."

"Yeah, something big did happen, but that isn't what did us in. For me, all these years of waiting for Nathan to get it, to get me, they wore me out."

Shawna said, "I know it has always been a source of stress that Nathan and Peter don't get along. How are things between them now?"

"Nothing has changed on that front. They are both stubborn and hold onto grudges. Sometimes I felt like a referee and what's worse, how can a mother make a call like that? Who could pick their fiancé over their child? It has been hard to deal with, but . . ."

"But what, Maddie?"

"Their relationship isn't what finally broke us. As hard as this is to admit out loud, Nathan isn't in love with me. I'm pretty sure he never was. I think he picked me because I was so different from his ex. When they split up, he was inconsolable. He needed someone and I happened to be there."

Shawna narrowed her eyes until they were slits. "You don't really believe that, do you?"

I thought for a moment before I replied, "It took some time to realize why things were so tough between us. He was trying to start a new life with me, but only doing it so he wouldn't have to face the loss of his old one."

Shawna stopped me. "I don't believe that. Why relocate to be with you then? He did that years after his divorce. Why try to get you back? He had to be over her by that point."

A sudden rush of anger coursed through me and I made the decision to tell her about the argument we had before I went to Atlanta. As I recounted the details of our beach excursion, I watched the expressions on Shawna's face range from empathetic, to miffed, and finally pissed.

When it was finally over, she took a sip from her glass before saying, "Wow, Maddie, that is messed up."

Not only was I feeling the heaviness of our talk about Nathan, but there was an added layer of guilt in play. Her reference to Nathan's behavior struck a nerve and I had a pang of guilt thinking about Travis. "I guess, but people forgive all kinds of injustices in the name of love."

"But not you?" she jabbed.

A little hurt, I said, "Touché. Do you think I'm giving up too easily?"

"I'm not saying that at all. It was my roundabout way of asking if you could forgive him. It's not completely out of the question. You have reconciled before."

As dreaded as it was, I knew I had to tell her the whole story about meeting Travis, and the weekend at the beach. I started from the beginning, and talked without interruption until the last of the wine was poured and my throat was dry. I was spent and deflated by it all.

"Madeline, I had no idea it had gotten this rough between you. I'm sorry you're hurting."

Insecurity got the best of me and I had to know. "Do you think I'm insane for leaving the beach that night?"

Shawna laughed. An ironic look was on her face as she said, "No. I can't believe you handled it as well as you did. A lot of people would have gone Jerry Springer on those two. What woman would allow her friend's husband to kiss her, under any circumstances? Then he had the balls to drive back with her. She actually dropped him off! That must have been awful. What a dick!"

A strange combination of hilarity and tears came over me and I managed, "Thank you for saying that. I've been kicking myself over the theatrics of leaving and wondering if I was out of line. I almost felt like I deserved Nathan's treatment after the time I spent with Travis, like it was my karma."

She stopped me. "I'll get to Travis, but first, let's finish up on Nathan. You are not crazy to be upset by his behavior. Look, we all know I rarely miss a good-looking face, but I would never mess with a friend's man, and my husband is the only person who will ever taste my lips." She chuckled suggestively. "Either set.

"I know what you've dealt with over the years, being stuck in the middle between Peter and him. I didn't always care for the way Nathan handled things, but I'm honest enough to understand where my allegiance lies."

She paused. "But this, him acting like a fool with that woman and brushing it off, that's not something I can excuse. Unless you can, then, for your sake, I will. You're my friend, and I support you."

I knew her impassioned speech and colorful language were brought out by the wine, and I also knew she was right. Somewhere in that lecture was a grain of genius. All I could say was, "Thank you."

She leaned to the side of her chair and looked at me, almost angrily. I wondered what she would say next. "And Maddie, if Nathan can't see how spectacular you are, he isn't the man for you."

I teared up and said, "I know that too."

Not letting up, she continued, "That Travis guy, he isn't either. He may see everything that Nathan is missing, but it does not matter. You wouldn't do well in a love triangle and you know it."

She shook her head and continued. "The timing and circumstances of you meeting him couldn't be worse. It was like the perfect storm or an outlandish episode from daytime TV. I'm sure that made the escape feel all the more intense, but you have to know, it isn't real. He has a family and you would never want to mess with that."

I had to stop her, she was making way too much of Travis and me. "Hold on a minute. I don't think Travis is *the* guy and I agree with everything you're saying."

How could I help her understand? "The thing is, it felt nice. We talked in such an open way and I could tell, he really wanted to know me. It highlighted everything Nathan and I were missing."

Shawna looked baffled. I could see her warring with the concept and I braced myself for what was coming. "Don't get hurt, Maddie. I know you, and your conscience. You won't fare well if you're the cause of that family coming apart."

I needed to reassure her and maybe myself. "He was kind to me and it opened my eyes, but that's where it ends. I'm sure we'll stay in touch, but he lives in Chicago and I'm here. Our paths really won't cross."

For a moment, I allowed myself to feel the truth and I said, "I'm actually grateful to him. Maybe if he and I hadn't had that connection, I wouldn't have been strong enough to see a life without Nathan." The breeze kicked up, tickling the ragged hem of my sundress. I closed my eyes and tilted my chin toward the sky. The late-summer sun heated my bare shoulders and I willed the words to be true. "There is nothing for you to worry about. Please don't."

Shawna half chuckled before saying, "Are you kidding? Worrying about this is going to become my full-time occupation. Now that the kids are launched, let me introduce you to your new helicopter mom. We need to get you back on track."

I replied playfully, "I didn't realize I was off track."

Blinking back a look of disapproval, she said, "That's just the problem."

❧

WE PULLED OFF OF THE 101 NORTH AND TRAVELED WEST THE last few blocks to their house on the cliff. The homes were snugged against one another with shrubs or trees dividing the yards, blocking even a glimpse of the ocean below. Living on this street was like owning a slice of the sea. Equipped with residents-only access, those with the golden key were granted entry to a private path and beach below.

Shawna clicked the garage door opener and pulled into her space. After I got my bag, we shuffled out of the garage and through a doorway. Flipping on lights before we descended the stairs, Shawna announced, "The housekeepers were just here, so everything is good to go."

From the bottom of the landing, I scanned the room and noticed the changes they made during the remodel. The space was awash with natural light. West-facing French doors filtered smoldering sun rays, brightening the white wooden floors in hues of pink and orange. The walls were also white, creating a sense of serenity. A muted teal rug centered the room, and was situated beneath a sleek white leather sofa. The coolest feature was the gilded mirror that doubled as a TV. "It looks fantastic," I said, "I may never go home."

Shawna's face brightened, and for the first time today, I could see her dimples as she said, "You like? Did I do a good job?"

"Are you kidding? This looks incredible. I love the little details you incorporated. The bits of brass against the stark white are spectacular, and that rug, don't get me started on that."

"Wait until you see the bedroom," she said, and tugged my elbow that direction.

We made a left through the door and I was shocked at

what I saw. They'd increased their basement to add this daydream of a suite. The white walls and floors continued, and the king-size bed was coiffed to magazine-cover perfection. Through the wall of windows, the Pacific Ocean appeared close enough to touch. Beyond the glass, suspended above the water, was a wooden deck with a set of chairs and a small table.

My breath caught at the sight of it. "Shawna, this is heaven. I can't believe you designed this."

The room was immaculate and I had to do it—mainly because I knew it would drive her mad. Like an errant child, I tossed my shoes and ran to jump on the bed. As if possessed by a five-year-old, I leapt up and down until the comforter was messy and the throw pillows had fallen to the ground.

Shawna did her best to ignore me as she unpacked my bag. I played while she smoothed my items and hung them in the closet. After one last jump, I landed with a thud on my ass and stared out at the bluest backdrop.

"Hey," I said, a wave of emotions tugged at me, "thank you for this."

She hung the last dress and came to sit beside me. "You have nothing to thank me for. Enjoy yourself here and stay as long as you can. I miss having you close."

I couldn't have agreed more. The sorrow that had been holding me was a little less, thanks to the kindness of my best friend. I squeezed her hand and she forcefully kissed me on the cheek, no doubt leaving an imprint of her lipstick.

She stood up and said, "Get the rest of your things settled and come upstairs. Chris is cooking us dinner tonight."

"Okay. I'll be right there."

"See you in a few," she said, and made her way out of the apartment.

When I heard the door close, I walked over to the bed and

smoothed the silken duvet. One by one, I replaced the pillows until the bed was restored to its original state. Next, I took my toiletry bag and put it in the adjoining restroom. Marble floors and countertops gleamed, and the oversized steam shower begged to be used. There would be time for that later.

I returned to the bedroom, removed the phone from my bag, and checked for messages. There was a text from Peter, which was a nice surprise. It said, *Hi, just wanted to make sure you got there ok.*

I tapped a response and wrote, *Hi baby. I'm at their house and I miss you already. It's strange with Kaylee and Jordan gone, but wait until you see what they did to the basement. I love you.* I snapped a shot of the view and hit send.

Peter's was not the only message. I saw a red indicator by Travis' name and clicked to open it.

Hello, Shorty. Are there any double stuffed Oreos in your Labor Day forecast?

I couldn't help but smile as I replied to him, *No Oreos in the forecast, but this is . . .* I added the picture of the ocean then clicked the green arrow.

I tossed the phone onto the bed and searched my purse for a hair band. Finding one, I put my hair into a ponytail then wound it into a bun. The phone chimed, indicating I'd received a text. I unlocked it and found a response from Travis. It read, *Wow, I had no idea the Oregon coast would look like that. Is that a palm tree?*

Of course, he would assume I was at the Oregon coast, since that was where I told him I'd be spending the weekend. I squirmed, but replied, *I'm in San Diego, Solana Beach to be exact. It's kind of a long story.*

Three dots indicated he was typing, and then the response came. *Is everything ok?*

I shook my head and puzzled to find the right words. *I*

don't know how to answer that in a text. I'm staying at my best friend's house. She and her husband are leaving on a trip tomorrow, but we're having a great time today.

I waited for his response and it didn't take long. *I won't keep you then. If you don't mind, can I call you tomorrow?*

I knew it was a bad idea, but my heart responded before my head could overrule and I typed, *Sure. Let's talk then.*

His reply was almost immediate, and he wrote, *I'll talk to you tomorrow.*

◈

WE SAT ON THE DECK, OVERLOOKING THE SEA. "CHRIS, THAT was the best meal I've had in a long time. You need to give me the recipe for your marinade."

Flickering light from the Tiki torch danced across his face, and kept the mosquitos at bay. The dusky sky held the last vestiges of color, a distant pink smudge against the darkening sea. Wind whisked the tendrils of Shawna's hair. I watched as Chris took the bottle of wine from the table, filling her glass then my own.

He replied, "Maddie, it's taken me years to perfect that masterpiece, what makes you think I would share it with you?"

Shawna watched the exchange. An imperial expression rested on her face as she sipped wine and stroked the dog who refused to sit anywhere but her lap. "For old times' sake?" I whined.

"Ha, not a chance. You'd have done better if you played the sympathy card." He joked, but the words cut a little too close to the bone. My expression must have shown something, since Shawna kicked him under the table. Before the moment got too awkward, he rebounded, "That was dumb, but you know what I meant."

Thoughts swirled in my head, but I used it to my advantage. I mustered an overzealous pout and said, "Oh, I know what you meant. Not only do you not trust me with your recipe, but you also think I'm pathetic."

Chris' chiseled face looked pained. "You know damn well I don't think you're pathetic, and I'm still not giving you the recipe."

I snorted half-heartedly and managed a barb. "Not only did I grovel, but you still turned me down. How is that not pathetic?"

Trying to put a smile on my face, in typical Chris fashion, he joked, "Who said anything about turning you down?"

Shawna socked Chris on the arm. Her ring added an extra bite that made him flinch and her words packed a similar punch. "This ain't no *Sister Wives*. You better watch your step, little man." The dog raised his head at the jostling, and a miffed expression showed on his scruffy face.

The ironic nickname of "little man" had been a joke between them since they met. Chris was oddly tall and at six foot six he towered over most. Though Shawna was only five three, she ruled him and I wondered if he was a little afraid of his wife.

Batting his girlishly long lashes, Chris blue eyes beamed at Shawna and he said, "Yes, number one. Please accept my apology."

My feisty friend was not to be messed with. If anyone should know that, you'd think her husband would. I watched without shock as Shawna doused Chris with the contents of her wine glass. Red streaks of liquid dripped down his face and onto his T-shirt.

Shrugging it off, he ran his hands through his wavy brown

hair and stood. Tossing his shirt on the deck, he took the few remaining steps before dropping into the infinity style hot tub. He quickly submerged himself then bounced up with a splash. Wasting no time in the water, he got out and walked back to the table. With a smile on his face, he shook his head and body like a dog. Water drops splattered us both as I watched their strange exchange adoringly.

Shawna squealed and tried in vain to be stern as she demanded, "Stop it or I'll cut you off."

This did nothing but increase his exuberance as he flung his head her direction. He teased, "We both know you can't cut me off, even when you want to."

Chris stopped shaking and walked over to Shawna. Pinning both of her wrists with his hands, he leaned in and said, "I wouldn't tolerate it anyway." With that, he swooped down and kissed Shawna senseless.

Their magnetism for one another awakened the breeze, and the torch's flame seemed to brighten in their honor. He released her lips and hovered. With a cheeky smile on his face, he turned and resumed his place in the chair. Shawna snapped out of her trance and walked over to the cabinet to get a fresh towel. After handing it to him, she took her seat and their eyes locked. As I watched my friends, I saw the truth of their bond. It became clear to me that together, they were love.

He looked my direction, the softness he felt for Shawna still shining in his eyes. He started by saying, "Shawna gave me the cliff notes on the situation between you and Nathan. How are you holding up?"

Now I was the one who wanted to throw her glass of wine. Instead, I looked over at Shawna and flipped her off.

She back-pedaled. "What? You know how he is! He knew something was up when you agreed to come on such short notice." The wheels seemed to be turning as she continued to defend herself. "Besides, we don't have any secrets between us."

I nearly choked on my wine as I stretched to believe that last part. "Ah yes, the mystery ingredient to your successful union is finally revealed."

Chris' voice dripped with innuendo as he came to her defense and said, "Don't hold it against her. She put up a good fight. I had to use some serious torture techniques to get it out of her."

Shaking my head, I couldn't help but be amused by their teenage antics and obvious chemistry. Spending time with them was like witnessing a miracle. Their adoration for one another poured out and warmed everyone in the room.

He cleared his throat, bringing me back to the topic, and said, "You'd better start talking or I may have to use some techniques on you."

Shawna slugged him on his arm and I watched as the area reddened. He tried a new tactic. "Are you ok?"

Resigned that we were going to have this conversation, and it may help to get the male perspective, I said, "I don't know how to answer that."

Chris nodded as if he understood and said, "Shawna told me about the casino incident."

His statement hung in the air. My heart sped at the recollection and I had to know his thoughts. "What do you think about it?"

He took a deep breath. His normally cheerful face lost any trace of humor. "I think it sucks and it makes me want to punch Nathan."

His reaction to protect me was sweet. I was happy to have an ally in Chris. I chuckled and said, "I'd pay good money to see that."

His tone was as direct as his reply and he said, "Maddie, I can't believe Nathan treated you so disrespectfully, and with a married woman on top of it."

His words matched my thoughts and I struggled to reply. "Then why minimize it and make me feel like a crazy person, like it was no big deal?"

Chris shook his head, and asked, "Have you ever heard of gaslighting?

"Of course," I replied.

He said, "He's probably done worse, but this situation leaves just enough doubt. If he's feeling guilty, or wants out, and you end it on this note, he can tell the next girl it didn't work out because you were crazy jealous."

This confused me. "Why go to these lengths? He could just break it off with me."

Chris explained, "He either can't face his own feelings or he doesn't want to. I can't imagine how hard it would be to sit across from someone you've spent years of your life with only to say, 'I don't see you in my future.' He's too weak to face you so he's doing things to force your hand. It isn't just the fact that he kissed that woman, but everything he's doing. It all adds up to the real Nathan, or sadly, the way Nathan really feels about you."

Chris words stung with their clarity. My eyes blurred a little, but I kept the tears at bay. I said, "I know you're right. Maybe I've known something was off from the very beginning. He said all the right things, and usually followed through, but there was always something missing. I think that's why I freaked out when I saw him with Lucinda. The frank male appreciation he showed her was something I'd never felt from him. It was like watching my worst fear come true."

Chris spoke with the kindness of an old friend. "Maddie,

take it from someone who has known you for years, you're incredible. I know you don't like to dredge up the past, but you were dealt some pretty tough cards, and look at all you've accomplished. You're an amazing mother, a caring person, and you know your shit in the business world. I'm going to be honest with you, but you can't hold it against me if you somehow decide to reconcile with Nathan. Do you agree?" He waited for my reply.

I braced myself and said, "Okay, what is it."

"The guy was a little cold, like he was missing something in the personality department. I never would have said anything, but all along I've wondered if he was the one for you."

Once again Shawna socked Chris. Her well-aimed blow landed in line with the last one. He moved his chair out of range, then turned his attention back to me before carrying on. "What I'm trying to say, but am fumbling awfully, is that you are a stunning and wickedly smart woman. You deserve someone who knows it."

His words caused an irreversible crack in my universe. Their notes singed the air, making a permanent record of his opinion.

SUNSET

The three of us stood by the trunk of the SUV as the overhead speakers warned that no loitering was permitted. When Chris removed the last suitcase from the car, he and Shawna turned. She squeezed me tight and when we released, she held both of my hands. "Thank you for coming down and for taking care of my fur babies."

"Don't thank me. You're doing me a favor. I'll take good care of them. Send pictures and bring me back something lovely." I gave her one last squeeze.

Chris was next; he pulled me into a hug and whispered in my ear, "You're a catch, remember that." He released me and I watched as they crossed the sidewalk and entered the round-about. Shawna waved one last time before she was out of sight.

I turned to look at the masterpiece of a ride that awaited, and felt like a kid left alone for the weekend. As I slid into the driver's seat I was engulfed by the aroma of new leather and Shawna's signature fragrance, Molecule 1. If nothing else, the joy of driving this car made me excited to meet the customer in Orange County. I opened the sunroof and tapped the Pandora app before gliding onto the roadway.

The harbor shimmered in the morning light, and the world looked hopeful through the lens of the exotic vehicle. Changing lanes, I made my way over and toward the I-5 on-ramp. After passing through a few intersections, I entered the highway. There was enough space, so I quickly accelerated and smoothed over a few lanes. Once I was established in the fast lane, I gave the pedal a tap. The back end lifted and we were off. I looked down at the speedometer and saw I was going 88 miles an hour. A sea of red brake lights halted the cars ahead, and the adult in me fell in line with the morning traffic.

Adam Levine's voice floated through the crystal-clear sound system as I listened to the Maroon 5 station. The song "Wait" was interrupted by the phone ringing through the speakers. Thankful for Shawna's insistence that my phone be paired, I found the accept button and answered. "Hi. This is Madeline."

"Well hello, Madeline. How are you today?"

It was Travis. His relaxed tone caught me off guard, causing my breath to hitch. I tried to sound calm and said, "Hey, Travis. How are you?"

He asked, "Are you outside?"

"I'm sorry, the sunroof is open. One second." I clicked the button and the glass lid sealed the car into silence. "Can you hear me now?"

"Wow. I sure can. Is this a good time to talk?"

I chuckled inwardly and wondered how to respond. I settled with, "It is. How was your weekend?"

He replied, "It was good, thanks. We had a full house yesterday and I had a couple of work fires to contend with, but otherwise it was uneventful. What about you? I thought you were going to be in Oregon. What took you to California?"

I was unprepared to respond, and stuck to the business aspect. "I had to come down to meet a customer, and it turns out there are several other accounts that need attention. I'm going to be here through next week."

He was silent for a beat, then said, "From reading your text last night, I thought something happened. Was there an emergency with the customer? Is that why you had to leave quickly?"

Apparently, I contemplated my response for too long.

"Are you still there?" Travis checked.

"Yes, sorry."

After a beat he said, "It seems like I need to pay better attention. You don't want to talk about this right now. Do you?"

Grateful for his awareness, I agreed, "No, I really don't."

"Got it." He changed the subject. "So where are you headed?"

"Today I'm going to Orange County. I'm taking a look at a few of the TransTruck sites there. You should see the view and my ride!"

"Your ride? What do you mean?" he asked.

It was impossible not to boast so I said, "I'm driving a Tesla and traveling beside the Pacific Ocean."

"Woah. That's one hell of a rental. Your company must have a liberal expense policy."

I chuckled and said, "Ha, ha, you have to be kidding. Nope, this is my friend Shawna's car. I get to use it while she and her husband are away."

"Now I understand why you rushed to get there," he said. "That's got to be a fun ride."

"It's a dream on wheels."

"I bet. Are you going to be staying at your friend's house while you're there? That picture you sent of the view was incredible. They must have done something right."

"Yes, I am staying at their place and I'm looking forward to it. Of course, it does come with a couple of strings," I said.

"Strings?" he asked.

"Yep," I teased, "their fifteen-pound Terrier, Harvey, and the twenty-pound kitty, Priscilla. I'm pet sitting in heaven."

He chuckled. "That sounds like a big cat and a small dog."

"They're cute. Harvey is a good little walking companion, and as you could see from the picture I sent, the house is right on the beach."

"Stop it," he kidded me. "You're making me so jealous."

I laughed and said, "It's easy duty for sure."

"Well, I'm glad to hear that you're getting to do that. After last week, you deserve something good."

I warmed at the recollection of his full cheeks and the way his nose crinkled at the bridge when he smiled. I absently replied, "And you don't know the half of it."

"What's that?" he inquired.

"Nothing, I'm sorry." I tried to steer the conversation away from my comment. "Don't be too jealous, you should see the traffic jam I'm approaching."

"Be careful." His vaguely familiar timbre vibrated through the speakers. "I should let you concentrate on driving. Can I convince you to send me a picture from your beach walk tonight?"

I wondered if that was a good idea, but dismissed my concern. He wasn't going to jump through the phone or anything. "Sure, I'll take a nice sunset shot and send it to you."

"I look forward to it. Drive safe out there."

"Thanks for calling, Travis. Bye."

As I drove the last few miles to my meeting, I thought of Travis. I remembered the way his finger brushed against my cheek when he wiped away the tears, and how my body zinged with the brightest energy at his nearness. These thoughts were such a welcome contrast to all the real life that had been happening lately. No wonder I was drawn to him. It was a sweet escape and it was harmless—at least that's what I wanted to believe.

A LONG AFTERNOON OF MEETINGS LATER, I WAS FINALLY making my way down the last stretch of Highway 101, nearing Shawna's house. I looked at the beaming ocean, and I couldn't wait to put my toes in the sand. As I pulled into the garage, I could hear Harvey's excited woofs coming from inside the house. When I opened the door, I was greeted by his cheerful demeanor and wagging back end. He was adorable and very happy to see me.

"Hi there, Harvey." I reached down to pat the little guy.

He briefly made eye contact, then looked past me as if waiting for Shawna to appear. "Sorry, Harvey. It's just me today."

He looked me in the eye, then once again toward the door before a resigned huff turned him around. "Hey, don't be so disappointed, I may not be the mamma, but I am the one who is going to take you for a walk."

Harvey's floppy ears perked at my comment and one of them stood at attention. His little body shook as he circled around my feet. "You like going for walks, don't you?"

He woofed playfully as he followed me up the few stairs and into the sprawling kitchen that hung over the sea.

Priscilla must have heard all the excitement, for she sauntered into the room and wove her way through my feet. Her sweet mews filled the space while her yellow-green eyes implored. She jumped to the barstool and sat regally, but the mewing never ceased. Someone wanted attention. I stroked her smooth grey fur and listened to her prattle on in that sweet kitty voice of hers. "Are you missing your mamma, big kitty?" The cat let out one final meow then purred.

I put their dinner bowls together and settled them on the ground. Harvey came running, but stopped shy when he got close to Priscilla. The cat looked at him, and a warning expression seemed to pass between them. I moved Harvey's a few feet from hers and this solved the problem. Harvey quickly gobbled up the contents of his bowl and Priscilla followed. "Ok guys, I'll be back after I change." The pets were unaffected by my words and they continued eating without so much as a backwards glance.

I left them to it and made my way back through the garage and into the incredible new world that was once a dingy basement. Removing my work clothes, I pulled on a pair of running shorts and a tank top before collecting my phone.

❦

WE STOOD AT THE GATE AND I COULD FEEL HARVEY'S anxiety as I fumbled with the golden key. It turned and the heavy door opened, availing us to the kind of view normally reserved for motion pictures. No matter how often I'd seen it, the scene still took my breath away. For a moment I watched as the rising tide rolled in, forcing the late afternoon sunbathers to retreat to higher ground. Early evening light illuminated the whitecaps in hues of gold as the pelicans flew by in perfect unity. The beautiful beach called and I joined Harvey in his rapid decent along the gravel path.

When we arrived at the base, the dog tugged at his leash and I let him lead the way. He had his routine and I wasn't about to change things. I stumbled to keep up as we took the final steps that placed us on the sand. Slipping off my sandals, I took them in hand and walked in silence as Harvey caused a stir with almost every passerby. He was a charming little guy with a stocky, determined stance, and oversized brown eyes nearly hidden by his dark muzzle. Though small in stature, Harvey kept a good pace and after the long commute I was thankful for the activity.

The bewitching sky glowed through fluffy clouds, casting an ethereal filter on the world. The beauty of the moment and Harvey's steady pace made it easy to be present. I breathed in the fresh air and felt the tension release from my shoulders. Unfortunately, my walk was interrupted by my phone buzzing. I removed it from my pocket and saw that Nathan was calling. The fleeting moment of relaxation vanished as I answered.

"Hello," I said.

"How are you?" Nathan's voice came through the line causing my eyes to tear involuntarily.

I managed to respond, "I'm doing okay. What about you?"

There was a brief silence, then he said, "Same here. How are Shawna and Chris doing?"

We left things so awfully that I never told him about their trip. "They're doing great. Same as always, disgustingly in love. They left this morning, though. Shawna joined Chris on a work trip to Germany."

"Oh, I didn't realize they were going to be gone." After a pause, he asked, "And the customers? How is work going?"

The distant cry of a seagull taunted and somehow articulated my sentiments. "Did you really call to ask about work Nathan?"

I heard him take a breath and he said, "I was calling to see how you're doing."

My stomach turned, as I considered his question. The waves rushed on, one after the next, leaving a string of bubbly foam behind. "I'll be fine," I managed.

"Maddie," he spoke as if to a child, "we tried and it didn't work out. We both deserve to be happy."

I knew the battle was over; Nathan raised the white flag, and it was done. Still, the painful truth slapped me as strongly as the waves against the shore.

Those hollow words had no doubt been spoken a million times, yet the basic statement did nothing to shade our truth. As easily as he'd walked into my life, Nathan was going away. He held the evidence of our time together as proof of our effort. I wondered if his words were true. Did we try? Did I?

I wanted to keep my wits about me, but my ragged emotions bested me. Through the veil of my tears I blurted, "Well, I hope you'll be happy now."

"Listen, Maddie, I know this sucks. I'm sorry for my part in it, but we can't keep going. It isn't good for us or our kids."

The finality of his words wasn't nearly as cutting as the certainty with which he spoke them. I couldn't hear any more and ended the talk without drama. "Take care, Nathan. Goodbye."

His voice was a whisper and he replied, "You too, Maddie. Bye."

My legs turned to butter and I collapsed onto the sand. Harvey was a little confused and wanted to keep going, but his human-like instincts took over. Those big brown eyes met mine before he tested my lap, one paw at a time. He walked in circles and his nails bit into my bare legs before he settled into a tight ball. The warmth of his breath grazed my thigh and grounded me. In my moment of need, this creature seemed to understand, giving me a fresh perspective of Shawna's obsession with the little mop.

No matter how good it felt to be snuggled up against the little guy, like the setting sun this moment signified the end of a dream. Ours was not a fairy tale, far from it. Still, I couldn't help but mourn the dying hope that once glowed in my heart for Nathan and me. He was different, or so I believed. No magical spark drew us, instead it was the mature coming together of two people who had things in common. Unfortunately, the threads we clung to were worn thin and unravelling, like our future together. In the flash of a weekend or the slow counting of five years, my universe had become alien.

The phone buzzed and I thought maybe he was having second thoughts. I unlocked the screen, but was surprised to find that the message was from Travis. I clicked to display the text. It read, *Did someone forget to send me a picture? According to the Weather Channel, the sun has already set in San Diego.*

His words mocked the stinging truth. In the waning light, under the last ember of a setting sun, I snapped the picture that captured my sentiments. Darkness was coming and I could do nothing to stop it. The sun had set on Nathan and me.

FORBIDDEN VIEW

Daylight shone through the glass and the ocean's rhythmic pounding became my natural alarm clock. I stirred and felt my sleeping companion, Harvey, snuggle even closer to my hip. Feeling as reluctant as he appeared, I stretched and somehow convinced myself to face the day.

Taking the phone from the side table, I unlocked it to check for messages. After last night's conversation with Nathan I had put my phone away for the rest of the night. I couldn't allow myself to sit on pins and needles, waiting for any notification that he was trying to contact me. I looked at the display and found only one new message. It was from Travis.

That is a gorgeous shot. I wish I was seeing it in person.

More than anything, I wanted to enjoy the attention he was showing me, but what good could come of that? I thought about him and how we met. Marveling at the cruelty of fate, I tried to fathom the reason for our connection. Why had he walked into my life as Nathan walked out? Tears overtook me. What an absurd sight I would be to a stranger. There I was, perched at the edge of the sea, being snuggled by a sweet puppy as we lay against 1,000-thread-count sheets, yet I was feeling sorry for myself.

Suddenly, I knew what I needed. I selected Peter's number from my contacts list and dialed. He was finishing his last year in college and worked most nights as a server. Though it was before 7 AM, he was likely up and getting ready for class. As I waited for him to answer, I hoped he would be happy to hear from me.

"E-lo." He spoke in a somewhat cheerful voice.

"Good morning, baby. How are you today?"

"I'm okay," he replied. "Getting ready to head out the door. What's happening with you?"

"Not much. I just wanted to hear your voice," I said.

"Cool. Well, everything is fine here. I kind of need to go, unless you want me to take you to the bathroom with me."

Though Peter hadn't lived at home in several years, the thought of his toilet sessions still haunted me. "That's all right, honey. I'll be back next week. Are you free on Friday? Maybe we can get dinner."

Succinct as usual, he said, "Yep. I have to go. Bye, Mom."

❦

I DIDN'T HAVE APPOINTMENTS UNTIL THE AFTERNOON SO I took advantage of my surroundings, in particular, the beautiful deck. I set my laptop up and enjoyed the freedom of "working from home." There were orders to manage and emails to reply to after the conference last week.

I was distracted by a dialogue box as my computer flashed a preview of a text message from Travis. Without hesitation, I clicked on the blue icon and read his message.

He wrote, *Good morning, Shorty. How's that view treating you today?*

A picture was worth a thousand words, so I took one of my open laptop with the blue ocean as the backdrop. I sent it with the caption, *Jealous much?*

His response took seconds—*Yes, but not for long.*

Not sure what to make of his message, I replied with the confused emoji and wrote, *Not for long?*

My phone rang and it was him. I answered, "Hello."

"Hi, Madeline. How are you today?" I could almost see him smiling through the phone.

"It's hard to complain when you're looking at this incredible view. Plus, the dog doesn't care to listen."

"You do seem to be working in paradise." The smooth bass of his voice came through the line.

"What about you?" I asked. "How are things in Chicago?"

"Chicago isn't my headache right now. I've got some stuff happening in your neck of the woods that has me occupied."

"Oh, is everything ok?" I asked.

"Some issues are going on between a few of the contractors and my new supervisor at our Orange County site. If it doesn't get worked out fast, it'll delay our launch, which'll cost us over a hundred thousand dollars a day in revenue."

I replied, "That is a big deal. What are you going to do?"

There was a brief pause, then he said, "I'm going to fly in and take care of it."

My ears were ringing and I gulped down a tad of nerves. Avoiding the obvious question, I tried for humor. "Superman to the rescue?"

"Nope"his tone was direct"just a guy who wants his project done on time. I leave tomorrow morning. With the time difference in my favor, as long as there are no delays, I'll be on site by ten, Pacific time."

I was dumbfounded. That was close, too close for comfort. I had to say something. "I suppose an expedited flight means nothing against numbers like that."

"Madeline," he tried.

"Yes?"

"Any chance you're free for dinner tomorrow night?" His maple tone lured me. "I'll come to you. Maybe you'll even let me pick you up so I can get a look at that view?"

This was such a bad idea, but there was no point acting coy. It would be incredible to see him again. "Okay, but under one condition—we are going to be friends. Can you agree to that, Travis?"

His deep voice sounded boyish and he sang, "I can tell that we are going to be friends."

He was so damn alluring, even as he teased. "Travis," I poked, "are we clear?"

"We are. Don't worry, Madeline. Does this mean you agree to have dinner with me?"

Knowing it was dangerous ground, but that I wouldn't let the opportunity pass, I agreed. "You can pick me up and have a look at the view, but no lingering and you're not coming in after dinner."

"I wholeheartedly accept your terms, Shorty. Well," he continued, "I'd better get moving. There is still a lot I need to finish before I take off. Have yourself a great day. I'll text you tomorrow."

"Okay," I said. "I'll talk to you then. Travel safely."

As the sun warmed my back, I looked out at the ocean and had an honest conversation with myself. The magic of this place was unmistakable. Though I wanted to share it with him, for obvious reasons, inviting him here was a risky move.

⚜

NEVER BEFORE HAD TIME MOVED SO QUICKLY. THE HOURS sped by as if the day were on fast forward. Within a matter of minutes, Travis would arrive. I stood at the vanity trying to apply lipstick with my trembling hand. I was nervous to see him again. I hadn't dated in over five years and I'd never dated a married man. This was a lot to take in. I scowled at myself in the mirror and said aloud, "What are you doing?"

The doorbell rang and Harvey sprang into action. His excited woofs alerted me there was a visitor. Wiping my hands down my blush-colored sundress, I smoothed the fabric and dried my palms. When I rounded the corner, I could see Travis' large frame through the beveled glass. The dog continued to bark incessantly, though at a lower decibel once I opened the door.

His grey eyes seemed to glow in the late daylight. I was enchanted. "Hi, Travis. Come in."

"Are you sure? That dog looks pretty ferocious." He couldn't contain the smile on his face as he reached down and showed Harvey his hand to sniff. Harvey gave him a few licks and Travis responded by patting his head.

Once their greeting was official, he stood and came through the doorway, stopping in front of me. When he hugged me, I noticed it steadied my nerves. Careful not to leave lipstick on his crisp white shirt, I pulled back and said, "Follow me." Turning around, I walked up the few steps then crossed the room, leading him to the sliding doors. From the doorway, I waved my hand and asked, "See anything familiar?"

He was obviously thrilled as he walked past me and to the spot where I'd taken yesterday's picture. When he turned to face me, he said, "This really is paradise."

Seeing him there was intense. Little more than a week ago, he was a stranger to me. We were too alone for my comfort and I decided it was time to get him out of the house. "Now that you've seen the view, are you ready for dinner?"

His shoulders lifted, signaling he could take it or leave it. That wasn't an option, so I took the lead. "Come on, let's go." Once we were inside, I closed the door, tossed Harvey his treat and spirited Travis out of the house.

We walked the short distance toward the hidden gate. When we arrived I said, "I thought we'd walk to dinner." After unlocking the door, I ceremoniously held it open for him to pass. I followed him and waited while he soaked in the second delight I had in store for him this evening. He stopped at the edge of the path and studied the sprawling ocean that was framed by wild bougainvillea.

When I came to stand beside him, he looked down and said, "This is truly a dream. I can't believe I am here with you. Thank you for showing this place to me."

I couldn't believe it either. A strange combination of emotions swirled between us and I knew I had to keep things on track. "I'm glad you like it. Follow me. We're taking the beach to dinner."

I walked ahead, navigating the curvy path with the practice of someone who knew it well. Travis was no slouch and his legs were almost double the length of mine so he had no trouble keeping up. We made it to the bottom and walked the last few steps until we were standing on the sand. I reached down and slipped off my sandals.

He did the same and said, "Now I understand why you suggested I wear these."

I teased, "I assumed you don't often get to walk on the beach in Chicago, besides it's easier than trying to find a parking spot."

"This is the best commute to dinner I've ever seen. Please" he touched my shoulder, "lead the way."

We walked along the glowing shore, watching as the birds raced in and out of the tide. They dug their beaks into the sand, searching for a quick meal. The after-work running crowd passed us by, focused on their heart rates and step count. Travis was quietly taking it all in. My emotions vacillated between tranquility and chaos. A drink was definitely in order. Thankfully I didn't have to wait, since we'd arrived at the restaurant.

I broke the silence and said, "This is us."

He was surprised and said, "That didn't take long at all."

We walked inside and were greeted by the cheerful young hostess. "How many will there be tonight?"

"Two," Travis said.

"Right this way," she replied.

We followed her through the restaurant and finally settled on a table near the window. Once we sat, she handed us our menus and said, "The best seat in the house for the cutest couple of the day. Your server will be right with you."

After she left, Travis looked at me and said, "Did you hear that? We are the cutest couple of the day. I like this place." He chuckled.

It would be easy and even fun to pretend we were a couple, but I couldn't allow myself to buy into the picture. I didn't yet know how to define our connection, but one thing was certain, we weren't a couple. Fortunately, I was saved from responding by the arrival of our waiter.

"Good evening, you two. My name is Eric and I'll be

your server this evening. Would you like anything to drink before dinner?"

Travis deferred to me and I said, "I'll have a glass of Pinot Noir."

"Excellent," Eric said, "and for you, sir?"

"I'll have the IPA. Thanks."

"Not a problem," he said. "Today's specials are noted on the insert. I'll give you two some time to look at the menu and I'll be back with your drinks."

When he left, Travis said, "I assume you've been here before. What's good?"

"Everything is great. If you like seafood, I'd go that direction. They also make a terrific burger, but I don't want to disappoint you after the one we shared in Atlanta. Maybe you should try something else," I suggested with a smirk.

He stopped me with his eyes. "The best thing about eating that burger in Atlanta was the person I shared it with." He knew he'd stepped out of bounds so he averted his eyes to study the options.

I picked up my menu and tried to ignore the frisson of nerves that ran along my neck. It was difficult to focus on food choices when I was floored by the fact that Travis was sitting across from me. Thankfully, Eric arrived with our drinks. I knew the wine would bring me down a notch.

He set our glasses down and asked, "Do you have any thoughts after looking at the menu? Can I get an appetizer started?"

Travis asked me, "Are you okay if we start with the cheese board? It'll give us some time to decide."

"Sounds great to me," I said.

Eric confirmed, "Okay, I'll put that in and see you guys in a few."

The moment he walked away, Travis leaned forward and

with a glint of excitement in his eye, he said, "I have something to tell you, Madeline."

Not sure what to expect, I hesitated for a second then said, "Dare I ask?"

"My name is Travis, and I am a cheeseaholic."

I had to laugh at his silliness. Between his joke and the wine, a tiny amount of tension dissipated from my shoulders. I replied, "Welcome, Travis."

He smiled and continued, "Seriously, I'm kind of a connoisseur. When I saw they had Humboldt Fog as one of the day's selections, I had to have it."

His excitement about the cheese was charming and unexpected. "I had no idea you were so into dairy." I stifled a laugh and took another sip.

He looked out the window, and I joined him. The waning sunbeams created a peach halo through the fluffy clouds and the water took on a monochromatic hue. A shiver ran down my spine as I imagined what it would be like to live in the dark sea. Another of my phobias was being stranded in the ocean at night. Hopefully Travis didn't have a game for that occasion.

He turned to face me, and with a serious expression on his face, said, "How are you, Madeline? Can we talk about it now, whatever it is that brought you down here so quickly?"

His candor caught me off guard. I tried to summarize the conclusion of my engagement, but wondered how to make it concise. I said, "I just needed a little space from the home Nathan and the customer here was a good reason to get here quickly."

Travis took my hand across the table and said, "I'm so sorry. You must be going through a lot of emotions . . ."

"We'd been struggling for a long time. It was finally time to end it."

"Are you okay?" he asked.

"That's a tough one. It feels like someone let the wind out of the sails. I'm pretty sad. Nathan was my first and only relationship after Peter's dad left."

"I was surprised to hear that Peter was fifteen when you met him. In all of those years, you never dated?"

"I dated a little, but never anything serious, not until Nathan."

"What was different about him?" He touched my hand again. "I'm sorry. We don't have to talk about this."

"No, it's okay. Getting to know each other is part of being friends, right?"

He leaned back slightly and said, "It is."

"What was different, was what we had in common. We were both parents and working in the same field. There were some natural connections."

"That makes sense. Relationships have started on much less than that."

As I sat there, under his watchful eye, I was torn in two. Nathan and I were the past and I was sitting across from a man who was here for a reason. A flash of anger swept over me and I realized it was directed at Travis. I spoke without filter, and asked, "Travis, what are you doing here?"

Before he could answer, Eric arrived with the cheese platter. He set it on the table and walked us through the day's selection. "Would you like to order now or should I give you a few minutes?"

Travis said, "We could use some time. Thank you."

When Eric was out of range, he turned back to face me. "I'm here because I wanted to see you again. I know it's wrong, but I couldn't stop myself."

His admission was spoken so plainly that it deepened our bond. I felt the same, and as much as I wanted to, as much as

I knew what I should do, I couldn't bring myself to leave him alone. I wasn't ready for it to end. I tried for a joke instead. "Wild Horses?"

He took a scoop of the Humboldt Fog, smeared it on a slice of bread and foisted it toward my mouth. "Something like that, Shorty. Take a bite."

And I did. I took a bite. I took a sip. We ordered dinner and drank and laughed and for the rest of the night, we were just two people. We talked about growing up, those awkward adolescent years, and how our lives had evolved.

The evening was winding down when he asked me the most evocative question so far. "What did you think you were going to be when you grew up?"

Now there was something I hadn't pondered in a long time. I thought back to my childhood fancies and I answered him with a snicker. "I thought I would be a singer and an actress."

He smiled and I braced myself for his response. "You would make an incredible actress. I'm not sure about the singing though. Maybe you can give me a little performance so I can judge for myself," he teased.

"You're right to be unsure of my crooning ability. The reason I didn't become a singer is because I have terrible stage fright. I can't stand in front of people and sing. I'm more of a shower or car singer."

"I want to hear. What will it take to get a live performance from you?"

I felt a little feisty and it showed in my reply. "I'll tell you what, if I still know you by the time your birthday comes, I'll sing 'Happy Birthday' to you, Marilyn Monroe style. When is your birthday?" I asked.

His smile was alarming as he replied. "Ha, ha. You should have asked that question first. My birthday is at the end of

October. I think you'll still know me by then." He was about to say something else when the waiter arrived.

Eric asked, "How are you two doing? Was dinner to your liking?"

We surveyed our nearly clean plates and I complimented, "It was delicious."

"Can I interest you in dessert? We have a very special pineapple upside-down cake this evening."

My eyes must have lit up because Travis asked, "Do you want to give it a try?"

"How can I resist?" I said. I instantly worried about the dual implication.

"Very good. I'll be back in a while." Eric smiled and made his exit.

I leaned closer to Travis and said, "I love all things pineapple."

He laughed and said, "Me too. I was so hoping you'd want it."

I raised my wine glass in a toast and said, "Here's to pineapple and cheese."

He chuckled and I liked the way it relaxed his entire body. His glass met mine as he chimed, "Cheers."

I wanted to stay in the comfort of that restaurant, of that evening, with his attention feeding my soul. My wanting didn't change the truth. He wasn't free and I would not be the catalyst of tragedy. Instead, I resolved to enjoy the way the flickering light danced around us. I got lost in the gleam of his eye as he told stories about childhood friends. We savored the sticky-sweet pineapple cake, and I rationalized that if this was our last memory together, it would be a warm one.

After a swift walk back, we stood at the top of the trail and revisited the ocean view, only this time under a night sky. The moonless evening cast an eerie haze on the beach below, and the water looked ominous. In contrast, the restaurants and homes lit a cheerful path along the sleeping coastline. We hadn't spoken a word since we left the restaurant, each of us in our own heads. It was as if the air hit our face and our chariot turned into a pumpkin, but neither of us could acknowledge it.

The wind kicked up and with it came a damp chill. He put his arm around me. He was warm, and also big. These random thoughts kept me from the real situation. Had this been a date, it would have been a hell of a good one. Had this been a date, it would end with a goodnight kiss. I wondered what I would do if he tried to kiss me? Please, don't let me find out.

He turned and for a moment I panicked, but he pulled me into a hug. We held each other for a long time, until my nerves finally settled and his heartbeat slowed. Through the feedback of his chest, I heard him murmur, "Thank you, Madeline. Thank you so very much."

TAKE ME OUT TO THE
BALL GAME

Morning light filled the room and I opened my eyes to focus on the clock. It was 6:45 a.m. I blinked and tried to acclimate to the daylight, but a minor wine headache tugged at my temples. The dog felt me move, for he inched even closer to my hip, a clear indication he wasn't ready to start the day.

My thoughts swirled back to the night with Travis. I lay there for a moment, recalling how natural it was to spend time with him. Even at the end of the night, our goodbye could have become awkward, but it didn't. When he held me, it seemed like he understood what I was feeling. It amazed me we could be so open with one another, yet somehow reserved. Knowing our time was limited, it felt like we needed to cram everything in, but that was impossible. Ours would be a chapter, not a novel. The clock on the dresser reminded me of how fleeting it all was.

Needing to clear my head, I decided for a run. I had time before my first appointment and the dog would appreciate it. I might as well work out my neurosis on the sand. I pulled on my running clothes, splashed water on my face, and dragged the dog from his cozy spot on the bed. "Come on Harvey. Let's go earn some breakfast."

At the bottom of the path, I stopped Harvey just long enough so I could put earbuds in. Opening Pandora, I selected the top 40 station and we were off. Taylor Swift's "Delicate" set the tone for my internal counseling session. How apropos, since the lyrics made me think of an affair.

I let those thoughts in and admitted to myself that I was having an affair. Maybe we hadn't had sex, but there was a building intimacy between us. There was no way around it—however physically innocent, we'd crossed a line. Most puzzling was the fact that I didn't feel particularly guilty about it.

We jogged at a steady pace and I was thrilled to find that the little dog had wheels. The air felt good against my face and the movement was rejuvenating. The ocean tossed and swirled leaving the foam of whitewash in its wake. A burst of gulls flew against the morning sky and somehow, I found ease.

My thoughts came back to Travis. Our fateful meeting in Atlanta was less than two weeks ago. I lived in Oregon, he in Chicago, and last night we dined on a beach in Southern California. His work brought him here, but he'd gone out of his way to see me. Destiny may have introduced us, but last night was definitely orchestrated.

A rush of butterflies played in my stomach as I recalled the way he held me. The nearness of him was so welcome and at the same time, disconcerting. His touch caused every nerve ending in my body to stand at attention. I knew I wanted to be even closer to him, but that could lead nowhere good.

Cardi B.'s powerful voice was interrupted by a buzzing

sound through the headphones. I took the phone from my pocket and saw I received a text message from Travis.

Good morning, Shorty. I hope you had the sweetest dreams. Thank you again for showing me around and for your company last night. Any chance you'd be willing to do it again? Tonight?

We hadn't discussed seeing each other again. I assumed he'd go home before the weekend. Besides, I couldn't remain in denial if our meetings were premeditated. Still, it turned out to be such a fun and easy night. He was the perfect gentleman and if he wasn't going to be home anyway, what was I taking from his family?

Before I changed my mind, I quickly scribed, *Good morning, Travis. You're more than welcome. I guess I would be willing to do it again tonight. :)* I wanted to add, *but only if we can stick to the program. We're friends and nothing more.*

His reply was immediate. *Well, don't let me twist your arm. I, on the other hand, am very much looking forward to seeing you again. I can make it to you by around 6:45. Will that work?*

I couldn't stop the over-the-top grin from forming at my lips, nor the excited skip of my pulse as I replied, *That'll work. I'll see you tonight, Mr. Baker.*

I felt a tug at the leash, and looked down at Harvey. His big brown eyes stared up at me and his head tilted to one side. I wondered what he would say if he could talk. Dismissing the question, I gave his leash a little tug and set the pace for our run back to the house. There was plenty of time to consider Harvey's perspective later. For now, I would be happy.

HARVEY AND PRISCILLA CROWDED AROUND MY FEET AS I PUT their dinner bowls together. Priscilla's sickly-sweet mews were maddening Harvey who was jumping in circles. Their anxiety heightened my own, and I felt flushed. The workday had flown by. It was already 6:40 p.m. The doorbell rang before I could settle their dishes. I glanced through the glass and saw Travis standing there. I set the food down, a few feet apart to prevent any food fights, and made my way down the steps. Collecting my purse, I slid on my baseball cap and opened the door to greet him.

Straight white teeth beamed at me and the fresh scent of verbena floated between us. I couldn't help but admire the way he looked in dark jeans, Nikes, and a blue T-shirt. I crossed the threshold, gave him a quick hug and said, "Happy Friday. Are you ready to watch some baseball?"

A huge grin was on his face, and he said, "No better words were ever spoken, and look at you all decked out in fan gear."

Closing the door behind me, I said, "Oh yes, we take baseball very seriously in my family." As we walked the few steps to the driveway, I gestured toward the Tesla. "Hop in. I'm driving tonight."

He skipped into action. His long legs cleared the distance to the passenger side of the car in two steps. Rubbing his hands together, he said, "Madeline, you are the coolest woman I've ever known."

"Well, that's something," I said.

We settled into the car, and I couldn't stifle a laugh when I noticed his childlike expression as he studied the control panel. I fired up the engine and we started our ride down-town. Since it was nearly 7 PM and the commuter traffic was over for the weekend, the trip went smoothly.

As we drove, I made idol conversation and said, "If we're lucky, we might still make it on time for the opening pitch."

Travis smiled excitedly. "Maddie, sitting next to you anywhere would be a dream, but speeding along the coast in this car, on the way to a baseball game, is pretty much X-rated . . . opening pitch or not." He quoted a line from *Pretty Woman*, "In case I forget to tell you later, I had a really good time tonight."

I chided, wondering if it was a little too direct, "Ok Vivian, as long as you're not expecting any frosting, we'll be ok."

"Rubies and diamonds aren't really my style." He continued the volley. "Baseball, on the other hand, now that's my idea of frosting. The only thing that would make this better would be a Cubs versus Padres lineup."

I kidded, "Oh, sorry, I couldn't realign the entire National League for you. I hope the Rockies will do as a stand-in."

He stayed in character. Holding a straight face, he said, "I guess I can live with it."

I liked his wit. My grandmother came to mind. I could almost hear her sing-song voice say, "He has a way about him." Travis did have a way about him. Only I didn't know if his way was the practice of a philanderer or something else.

My silent rant was interrupted when he touched my elbow. I turned and our eyes clicked. He cleared his throat and glanced ahead, my signal to concentrate on the road. After a moment he said, "I'm sure you have some thoughts about me, about this situation."

Unprepared for the segue, I braced myself and said simply, "I do."

"This is unchartered territory for me so I hope I'm not over-stepping." He paused and ran his hand over his hair before saying, "I think I should tell you about my marriage." He looked pained, but went on. "This may not be logical, but I feel that if I talk to you about my wife, it is disloyal to her and also not kind to you. On the other hand, you're probably wondering why I'm worried about that when I'm spending time with you."

He looked down at his hands. I could tell he was struggling, and there was nothing for me to add, so I waited. He said, "This is pretty confusing and I just want you to know, I'm thinking about it."

Until that point, he'd shared little about his marriage and I didn't care to ask. I was in no position to form an opinion about his wife nor should I be trusted to give him advice. Nothing good could come from that kind of dual agency. Still, I wanted to learn something that justified his actions. I wanted to believe in him.

I was trying to process his words, and before I could respond he blurted, "We haven't slept together in nearly a year."

I was stunned into silence. He took an audible breath and said, "I'm not telling you this for sympathy or to justify my actions." He slowed his speech and continued, "I'm also not suggesting that's what's going to happen with us. It's just that the conversations we've had, and walking near you, it's more intimacy than I've had in a long time. I want you to know, this means something to me. In many ways it's wrong, and I don't want to hurt you, but this is the best I've felt in years."

His words rang true. Not only did I believe him, but I could relate. The last thing I wanted was to find myself in a relationship with a married man, but I couldn't turn a blind eye to the truth. He was there when I needed someone. Maybe I would have found my way back to the hotel without him, but that's not what happened. I didn't go looking for the guy, in fact, I did my best to give him a wide berth that evening. Regardless, in the end I found myself crying on his shoulder and opening up in ways I hadn't before. He deserved an honest response, but I needed a retreat to compose my thoughts.

Fortunately, I had to navigate the last few turns before finding the parking lot. I maneuvered into the driveway and up the ramp until we found a space. After cutting the engine, I turned to Travis and said, "Thank you for saying that. I've been struggling with this too. Maybe we found each other right when we were supposed to." I put my hand on his knee and nudged him. "One thing I know for sure, if we don't get our butts into gear, we're going to miss the opening pitch."

His face relaxed at my last comment and he said, "We wouldn't want to miss opening pitch."

AFTER A SHORT JOG, WE FOUND OURSELVES AT THE ENTRY. I unlocked my phone for the attendant to scan the tickets, and we passed through the gate just as the national anthem began. We rushed to stand at an overlook Hands over hearts, we listened as the patriotic ballad reverberated through the stadium. No matter how many times I'd heard it, the song always brought tears to my eyes.

When it ended, I inhaled and asked, "Drinks?"

"Yes, please," He agreed.

"This way," I said.

We moved up the escalator and to the concession stand. Travis looked down and asked, "What do you want to drink?"

"Hmm . . ." I studied the choices. "Red wine for me, please."

He ordered and within a moment our drinks were up. He handed mine over and said, "Lead on."

"This way," I replied, and we started toward our section. We paused at a landing that overlooked the field. I watched as Travis scanned the park with an impressed look on his face. I finally said, "We're on this side," and we walked down the flight of stairs.

Our seats were in the front row of the second tier, over-looking home base. We could see the entire stadium from this vantage point. The only thing separating us from the 90 miles-per-hour pitches was a net barrier, and I knew it would be an eventful night. The scoreboard was alight with images of the players and their statistics. The roving audience cam was in full swing, embarrassing couples and spotlighting excitable kids who were hoping to get noticed.

Travis looked at me. "These seats are incredible. How did you get them?"

I replied in my cheekiest tone, "Mister, I can't tell you all of my secrets. Got to keep it interesting."

His full brows rose, crinkling his forehead, and he said, "Madeline, there's been no shortage of interesting from the moment I first saw you."

Crack! The crowd went wild. The opposing team's player landed a solid hit to a dead zone in the outfield. The ball bounced once and the center fielder caught it. He quickly threw it to second base, but the runner was too fast and slid under the tag. I looked at the scoreboard. It was 0-0, with two strikeouts.

The next man up tested his swing at the sideline before taking his spot at home plate. Number 28 stepped onto the dirt, and the crowd booed. Unaffected, the player trained in on the pitcher and waited for the throw. The first ball sped by at 91 mph, but was just outside. The player on second stepped bravely away from the bag, attempting to gain a hefty leadoff, but the pitcher wasn't having it. He shot the ball to the second baseman, but the runner beat the throw back.

Now that second base was under control, the pitcher returned his attention to the catcher. A few hand gestures passed between them until the pitcher's nod set the strategy. Their silent plan complete, the pitcher wound his arm and sent the ball flying. It flew over the center of the plate at 92 mph. The batter was dumbfounded by his miss. The scoreboard flashed, 1 ball, 1 strike and it was time for pitch number three.

Pulling his cap down further, the pitcher decided the next throw. His nod to the catcher confirmed. He wound up and with a mighty lift of his leg, sent the ball down the pipe. It was straight and definitely not a meatball. Number 28 swung and the crack of his bat reverberated through the stadium. The ball launched forward, once again landing in the outfield, this time closer in. The second baseman ran to the ball. After a speedy assessment, he threw it home, hoping to stop the aggressive runner from scoring. The catcher stood to his full height, snagged the ball easily and tagged the runner. The ump called the third out and the crowd went crazy. It was the Padres' turn to bat.

Travis and I had been so immersed in the game that we hadn't spoken while the action was happening. As the players switched sides, I asked, "What do you think so far? Nice stadium, huh?"

"Oh, it's gorgeous. I can't believe the views from every angle. I heard the bar was pretty terrific here too."

I pointed to the old brick Western Metal building and said, "It's in there. The building was constructed in 1909 and there was a big debate about knocking it down for the proposed new ballpark. Ultimately, they decided to incorporate it into the design. Do you want to go check it out or are you someone who can't stand to miss even one pitch?"

He chuckled and said, "Baseball is a pretty long game and we're at the start of it. I think we can take a chance. Besides, from what I noticed on the way to our seats, they have monitors everywhere. I don't think we'll miss a second of the game."

"Okay," I said. "Let's go."

He stood and I followed him up the stairway and to the escalator. In no time, we rose to the top of the stadium and stepped off. Travis walked to the edge of a balcony that jutted out over the city skyline. The bay was dark beneath the evening sky, except for the reflection from the buildings. Their decorative lights created a mirrored effect against the water. A gentle breeze danced along my arm. Travis leaned forward and rested his forearms on the railing. He looked like a king, surveying his domain.

When he turned to face me, he asked, "Is everything beautiful in this city?" His eyes were serious and slightly hooded.

I blushed past the suggestion that hung between us and said, "It is an incredible place."

His attention remained a beat longer, then he shifted himself to standing. "Come on, Shorty, let's get you to the safety in numbers place."

We followed the signs the last few steps to the bar and entered the industrial-style structure. Concrete floors met original brick walls in the combination sports bar and memorabilia store. We wove past the shoppers and I peered out to the balcony. Much to my surprise, at the very edge of the patio was an open table. Only one of the chairs had an unobstructed view of the field, which explained the vacancies.

I pointed at the table and asked, "Want to grab that spot?"

He nodded and we walked through the glass doors. Travis saw the difficulty with the view so he rearranged the chairs slightly. He gestured for me to take the seat near the rail and moved the second stool closer to my right before sitting. Since he was tall, the wall that presented an obstruction for most was below his sightline.

He leaned in dramatically. His knee smashed my leg against the rail, as he pretended to crane his neck to see. The act, though not repelling, was unnerving. My natural instincts were to lean in. The thought crossed my mind to kiss his cheek, but I stopped myself. Instead, I gave his shoulder a push with both of my hands, and in a laughing tone said, "Would you care to switch sides?"

He straightened and smirked, but couldn't reply before our server arrived.

"Hi, I'm Sherry," she chimed. "Can I get you two something to drink, or maybe a referee?"

Travis replied, "I think we'll stick with drinks and food for now."

She looked over at me and I said, "I'll have a glass of red wine."

"All right, and for you, sir?" she asked.

Travis said, "I'll take a large IPA and can we get something to eat? Madeline, is there anything that sounds good to you?"

"Nachos?" I suggested.

"Okay," he said, and redirected his attention to Sherry. "We'll have the nachos with chicken, please. Thank you."

She smiled and said, "Great, I'll be back shortly, kids. Try to stay out of trouble."

When she left us, we looked at each other and laughed. Our silliness was interrupted by a loud crack as bat met ball. We looked at the field in time to watch it soar to the sky.

Unfortunately, it went so high it gave the centerfielder plenty of time to assess where it would land. After a few minor adjustments, he stood and waited for it to drop into his glove. That catch retired the inning.

As the players switched sides, I thought of Peter. He loved baseball. Suddenly, I missed him very much.

Travis must have noticed my expression. He asked, "Madeline, is everything all right?"

I turned to him and said, "Yes. Baseball makes me nostalgic. It reminds me of when Peter was small. He played for years when he was a kid."

Travis nodded in understanding and said, "My oldest played too. It was quite a time commitment."

"It's funny," I said, "I thought the same thing at the time. Two nights a week of practice and half of Saturday for games. It was a lot. Who knew how much I'd miss those times?"

"They do grow fast," he agreed.

"I see you two have settled down." Sherry's voice came from behind and she set our drinks down.

Travis held his hand up as if taking an oath and said, "We promise to keep it down. You have my word."

Sherry looked at him with a doubtful smile on her face and said, "I'll be back with your nachos."

I laughed and said, "I don't think she believes you."

He feigned an annoyed expression and agreed, "I think you're right."

After watching the game for a time, he broke the silence. "Maddie, there is something I've been wanting to ask you."

I took a sip of wine in anticipation of his question and said, "Yes?"

"Exactly when did you become a die-hard Padres fan?" he

chided, and looked me up and down, a jab at my team shirt and baseball cap.

I was about to filet him with a saucy response when Sherry arrived with the platter of nachos. "So far, you're keeping up your end, but I've got eyes on you," she joked. "Do you need anything else at the moment?"

We already had hot sauce and napkins, so I replied, "We're good for now. Thanks, Sherry."

The moment she left, Travis snagged a loaded chip and gobbled it up. When he finished chewing he said, "Seems to me someone asked a question."

I swallowed my chip and took a sip of the wine, it wasn't the best combination, but we were at a ball park. I said, "Shawna and Chris moved down here from L.A. when Peter was about six. Their kids are really good friends with Peter, more like siblings, and Shawna has been my best friend since college. After they moved, we came down a lot on the weekends and for vacation. During baseball season, if the Padres were playing I'd always find time to take him to the games. It was our thing together. This started long ago, before they built this stadium. Back then you could get the kind of seats we have today for a lot less."

"That is a nice memory. Does Peter still like baseball?" he asked.

"He does," I said. "He's a little fanatical at times. Although Oregon has no team, he still watches and roots for the Padres."

Travis looked puzzled and asked, "Why not the Dodgers or Angels? Did you never make it to their games?"

"Very observant, Mr. Baker. The first security company I worked for in L.A. was a boutique, referral-only kind of firm. We specialized in handling 'who's who' type of clients and mainly estate security. Though we were based in L.A., the owner took on projects in other areas. One of his clients was Trevor Hoffman. Do you know who he is?"

Travis looked at me as if my head was spinning in circles and said, "Of course I know who he is. He was just inducted into the Baseball Hall of Fame."

"That's right," I said. "Well, a funny coincidence ended up happening. Since Peter and I were pretty much regulars at the ballpark, I ended up getting us season tickets. Our seats were right past first base."

"Nice vantage point. Peter sounds like a lucky kid."

"Yeah, he used to love it," I agreed. "Anyway, at work we had a company picnic. All the employees and their families were invited for a barbecue. The special treat was, Trevor Hoffman was going to join us and would be signing autographs. Of course, Peter was excited to meet him in person."

"No doubt," Travis agreed.

"They set up a table for him and everyone lined up to get an autograph. When it was finally our turn at the front, Trevor Hoffman looked at me and said, 'You guys go to the games all the time, don't you?'

"I said, 'We do.'

He followed with, 'And you sit right off the first base bag, don't you?'

"I was floored and so was Peter. I answered him, 'We do.'

"He nodded and started talking to Peter asking him if he played and what position. It was terrific. You can imagine the conversation Peter and I had later. He was so excited to be noticed by the famous pitcher who was known for using binoculars to watch the game and study the players. Since we always sat near first base, I guess we were in his view. From that day forward, the Padres were his favorite team."

Travis chuckled and said, "What a cool memory for you both. I bet he looked forward to seeing you two there. He probably couldn't take his eyes off you. You just might have distracted him from the game and who could blame him?"

"It was great. All of those outings with Peter, so many years of baseball and I never got tired of it. People think being a single parent must be so hard. To tell you the truth, most of the time I was really happy. He was such a cool kid and it was fun hanging out with him."

"People think being a single parent is hard, because it is. Being a parent is hard even when you're married and there's two of you doing it. I can't imagine how it was for you, especially when he was small."

"I never thought about it being hard. I just loved him so much that I wanted him to feel happy and safe. That was all that ever mattered."

"Still, it must have been lonely," he said.

"Sometimes," I agreed, as I surveyed the decimated platter of nachos. Hoping to change the subject, I asked, "Do you want to give up the table and head back to our seats?"

"Sure, as great as this is, I'd love to see the finale from behind home plate."

He left cash to pay the bill and we stood to leave. His hand pressed the center of my back as he guided me to walk in front of him. I was thankful he couldn't see my face. I knew it was flushed. As we retraced our steps through the bar and down the escalator, I was careful not to act on my impulse to lean in to him.

We returned to our seats and, after a while, got comfortable with one another. Between cheers, we found any reason possible to touch, exchanging a friendly poke of the arm or the occasional high five. Our ankles grazed each other's on the ground. He tugged my cap down over my eyes and I stuck out my tongue. I learned he could whistle. He learned I could not. To anyone watching we looked like a cute couple out on a date.

Finally, it was the bottom of the sixth inning, with two outs. The Padres batter, number 22, had stepped off the plate for a quick test swing. I looked at the field and saw a man on second and another on third base. The crowd roared as number 22 returned to the plate. After a brief exchange with the catcher, the pitcher wound up and catapulted the ball down the center.

Number 22 swung beautifully. That rare and magical sound of a home run echoed above the screaming crowd. The sky exploded to life, as colorful fireworks spiraled from behind the stadium, creating a kaleidoscope against the black sky. The scoreboard flashed digital confetti, alternating with bold letters announcing, "HOME RUN." Everyone was on their feet, cheering as the runners made their victory step across home plate.

Travis looked at me. I tried to ignore the pull, but the moment conspired against us. He leaned down and I knew I would let him kiss me. When his lips touched mine, the softest whisper of electricity pulled me in. His tender mouth coaxed mine into a state of confusion. An involuntary sound escaped my throat. It was too much and I had to pull away.

For a moment, I couldn't move. The screaming fans and explosions from the fireworks did little to drown out my scattered thoughts. That just happened. Travis and I kissed. It had been five years since I kissed anyone but Nathan.

A woman to my side jumped up and down and playfully bumped her hip into mine. Her joyous expression could not be contained as she raised her hand to give me a high five. I tried to match her enthusiasm and slapped her hand in automatic response. Though celebrating felt inappropriate, it was probably a better choice than running from the park.

MY ENTIRE BODY WAS STIFF AS I DROVE US HOME FROM THE game. We left shortly after the seventh-inning stretch when I suggested the traffic might be difficult if we waited. From the time we'd kissed, the strangest darkness had come over me. I needed time away from him to process what had happened. It was time for the night to end.

Travis tentatively cleared his throat. "Madeline."

I stopped him before he could say anything more. I needed to lead the conversation. "How did you like the game?" I asked.

After a beat he said, "It was the best surprise. I really appreciate you taking me."

Keeping to the safe subjects, I said, "No problem. You can't visit San Diego during baseball season and miss out on a Padres game."

"It would be a shame," he agreed.

I could feel his attention on me, though I didn't dare look his way. I didn't have the words or the courage to address the most important topic. Travis picked up on my cue and remained quiet for the last part of our drive.

After what seemed like an eternity, we exited the highway and wound our way west. The street lights were in our favor, since each one lit green as we approached. Soon, I made the last turn and we pulled into the driveway.

Travis stayed seated, looked over and said, "I hope I didn't ruin anything."

My mind raced. I knew it was best to sweep that kiss under the rug and extract myself quickly. "Travis, I had a great time. Thank you for coming down and for listening to all my stories. It was fun."

"You don't need to thank me, Madeline. I wanted to be

here. I know it doesn't make sense and I'm sorry I've upset you."

I resolved to handle this with the nonchalance that only a trained actress could muster. Settling a smile on my face, I said, "I'm not upset, just tired. It's been a long week."

With that comment, I opened the car door and got out. Travis did the same and walked over to my side of the car. He stood in front of me and I couldn't look at him. I shuffled my feet until he pulled me into a tight hug. At first, I stiffened, but the tempting fragrance of his cologne against his freshly laundered T-shirt seduced me. His gentle hands rested at the center of my back and my arms naturally circled his waist. I shut my eyes and let everything else fall away.

We lingered until Harvey's insistent woofs brought me to reality. I stepped back and said, "That's the sound of my curfew."

His expression was pained. "Indeed, it is."

He walked with me to the front door and when I turned to say goodnight, he did it again. His mouth found mine in a determined, though brief, kiss. When he pulled back, he didn't speak. He just turned and walked away, leaving me breathless.

IT'S JUST BUSINESS

Monday morning started with a flurry of to-do items. I was already on my third cup of coffee and it was only 7:30. Per my now standard routine, I started the workday early to tackle emails ahead of the day's meetings.

I was about to head for the shower when another email came through. This one was from Robert. I opened the message and saw that John West was also copied. The subject said, "Ride Along." I quickly read the message.

MADELINE,

John West will be in Portland this week. He wants to spend Thursday and Friday with you and in front of customers. I'll be coming down on Thursday afternoon. Plan on having dinner with us that night.

To prepare for his visit, set appointments with Mandray Enterprises, Fright Flight and Shae Manufacturing, and two additional prospects you've been working with. He lands at 9 a.m. and you'll need to pick him up at the airport before the appointments. John will text you the flight information; until then, please get your schedule in order.

THANKS,

   Robert

I WASN'T SURE HOW TO REACT TO HIS MESSAGE, AND I DIDN'T have time to ponder the meaning behind John's abrupt visit. The additional meetings meant I had to shift my schedule around. With everything I'd already planned, this week would be another long one.

༒

THURSDAY MORNING ARRIVED AND WITH IT CAME A STEADY level of anxiety. As I drove to the arrivals section of the airport, I glanced at my phone. John's text said he'd be waiting by the Alaska Airlines terminal. I inched my way there and saw him standing at the curb. His blue suit and white shirt were so crisp, it was as if he'd had them pressed after the flight. Taking a deep breath, I pulled up to the walkway, put the car in park, and got out to greet him.

"Hi there," I said and opened the trunk. "How was your flight?"

His forced smile was transparent, and his cold, dark eyes didn't shift when he replied. "Fortunately, it was uneventful so I was able to get some work done on the plane."

Such a warm and friendly guy. I placed his bags in the trunk, closed the hood, then circled around to the driver's seat. When his seat belt was fastened, I pulled from the curb.

John began the conversation, while studying the road ahead. "Where are we going first?"

"We're headed to meet Mike Quick, the VP of Facilities at Iron Run. I met one of the directors at the SSI conference and he's arranged a meet and greet."

He was quick to respond, "What is your agenda for the meeting?"

Through this brief exchange, I was already starting to see a "leadership style" resemblance between Robert and him. "Hmm, I thought I added it to the calendar invitation I sent on Tuesday. The agenda is pretty straight forward. First and foremost, it's a meet and greet. Shane Freeman, the director I met at SSI, would like us to look at replacing a few of the cameras at their local facility. They have four manufacturing sites in the region, all with aging systems. The end game is us getting our equipment in those sites, and today is the first step.

"If you take a look at the emails I sent last night, you'll find one regarding Iron Run. There are notes about Shane, and some information on their standards and procurement process."

I glanced at John and saw his jaw clench as he unlocked the phone to read. The silence was awkward, but not as strange as the robotic volley we'd been having. He was either extremely unfriendly or, for reasons unknown, the man disliked me. Maybe it embarrassed him that I'd planned the meeting and he missed the message, but it should demonstrate my competence. I wasn't a rookie.

After a couple of minutes, he looked up and said, "Good detail here. Let's kick the door down."

He spoke in such a flat tone that I almost laughed, but the necessity for a paycheck stopped me. I said, "I'm in. You do the kicking."

❧

THE MEETING WAS ABOUT TO WRAP UP. MIKE QUICK, THOUGH courteous, was squirming in his seat. From the moment we shook hands with the men, John hadn't stopped talking. He went so far into detail about the product line and new offerings he left us no time for discovery.

Shane made eye contact with me several times and I was at a loss. What could I do to stop John's verbal diarrhea, kick him under the table? Noticing the time and that we were expected at our next meeting in thirty minutes, I interrupted. "I hate to cut this short, but John and I are on a bit of a schedule today."

The relieved look on Mike's face was evident. He said, "Thank you for watching the time Madeline. I have another meeting in a few minutes myself."

He stood and we all joined. As we walked down the corridor, we paired up. Shane and I went ahead while John and Mike hung behind. When we were out of range, Shane said under his breath, "Your boss is kind of a talker, huh?"

If only being embarrassed in front of clients were new. Unfortunately, I'd witnessed this type of meeting before. The big bosses fly in to throw their weight around, but rarely lend anything substantive to the sessions. From what I could tell, many of the people who advanced into management had a similar make up. Most were shameless self-promoters who spent more time talking than listening.

I wanted to reassure him and said, "Don't worry Shane, he's just here to shake babies and kiss ass. I'll be the one you work with in the end."

Shane snickered and said, "I understand. Good luck this week."

We arrived at the lobby and waited as John and Mike

made the last few steps. John took two business cards from his pocket and gave one each to Mike and Shane. "It was a pleasure to meet you both. Please keep me in the loop on anything you need."

Mike shook his hand, then mine, and said, "Thank you both for coming in. Shane will be Madeline's point of contact for this project. He'll keep me up to date with the results after the cameras are replaced."

I shook Shane's hand and said, "Thank you for arranging this. I'll get back to you soon with the details for the camera installation."

Next, I took Mike's hand and said, "Mike, I really appreciate you taking the time out of your busy schedule to meet with us."

He smiled, and I thought I saw a trace of humor on his lips. "My pleasure, Madeline. You guys have a good day."

❧

Two meetings later, the sound of John's voice grated against my nerves. It didn't help that I was sitting in a major traffic jam, or that I was stuck with him, and Robert, for the evening. The day had already been quite long and now there was the dinner to face.

I maneuvered the last few blocks and found parking in front of the restaurant connected to John's hotel. We got out of the car and he took his suitcase. "You go ahead to the restaurant. I'm going to check in and drop my bags. I'll join you and Robert shortly."

When he left, I took a moment to check my phone for messages. As expected, there were several emails that required my attention. I responded to the ones I could, then looked at the text notifications. There were two from Travis.

2:48 PM. *I hope the meetings with John are going ok.*

4:08 p.m. *Call me later if you have the time.*

At 5:18 I quickly scribed a reply. *I'm not sure if I'd describe this day as okay, but I'm stuck for a while. John and Robert want me to have dinner with them. Text back if you'd still like me to call when we're done.*

After replacing the phone in my purse, I crossed the street and took the few steps into the restaurant. Scanning the room, I saw Robert was already there and seated. He stood as I approached and said, "Hey there."

We shook hands and I asked, "How are you? Was the drive in ok?"

He cleared his throat and spoke. "It was. I slid in under the traffic so it worked out. Where's John?"

"He went to check-in to the room," I said.

"How were the meetings today? Do we have a shot at the Iron Run account?" he asked.

I wouldn't confide to him how I felt the meetings really went, so instead I kept it safe and said, "We do. The first step is to upgrade a number of their oldest cameras at the facility here. If they perform well, we'll be considered for the other projects."

Robert didn't look pleased, and said, "Baby steps. What about the meeting with—"

He couldn't finish his thought because we were interrupted by the arrival of John and our server. Robert stood and shook John's hand, while the server stood back waiting for their exchange to end.

Once John sat, she asked, "Can I bring you both something to drink? Another round for you?" Her eyes rested on Robert.

I noticed he was drinking brown liquor, which was a

relief because I wanted a martini. Robert answered first, "Yes, I'll take another."

John looked my direction and I went for it. "I'll have the Classic Martini, please."

"And for you, sir?"

"I'll have the Classic Martini as well."

"Very good. I'll get this started and leave you to study the menu."

When she left, Robert resumed his questioning. "Madeline gave me her perspective on the Iron Run meeting. What did you think about the meeting, John?"

He sighed and said, "It went pretty well, but I'm not sure they're serious. We didn't have enough time to find out if they have a budget for the upgrades or if they're just putting feelers out."

His lackluster reaction toward the first meeting I secured caused a flash of heat across my chest. Iron Run was a new prospect and a major shoe manufacturer. Did John believe that Directors and VPs at companies like Iron Run took meetings for fun? If their account wasn't a good enough opportunity, I wondered what would be.

Robert looked at me and asked, "What about the rest of the day? How were things at Mandray and Fright Flight?"

As I had grown accustomed, after the long day I spent with the man, John was quick to reply. "Mandray and Fright Flight need support. I've tapped Lane Fine in the product department and he will follow up directly with those accounts."

Robert looked anything but pleased. Fortunately, his expression softened at the arrival of our cocktails. The server set each drink down and swept her eyes over the group. "Would you like to order anything right away or should I give you time to settle in?"

John said, "We haven't eaten anything all day. Can we start with the fried calamari and also the caprese salad?" He looked toward me and asked, "Does that work, Madeline?"

What was it with men, business dinners, and fried calamari? It seemed to be mandatory at every function. Not that I disliked it, but we were in the Northwest and there were so many options on the menu. Still, I agreed as if it were my choice. "Terrific."

"Great," she said, "I'll put this in and check back on you."

She left us and we reached for our drinks in synchronicity. At least there was one bit of common ground between us. Robert's gravelly voice commanded us in a toast, "Here's to one of the perks. Cheers."

The perfectly constructed martini met with my empty stomach and I knew the effects would soon be felt. I'd expected to get lunch between meetings, but John's long-winded speeches caused us to overrun time at every sit-down. After a long day with him, I was becoming used to sitting quietly while he talked. It seemed this dinner would be no exception. I listened as he and Robert discussed some of the other accounts and was comforted by the sensation of a quick buzz.

In no time, our server returned carrying the appetizers and a basket of bread. She set everything down and asked, "Do you want to order dinner or should I come back?"

John replied, "We'll be good for a while."

She left and I watched as the guys dug into the fried tendrils. I forked a wedge of cheese covered with tomato onto my plate and pulled a warm slice of bread from the basket. The food tasted incredible after the day's fast.

Before long, John sat back, wiped his mouth with a napkin and asked, "How are you feeling about the company so far, Madeline?"

I swallowed my bite and replied as expected. "I'm learning a lot and everyone has been great."

"I'm glad you feel that way." He paused as if deliberating and began again, saying, "Listen, Robert and I wanted to meet with you because we have some concerns. Don't be alarmed, we aren't doing a written warning or anything, but some things have to change for us to move forward."

Whatever buzz I had, it instantly vanished. I was terrified by his words. Literally at a loss for a response, I couldn't imagine what was coming next.

John didn't let the silence last long and said, "There's no need to become emotional. We just want to establish some protocol with you. If you can honor it, things should be fine."

His sexist stab nearly got the response it deserved. Oh, how I wished I could dump the dregs of my drink in his bloated face and walk the fuck out of there. Instead, I set my ego aside, willed my face to be contrite, and asked, "Please, what I can do?"

John replied, "Have you ever heard the term, '*chain of command*'?"

Who hadn't? I thought, but responded simply, "I have."

"Do you understand what it means?" he asked.

"I do."

"Then you *do* understand the importance of following a *chain of command*?"

The moment was surreal in a way I likened to a movie scene. I felt like a child being scolded by my father. I started to respond, but he held up a hand, a rude indication he wasn't finished.

"We're all just getting to know one another, and it's important to set the right expectations from the start. Do you agree, Madeline?"

I replied as expected, "Absolutely, John."

"Good," he said. "Here's what I need from you. Moving forward, I want you to document your work, and anything additional Lori assigns, in your calendar. When she requests something from you, immediately send a written summary of the assignment, copying Robert and myself on the email. You and Robert will meet every day to review your activities. Does that make sense so far?"

My throat was dry, but I managed, "It does."

"Excellent," he said and continued, "and we three will meet every Friday to review your progress."

"Okay," I confirmed.

John leaned forward and said, "I'd also like you to complete an in-depth market analysis as a part of your training process. Can you have that to me by Monday?"

My market involved six states. To do it right, the project would take all weekend. I was seething inside, but I presented the demure face of a porcelain doll. "I will do my best on the report, and I think I understand your expectations now."

His disingenuous smile sickened me. He wetted his lips and spoke as if he were conspiring. "I want you to know, you have an advocate in me. I love hiring women into non-traditional roles, and bringing them into the sales ranks. It helps me reach my diversity metrics, and the customers appreciate it. I want it to work out as much as you do. What do you say we start off on a new foot?"

It felt like I was in a bad dream. His words were out of line, yet he actually believed himself to be a kindly benefactor. This man was one the most overtly sexist people I'd ever encountered in business, and that was saying a lot.

Robert found his voice, and his empty expression was so telling. "I'm game if you are, Madeline. I hope we can work together."

With my back against an invisible wall, I now understood

the reason for the abrupt dinner. Their in-person warning placed me at the edge of a blade, and I realized these men were in charge of my destiny. I thought of a poem written by Paulo Coelho; one line came to mind. "A warrior thinks about both war and peace and knows how to act in accordance with the circumstances."

In the spirit of Mr. Coelho's poetry, I summoned my composure and said, "I know we can."

"Great," Robert said. "Now if you don't mind, John and I have a few other things to go over. Maybe you can take off, have an early evening?"

Not that I wanted to stay, but it was the final insult in a string of them, and further proof that I was not long for their world. I set my napkin on the table, took my purse from the chair and politely said, "Of course. Thank you for dinner and John, I'll pick you up at eight."

"Thanks, Madeline," he said without a trace of sincerity. "I'll see you in the morning."

With that dismissal, I stood up; neither Robert nor John felt the need to. Before I left, I said, "Goodnight."

I heard them both say, "Goodnight," as I walked away.

❧

I STEPPED OUTSIDE, AND A RUSH OF CITY NOISE UNDERLINED reality, proving this wasn't a dream. Cars whizzed past, while a man sat on the walkway in front of the restaurant. His dog, cat, and mouse all joined him at the sidewalk pop-up he'd created. The sign that rested at his knee said, "We're hungry. Anything helps." The animals were an unfair prop. I only hoped he took care of them, after all they were his big draw. Reeling from the unsettling "dinner" I'd just left, I was compelled to show this man the mercy I needed. I pulled some cash from my purse and dropped it in the hat before jaywalking across the street.

As I walked away, I heard him say, "God bless you, blonde angel."

His words felt more like stabs, since it seemed as though God had recently abandoned me. I got into the car and for a moment, was stoic. The shock of John's aggressive and barely veiled threat was still sinking in. I was on thin ice at work, and I'd done nothing but follow the instruction of my superiors. There was no point in defending myself with John or Robert. Obviously, the politics ran deep in my new company, and I was at a disadvantage. Having been on board only a month, and with the disparate nature of our offices, how was I to know the history and strategies of these people?

Today showed me more than I wanted to know. Throughout the day, I watched as John talked over me and every person in his audience. His rudeness knew no bounds as he held his hand up in a gesture to silence me. The sexism that exuded from both him and Robert, spoken aloud and brushed aside as a natural occurrence, was like a fart in an elevator. To say I was defeated fell short of the truth. John had been with the company for more than twenty years, and Robert over ten. If they were the example of leadership that the company retained, I wasn't going to fit in.

Sadly, finding a security company with female leadership at the helm was almost worse than the other companies I'd worked for. It seemed as if the disdain for her command bled into the field, creating jealousies and a cut-throat atmosphere. I was shocked by the comments of some of my new team-mates. Several told me that Lori was promoted after a relationship with the Product Line Director. Their theory made no sense. What impact could a Product Director have over the executive leadership board of a publicly traded company, and why would they take his advice in appointing a sales VP? I said that to a few and it seemed to dissuade further comment. After tonight, there was no mistaking the culture, or lack thereof, at World View International..

A combination of panic and rage intertwined and I felt disoriented. What had I gotten myself into by accepting this job? This sense of helplessness was the very reason I wanted to strike out on my own. A wave of resentment washed over me and I wondered if Nathan could feel the invisible daggers poking his flesh.

With my thoughts so hectic, I knew I needed clarity and to put things into perspective, but how could I? Then I remembered my promise to call Travis after dinner. I pulled the phone from my bag and scrolled to see his text response.

At 5:33 Travis wrote, *Yes, call me after dinner. I'll talk to you then.*

I switched on the ignition and once the services were active, dialed his number. As the phone rang, I maneuvered from the curb and onto the one-way street. By the third ring he answered.

"Hello, Madeline." His deep voice sounded so cheerful in stark contrast to my sentiments.

"Hi, Travis."

"How are you?" he asked.

I couldn't formulate an eloquent response, instead I snickered oddly.

"That good, huh? Want to tell me about it?"

I paused, trying to find the best summary for how my day went, and decided to give him the whole story. I told him about the customer meetings and the conversation I'd had with John and Robert over dinner. Travis listened in silence. At one point, I checked to make sure we hadn't been disconnected. He was still there.

When I got to the part about the homeless man calling me angel, Travis finally spoke. "Maddie, let that be the one thing that stands out for you today."

I sniffed. "I'm not sure I can overlook the less than veiled threat that John and Robert issued."

"No, and you shouldn't. Have you considered talking to HR about the matter?" he asked.

His intentions were good, but I knew Travis didn't understand the stakes. Though he also worked in a public company, Swift had been in business for less than twenty years. As a result, they had a more politically correct culture than the hundred-year-old conglomerate I worked for. If I went to HR, I would be blacklisted, and they would terminate me at the first opportunity, likely slandering me in the process.

Without going into detail, I said, "I'm not going to report them to HR. That wouldn't do any good, besides it would be their word against mine. With their tenure at the company, who do you think HR would support?"

He was silent for a moment, then he said, "I have the answer."

I didn't know what was coming next and inquired, "You do?"

"I do," he said. "And I don't want you to worry."

I chuckled and wondered what he could have in mind. "You're scaring me a little."

"Shorty"his voice sounded serious, in contradiction to the playful nickname he used"I have an idea that just might help the both of us. Give me until tomorrow and we'll find out together."

AFTER ANOTHER SLEEPLESS NIGHT, I WOKE BEFORE 6 AM. A sense of dread swept over me, but regardless of how I felt, I knew what I needed to do. Throwing back the covers, I put one foot in front of the other and got out of bed. Once downstairs, I took the day's supply of peanuts from the cabinet, and threw them unceremoniously out the front door. Still dark outside, it was a little early for the birds, but I knew they'd be here soon enough. I entered the dark kitchen and berated myself for forgetting to make the coffee last night. With everything that happened yesterday, I was so exhausted that I went straight to bed when I got home. I haphazardly poured coffee grounds into the filter and added water to the side before switching the machine on. If nothing else, I was tackling my routine with consistency.

With a steaming cup of coffee in hand, I sat at the dining room table to review the day's email when an ungodly screeching erupted from outside. I rushed toward the front, where I thought the noise was coming from, and pulled open the door. A flurry of birds, a mass of action, and a choir of guttural pleading flooded the air with adrenaline. I homed in on what they were concerned with and watched in horror as a giant hawk wrestled with a Steller's Jay. The flock of Scrub jays teamed with the Steller's in a joint war against the two-foot giant who was killing one of theirs. Still, twenty or more of these small birds were nothing compared to the dominant predator.

I screamed and the hawk turned. Our eyes met, and I was silenced. His composure proved this was his moment, and he wanted me to know his glory. Pulling my attention to his prize, I saw the listless creature trapped in his talons and knew there was nothing I could do. It took no effort for his five-foot wingspan—the bird pumped once, then twice, and was skyward. His prey dangled loosely, for little effort was required to carry the measly freight. One determined jay screamed and followed the hawk while the other birds hung back and cried in mourning.

The graphic scene shook us all. The powerful hawk fought desperately for his cannibalistic feast, demonstrating the power of determination, for he would go to any length to live. The others tried to fight, but even together they were no match for his strength and survival skills. It left me feeling hopeless, and I prayed it wasn't an omen of things to come.

❧❧❧

WITH THE INSANITY OF THE MORNING, MY FLOCK SET ME behind schedule. I pulled up to the hotel at 7:45 AM and was finally getting to my messages. I opened the text icon first.

There was a message from Travis at 7:01 that said, *Good morning. Surprises sometimes come in the form of email.*

I wasn't sure what to make of that, but hurried to check. I scanned my email, scrolling past several of the daily reports, until I found the one from Travis.

DATE: SEPTEMBER 28, 2018 06:59 A.M. PST
> ***From:** TravisBaker@swiftco.com*
> ***To:** MadelineCraig@WVI.com*
> *LoriHaines@WVI.com*
> *RobertGrain@WVI.com*
> *CharlesBradford@swiftco.com*
> ***Attachments**: Meeting Schedule / Construction Schedule / Bid Criteria / NDA*
> ***Subject:** SSI Conference and Support Needed*

· · ·

Hello WVI Team,

I intended to reply message to your follow-up after the conference but time got away from me. It was a pleasure to meet with you during the show. Not only was your event outstanding but there could be some immediate business opportunities as a result. I want to specifically thank you, Lori, for taking the time to share WVI's roadmap for future technologies, and Madeline, for your contact after the conference.

We enjoy working with likeminded, innovative, and customer-centric companies. Because of that, we've decided to put you to the test. We have several locations needing support or ground up solutions. Two of the sites will be handled by Charles Bradford (copied) and the other by myself. They are quick turn projects and one will be a high-profile construction project. We've already received two competitive estimates. The award criteria will be based on the best price and the supplier's ability to perform against aggressive schedules.

I request that Madeline Craig be my point of contact over the three projects. This simplifies matters for me and will help streamline communications. She and the appropriate technical engineer will be required to attend a full-day site walk with the electrical contractors and myself at our New York location.

Attached, find the meeting details, the construction schedule and bid criteria. After review, reply with your interest and the signed non-disclosure agreement. Should you decline, please do so by end of day, today.

Sincerely,
Travis Baker
Swift Projects Director

. . .

I QUICKLY REVIEWED THE ATTACHMENTS AND NOTICED THAT the New York dates coincided with Travis' birthday. The timing of his business need was certainly fortuitous. No doubt our budding "friendship" was at play. Still, I justified, this opportunity could buy me the time to look for something else, even leave on a high note, and who doesn't want to go to New York in October?

I didn't have much time before John would arrive. At 7:50 I texted Travis. *You are a lifesaver. I owe you one. Thank you so much.*

Three roving dots showed me he was replying. The message came back a second later. *You don't owe me anything. I am looking forward to seeing you in New York though.*

I quickly typed, *Thank you again. Meeting John in a minute. I'll text you later.*

I started a new message to John. *I'm parked on 6th Avenue across from the restaurant entry. See you in a few.*

While waiting for John, I worked through my other emails and even found time to review the reports. After a while, I looked at the clock and saw it was already 8:05. John was nowhere in sight. I called him. The phone rang once, twice, and on the third ring it sent me to voicemail. Polite as he'd proven thus far, I assumed he was close and didn't want to waste the time answering. A couple of minutes later and still no sight of him, I reluctantly dialed again.

This time his raspy voice answered. "Hel, Hello," he grumbled.

"John," I ventured, "it's Madeline. I'm waiting downstairs."

A loud bang occurred, and I asked, "Hello, John? Are you there?"

There was a wrestling sound and finally he reclaimed the

phone. "Madeline, I can't go with you. I'm sick. Food poisoning, I think."

My manners were automatic, and I asked, "Are you ok?"

A high-pitched giggle emanated from behind John's snappy response, and there was no mistaking, he had female company. "I'm fine. Be prepared for our call at four. I have to go." With that he disconnected the line.

I sat dumbfounded for a moment and I wondered if he was even aware of my news. Per his explicit instructions the previous evening, I'd forwarded him the email from Travis as soon as I read it. I'd expected to talk about it in person today, but that wasn't on the agenda this morning.

Before I could pull from the curb, my phone rang. I wasn't familiar with the number, but answered anyway. "Hi, this is Madeline."

"Good morning, Madeline." Her firm, but bright voice came through the surround. "This is Lori Haines."

"Yes, of course. How are you, Lori?" I asked.

She replied, "I'm pleased. Great teamwork getting our foot in the door at Swift. I want you to know, I'm keeping an eye on you and I like what I see. Is John there with you?"

Another day, another feather ruffled. How could I answer her without making a tenuous working relationship worse? "He and I spent the day together yesterday and we're meeting later."

Lori was quiet for a moment, and finally said, "All right then. I've replied to Travis with the NDA, thanking him for the chance to support their projects. I'll send John my approval for the travel expenditure and resource allocation. Please update me by next Wednesday with your agenda and the anticipated budget."

"I will, Lori, and thank you for your support."

"Goodbye," she said, and the line went silent.

I drove to my first appointment thinking about all that had transpired since I joined the company, and everything I needed to accomplish by next Wednesday in order to keep my job. The relationships between my supervisors and executive leadership were confounding, as was the culture, or lack thereof, at WVI. I thought of the people I'd met thus far and, Lori aside, the organization looked like the class of 1980's Young Republicans convention. The group—comprised of aging white men, their lecherous glances, and disdain for women in the workplace—was so outdated, yet nothing would change them. It was impossible to relate to their psychology or this antiquated company where status quo was valued above progress. These weren't the visionaries who understood how a strong company culture could translate to sales growth.

⁂

At 3:57 PM I raced through the front door and to the dining table. Opening my laptop, I quickly logged into the conference call that John and Robert scheduled. The process was complete with a minute to spare. I waited while listening to the annoying elevator music that played until the call was activated.

Time passed and it was now 4:02 p.m. I sent a text to Robert. *Hi. I'm waiting on the conference line. Just wanted to make sure nothing went wrong.*

At 4:04 Robert replied. *John and I are wrapping something up, hang tight.*

The cheerful—if spastically composed—hold music continued to torture me for the next nine minutes. At 4:13 John's voice finally came through. "Hello, Robert and Madeline, are you there?" In the background I could hear an announcement over a loudspeaker. Clearly, he was at the airport.

I unmuted the connection. "Yes, Madeline is on."

Robert did as well. "Here, boss."

"Okay," John said. "Before we talk about today's appointments, I need to understand something from you, Madeline."

I waited for his question.

"When were you going to inform Robert and me of your follow-up efforts with Swift? Why are we learning of this opportunity from the customer and not you?"

My blood pressure spiked, but I talked myself down with a deep breath. Buy yourself time, I thought, and I expelled the dirty air. "I have updated my activities in our system. I followed up with every customer and prospect we met during the conference. There wasn't much to report until his message came this morning."

John replied snidely. "It is my understanding that you invested quite a lot of time with Travis Baker during the SSI conference. Are you suggesting that this is the first communication you two have had since Atlanta?"

I didn't reply quickly enough and John stopped me. "Never mind. It is what it is, and here we are again. Lori has given her preliminary approval. I'll need the travel schedule and budget from you by Monday. I've got to cut this short since we're boarding soon. Send me a synopsis of the meetings from today and we'll reconnect next week."

With that, Robert said, "Have a safe trip home, John. Say hello to Heidi and the kids for me."

"Thanks," he said, "I will. Goodbye." The conference call disconnected and I didn't even have the time to be pissed. My weekend was booked solid with work.

SIGHT SEEING IN NYC

"Good evening ladies and gentlemen, this is the Captain. We are making our final descent into La Guardia where the weather is fifty-six degrees and the time is 7:42 PM Please follow the attendant's instructions as they make their rounds through the cabin. As always, we know you have a lot of choices when you fly, thank you for picking Southwest. We hope to see you again soon."

I looked out the window and watched in wonder as we circled the great city. Even as we hovered some distance away, the unmistakable skyline was emphasized by the colorful lights that outlined the otherwise dark buildings. They all seemed to conspire toward the most recognized and orgasmic of them, the Empire State Building. Enormous bridges glowed against the murky night and stood formidably above the water, connecting busy roadways to foreign lands like Brooklyn and Queens. My pulse quickened at the reality of this endeavor.

The weeks leading to the trip had flown by, and all the effort was about to prove out. There was more hanging on this meeting than I cared to address. For weeks I was focused on the business planning while doing my best to placate the egos of Robert and John—my ever-bullying middle managers. When they got tough, I called up the image of that hawk, willing myself to be as formidable and strategic as he.

I had doubts about the propriety of WVI's opportunity towards these projects. The purpose of going to conferences was to make new connections, and promote your offering. That was how it started, but I had to wonder would it have come to this had Travis and I not become friends? Not that he committed to awarding us the contracts. We still had to offer the best price and terms, but his influence might give us some small advantage. That didn't sit well with me and I intended to set the record straight when I saw him.

After a smooth landing, the plane taxied and soon we were at the gate. I stood and stretched to get my bag from the overhead shelf. That short tussle behind, I made my way through the airport and followed the signs toward ground transportation.

I passed security and was trying to decipher which way to go when I saw my own last name. Travis stood at a distance, holding a sign that had "CRAIG" written on the front. My nerves melted a little, seeing his soft grey eyes and those fluttery lashes that seemed to brush a bit of mist away at the sight of me. We met halfway and he swallowed me into a cozy hug. He smelled and felt like coming home. For a moment, I lingered in his arms.

When we pulled back, he said, "You're a vision, Shorty." His eyes never left mine, but I knew he appreciated the effort I'd put into my outfit. For the occasion, I wore a grey sweater dress and a new pair of black booties.

"It's nice to see you too, Mr. Baker." He was wearing his usual dark denim and a navy V-neck sweater.

He rested his arm around my shoulder and we walked

companionably, navigating through the airport and to the taxi stand. Within no time, we were at the front of the line. Travis took my bag and handed it to the driver before giving him our destination.

As we started the drive into Manhattan, I was contemplative. I'd spent the weeks planning the work. Tonight, I was confronted by the other facet of this journey, namely, the man whose knee rested against mine. I didn't want to warm into the conversation. It would be best to get it out in the open.

I swallowed and started by shifting to face him, "Travis."

His attention was on me. "Yes?"

"Listen, I know we kind of discussed this already, but I want to make sure we are on the same page."

He pursed his lips and waited to hear my next statement.

"It has been so good getting to know you, and I can't tell you how much it means to me that we've become friends." I paused for a breath and he took my hand. "The thing is, while I am grateful for the chance to work on your projects, it's important that we are weighed equally against the competition."

He squeezed my hand and said, "I understand how you feel and you need to know that the contract will be awarded to the best company. As much as I want you to do well, I have to recommend the right solution for our business needs. I can't let my feelings influence the outcome, so we have nothing to worry about."

"Thank you," I said, comforted by his words.

"Madeline, we aren't doing anything wrong. People go to conferences for the sole purpose of finding business. Just because we ended up liking each other, that doesn't mean we are doing anything unethical."

If only that were true, I thought, and said softly, "Your wife might feel a little differently about the subject."

He flinched at my comment, and I felt awful for confronting him. Still, it was impossible for me to ignore the conscious decision we were making. He was a married man, and one who'd come to collect me at the airport. The gesture was so romantic I wanted to jump into his arms the moment I saw him. Reality stopped meI knew it wasn't my place.

Before he could respond, we pulled up to the hotel. Travis paid the driver and collected my bag. A moment later we were inside and standing at the reception desk.

A slender young lady greeted us, "Hello again, Mr. Baker. How can I help you?"

He said, "Hi, Sheila. This is Madeline Craig. She's checking in."

"Of course. How are you this evening, Ms. Craig?"

"I'm well, thank you." Anticipating her request, I handed her my driver's license and credit card.

After a few clicks at the console, she slid my identification back and handed me two room keys. "You are on the twenty-seventh floor in room 2711." She smiled at Travis and he looked away as if he were avoiding eye contact.

"Thank you," I said.

Shelia replied, "I hope you enjoy your visit. Please let me know if there is anything else we can do."

With that, we turned and Travis guided me to the elevator. Once inside, he pressed the button and we began our ascent. After several stops, we arrived at the twenty-seventh floor. He led the way confidently, as if he already knew where we were going. I followed since the signs seemed to indicate we were heading the right direction. In no time, we were in front of my room. Using one of the cards, I slid it into the lock and he held the door for me to pass.

No lamps were on, yet the room glowed with the ambient lighting that was New York City. I couldn't wait to see more, so I crossed the room and slid the sheer curtains aside. That action bathed the room in a shadowy white light, as if someone turned a dimmer up on half the space. Times Square sparkled, and a rush of people, like fish swimming in a giant school, flanked the streets with life. I couldn't pull my eyes away from the glistening scene.

I sensed him behind me, then his arms were around my shoulders. He held me for a time as we studied the view in silence. The sensation of being alone with him, so close I could hear his heartbeat, was arousing. It would be easy to melt into the scene, into him, and forget the world outside. My resolve was weakening, and it had taken little.

To my chagrin, Travis released his hold on me. He stepped back a few paces before saying, "Why don't I give you a few minutes to get settled then we can get out for a while? Are you game for a walk?"

Maybe some space was in order, I thought, and agreed. "I'd love that. Give me fifteen minutes? Where should I meet you?"

He chuckled and I wasn't sure what to think about that. Travis walked a few paces to the middle of the room and said, "Fifteen minutes is great. I'll pick you up." With that, he switched the lock on the adjoining door and turned the knob. "I'll see you soon, but don't worry, next time I'll use the front."

He disappeared through the opening, shutting the door behind him.

❧

THE KNOCK AT THE DOOR SPIKED MY ALREADY FRENZIED nerves, causing me a jolt. I exhaled and went to open it.

Travis filled the hallway as only he could, and I noticed an extra hint of his cologne as he smiled down at me.

"Hi," I said. "Let me grab my coat."

"Sure," he agreed, and held the door open while he waited.

I went to the closet, put on my motorcycle jacket, and got my bag. "Okay, I'm set," I said as I approached the doorway.

"Are you ready for a little adventure?" he asked, while walking decisively toward the elevator.

I wasn't sure what I was ready for, but the action of walking away from our adjoining hotel rooms was helping to calm me. I kidded, "That all depends on your plan. If it involves another Ferris wheel, you're on your own."

"No Ferris wheels this trip, I promise," he said.

We entered the elevator and after a few stops, were in the lobby. Before we stepped outside, Travis pulled something from the pocket of his jacket. "You might need this." He unfolded a white knit cap with the Chicago Bears logo at the top, and a fluffy ball at the end. "Wear my toboggan, it could be chilly where we're going."

I had two immediate questions, and had to prioritize. "Wear your what?" I asked.

He smiled, carefully placing the cap on my head. "My toboggan."

"I'm confused, isn't a toboggan something you sled on?" I asked.

"It is, but where I come from, we also call these toboggans." He tapped my forehead, as if to emphasize.

"I've never heard that term used for a ski hat before. I learned something new today," I teased. "Why do I need this?"

He didn't answer. Instead, a wide smile brightened his face, and he touched the center of my back, an indication it was time to move. The doorman greeted us as we exited, and suddenly we were in the mix of it all. Throngs of people moved with determination over courtesy, and we fell in step with them.

Cutting through the crowds, we somehow blended into the mayhem that was New York City. Our way was paved by the shiny bulbs of the infamous theater district, the heart of Broadway. I followed in amazement as Travis walked with the pace of a man on a mission. Along the way, we passed street performers and beggars, all who shared equal footing on the expensive real estate of Manhattan's sidewalk.

The visual feast was overpowering, and the sound was like nowhere else in the world. Traffic rushed all around us. Car horns beeped and blended with a myriad of music and other kinds of outbursts. Everything was composed above the din of a thousand conversations.

Like a beacon, Times Square was calling. Impossibly, the scene became even brighter. It was as if everything were in Technicolor. The mighty buildings, one after the next, clicked neatly into place, like microchips on a hard drive. Virtual billboards assaulted us from every angle. It felt as though we were traveling through a video game, or a giant electrified Lego world.

One voice rose above the action, and called us out. "Hey, big man." He was a short, wiry-looking guy, carrying a boom box. "What did you do to land Miss America?"

Travis pulled me nearer and said under his breath, "There you have it, your first New York admirer. The first of many, I presume."

We arrived at a busy corner and he asked, "Are you ready?"

I looked all around, but nothing stood out. "Ready for what?

"Wait here a minute." He left me, to talk to a guy carrying a megaphone. As they spoke, I kept my eyes on him, realizing how dependent I was. The walk here, though short, would be difficult to retrace. We left the hotel and got swallowed into a rowdy maze. I felt slightly disoriented and a little vulnerable—something I rarely experienced.

After a brief exchange, he returned to my side. "This way," he said.

I followed him across the walkway and toward a red double-decker bus. He handed a ticket to the attendant and stepped aside. "Ladies first," he said with a smile.

What a sweet idea, I thought, and stepped onto the bus. "All the way to the top," Travis said from behind.

I walked to the small spiral stairway at the center of the bus, and wound my way up the tiny steps. The front rows were already full. He leaned forward and said, "Back of the bus."

I walked the last steps down the aisle and settled into a bench at the rear. Travis sat next to me and asked, "What do you think? Ready to do the tourist thing?"

"This is so unexpected," I said, "and a lot less hectic than it was down there." I surveyed our surroundings and though we were still in the thick of it, from twenty feet up, it all seemed a little less frenetic.

"Yes, and we get to see most of the city. We can hop on and off anytime. I thought we'd ride a while and end up at pizza in Greenwich Village. Does that sound okay?"

"Are you serious?" I asked. "It sounds like something out of a movie." I rested my attention on him and for a minute, all the noise fell away. Our connection could silence even the raucous sounds of New York City.

Cracking into my mental sidebar, a boisterous voice emanated from the speakers. "Good evening, ladies and gentlemen. My name is Tony and I'll be your cruise director this evening. Below deck, please give a warm welcome to our captain, Mr. Bling-Bling Bastian."

The group cheered and Travis leaned in to say, "I forgot to tell you, it comes with a little entertainment."

"This is such a cute idea. Thank you."

"Okay everyone, we are about to take off," the tour guide warned, as the vehicle jerked into motion.

For a minute we sat quietly taking in the surroundings. I half listened to our narrator, but found it hard to focus on the sites. From the moment I'd seen the New York skyline, until now, I had been a boiling mass of nerves.

The breeze kicked up and it was like an instant cold shower. My thoughts realigned as the cold wind cut through my unzipped jacket. Had I known we'd be doing this, I'd have chosen something warmer.

I shivered and Travis asked, "Are you cold?"

"A little, just the wind when we turned," I rambled lamely while tugging at the zipper.

He slipped his left arm out of his coat and wrapped it and his arm around me, snuggling me close. "Is that better?" he asked.

"Better" wasn't the word to describe what I felt. Yes, I was warmer, so much warmer, and I was comfortable, more than I should have been. It felt good to be swallowed up in his arms, the wind blowing at my cheeks and his breath at my ear. My heart was full and overflowing with the feelings I'd kept it at bay until now. His arms created a cocoon of heat. I wanted to be as close to him as possible, closer than possible.

My steady voice seemed to come from someone else. "Much warmer," I said. "I would have changed into something else if I knew what we were doing."

He chuckled, and in a conspiring tone said, "That's exactly why I didn't tell you."

His hand circled my ribs, and he eased me impossibly nearer to his side. I knew I should scoot away, give us both some breathing room, but I couldn't bring myself to do it. My head rested under his chin and the wind swirled around us.

"That's not fair," I said.

His tone wasn't light as he replied, "All's fair in love and war, Maddie."

I tilted my chin to meet his eyes. "Which is it then?"

His gaze didn't falter. "It's something."

It was a heady feeling to be with him, surrounded by the city. The world around was a muted backdrop compared to the intensity we shared. I was so wrapped around him, mind and body, that it was almost unbearable. For a long time we were quiet, each to our own thoughts as we listened to the announcer's stories about the passing landmarks. Our romance simmered as we drove past marvels like the Flatiron Building, Greenwich Village, Little Italy, and finally, over the Brooklyn Bridge.

I broke the silence and said, "We're just about to the spot."

"What spot?" he asked.

"From *Sex in the City*. You know, the famous scene where Miranda is supposed to meet Steve if they agree to stay together. You don't know it?" I insisted.

"Guess not." He chuckled. "How did it work out for Steve?"

His smirk was disarming and challenging at once. "It worked out," I said.

"Good," he replied, and pulled me back toward him. This time both arms were around my waist, and he held my hand in his.

As we hovered across the narrow bridge, guided by the shining strings of lights that reflected against the black water below, I endured the sweetest torture. Without the shelter of the buildings to protect us, the stiff wind sliced through the open space and my need to be close to him was two-fold. Not only did it feel like a silent reunion with our bodies touching, but without it, I may actually freeze.

We pulled off the bridge and he said, "Sorry it was so cold. Unfortunately, we have to do it one more time to go back, but as soon as we do, we'll get off for dinner. You okay?"

It was cold, but now that we were back on land, the wind wasn't as brutal. Still, I knew my embarrassing tell was shining bright, and thought it best to address the elephant in the room. "I'll survive, even if my Rudolph nose doesn't make it."

"What do you mean?" he joked.

"I know it's red. Since I was a kid it's always embarrassed me how my nose turns red when I get cold."

"We could pull the toboggan over your face if you'd like," he teased.

I spoke like a bratty child. "Not funny."

"Hold your nose, Shorty, we're about to make the return lap." He said it as we once again drove onto the bridge, only this time facing the city that never sleeps. After crossing, Travis said, "Why don't we make our way downstairs so it will be easy to get out?"

"Sure," I said, reluctant to release myself from his coat. He must have sensed it, as he slipped out of his jacket and wrapped it around my shoulders. I stood and walked toward the stairway. We made it to the bottom and the temperature increased by at least ten degrees. I wiped the tears from my eyes and shivered with delight as I adjusted to the warmth.

He leaned over and whispered, "Sorry," then took my hand. We walked toward the front of the bus and after a few minutes, got off. "We don't have far to go," he tried to reassure me.

"It's okay," I said. "I got a little chilled on the bridge, but I'll make it."

We crossed the street and were soon at the front of the pizza place. He held the door and walked toward the line where orders were placed. The warmth from the ovens and the aroma of garlic and fresh dough consumed the space. I felt simultaneously cozy and starved.

As we waited our turn in line, he asked, "What do you like on your pizza?"

I looked up at Travis; his eyes were clear and hair mussed. I couldn't stop the compulsion to flirt a little. "That's not a question." I spoke in a halted, come-hither tone, "I am one hundred percent, without a doubt, a lover of pepperoni."

His sharp intake of breath and flushed cheeks were either a result of the coal oven or my tease hit the mark. "That makes two of us," he agreed. "I'm kind of a fanatic. You're in for a treat."

While we waited, I looked around the pizza parlor. There was a counter where you placed your order and two dining rooms with old wooden booths. The walls were covered by faded murals and photos of people enjoying oversized slices of the house-made pie. The lighting was dim and everything was bathed in a slightly reddish hue. Scarred tile floors and walls etched with names of patrons told stories of long ago.

It was our turn at the counter. We were greeted by a young, dark-haired guy. "What'll it be for you this evening?"

Travis took the lead, "A large double-pepperoni for here."

"Okay, and to drink for you'z?" His brogue was adorable.

I replied first. "I'll have a glass of the house red, please."

Travis said, "Stella for me."

"Great, here's your number, guys. The drinks'll be right up. The pizza'll be a while. Sit anywhere you like."

"Thank you," Travis said.

He pointed toward a doorway and I walked that direction. There was an open booth tucked along one side of the room and we took it, settling in across from each other. I shrugged off Travis' jacket, then mine, and studied the photos on the wall. There were regular people, famous people, and lots of pictures of pizza.

Travis leaned forward, arms resting on the table. "First impression?"

I looked at him and was about to answer when we were nicely interrupted. A cute brunette carrying our drinks arrived at the table. "Here are your drinks, guys. Catch my eye if you want another round."

"Thank you," I said.

I raised my glass in toast, "Here's to New York pizza."

"Cheers," his deep voice agreed, and he downed a good amount of the bottle.

The wine overtook my taste buds and warmed me from throat to belly. "Seriously, I want to tell you, this has been a terrific night. Cold aside, that bus ride was a great way to see the city. Thank you for planning it."

"I'm glad you liked it. I didn't think it would be quite that cold, or I might have warned you, or maybe not. I have to confess, I like having you close."

His frankness changed the moment from a simple pizza dinner to one of the most intimate of my life. All I'd ever wished from Nathan was transparency, and here I was, finally experiencing it. The truth wasn't all that pretty, in fact, it was less than idyllic. He wanted to be near me. I knew his circumstance, and I wanted to be near him. Our truth was sullied, like most truths are, and we were naked with it.

I matched his posture by leaning forward, and said, "I didn't mind either."

With that comment, he suddenly jumped up and joined me on my side of the bench. The action squished the jackets against the wall, putting us hip to hip. Travis was unfazed by our proximity. It was part childish and part honest, the way he smashed against me. We weren't ready to let each other go yet.

"So," he started in a serious tone, "when did you first know you were a pepperoni addict?"

I chuckled, took a sip of my wine, and thought back to my childhood. "I was about five. We lived near a great deli so we always had nice cold cuts and things like that. One morning, I woke up before my parents and I was hungry. I looked in the refrigerator and saw there was a pepperoni log. I knew I wasn't allowed to use the sharp knives, so I got a butter knife and tried to saw a slice off. I ended up slipping and I dropped the knife. I was afraid the noise would wake my parents so I hurried and put the pepperoni away.

"When my parents woke up they saw the knife out and the pepperoni unraveled, so they asked me about it. I told them I knew I wasn't supposed to use the sharp knife and that explanation got me off the hook. My mom teased me about loving pepperoni and said that it wasn't for breakfast. I remember insisting I would eat pepperoni for breakfast when I grew up."

Travis deliberately bumped my side, just enough for me to look up. Our eyes met and he said, "You're adorable, Madeline."

Before I could respond, his lips grazed mine in the lightest touch. The unequaled fit of our combined mouths seemed impossible. With the hope of lovers, we shared everything we couldn't say with our silent caress.

"Ahem." A voice above was like a bucket of ice. "Your pie." The young server smiled knowingly as she placed it on the rack and set the plates down. "Another round before I go?" she asked.

"Sure," Travis took the liberty.

"Enjoy." She smirked and left us to our own devices.

His eyes shone with mischief. "We got busted."

His joke wasn't all that funny and I said, "Let's hope not."

He stood and walked to the other side of the booth, announcing, "It's time to get serious." I watched as he expertly smoothed a slice of the bubbling pie onto a plate then slid it my way. He did it again and took the next piece for himself.

After adding a liberal amount of red chili pepper, I tackled the slice by folding it in half. The steam from the sauce and grease from the double helping of pepperoni married the creamy cheese and crust into a flawless combination. When the last delicious morsel of my first taste melted, I said, "Pinch me."

Travis asked, "What?"

"Pinch me," I replied. "I think I've died and gone to heaven."

He gave my bicep a zinger of a twist, and said, "I know I have."

I couldn't help but enjoy the way he looked at me or how it felt when his lips stole a kiss. Instead of laboring over the fault in our actions, I relaxed. I drank wine and ate the best pizza, sharing the kind of ease I'd rarely experienced.

If the remaining dregs of pie and our drinks were any sign, dinner was winding down. Travis patted his stomach. "This bear is pretty full. What do you say we walk for a bit, maybe see a little of Greenwich Village, and then we can take a cab back?"

"That sounds great," I agreed. "If I eat another bite I'm going to blow up."

We stood and I slipped on my coat and handed his over. "Since we won't be in the wind zone, I guess I can relinquish your jacket."

He slipped it on. "Just say the word and it'll be at your service. This way."

I followed him out the exit and was surprised to see the line was still in full swing. "Thank you again, Travis. That was the best pizza I've ever tasted."

"Don't mention it," he said.

We walked down the quieter streets and he navigated like a man who knew his way around. The brick row houses with their carefully painted doors stood unchanging for a century, like the pizzeria around the corner. Brightly lit porches boasted tiny details in potted plants or hanging lights, in an effort to stand apart from the rest. The beauty of this neighborhood, in the midst of the greater city, was something to be cherished. A tiny respite in the center of it all, a place to call home.

One door stood out. It was decorated with the most beautiful fall wreath and a netted glass globe hung to the side; a flickering candle shone softly through the glass. I couldn't stop myself. I had to take a picture. Kneeling a distance from the front steps, I centered the frame and snapped the shot. To my surprise, I heard Travis do the same. I looked over to find he was taking a picture of me, taking a picture of the house. "What are you doing?"

He showed me the screen. It was a profile of me. My face was hidden by bangs and the grainy lighting. When I looked at him, he didn't smile, but slid the phone into his pocket and his arm around my shoulders.

We continued down the street, enjoying the classic architecture, until we found ourselves in front of a very modern building. We peered through the floor-to-ceiling windows and saw a variety of high-end vehicles ranging from Maserati to Ferrari and more.

Travis seemed to know the business. "It's a cool idea. You pay a monthly membership and you get to use any car you'd like. One day . . . " He sighed, feigning melancholy.

"The black convertible over there looks like something a spy would drive," I said.

"Yes, it does," he agreed.

"People might think we were spies if we rented one," I kidded.

"People might think we're spies anyway. If big brother is watching, they'd know we've visited three states together in sixty days. You've got a security background and I work for the largest communication company in the world. We've got spy written all over us."

I took the scenario and ran with it. "Yeah," I said, "the only thing missing is the trench coat."

"No," he chided, "we can't wear trench coats. That's not our style, too passé."

"True," I agreed sarcastically. "We're much more discrete with me wearing your—what is this called again?" I pointed toward my head, "Toboggan?"

"You're messing with me, Shorty." His arm pulled me closer to his side.

"You're kind of a big target," I said.

"I may be big," he said, as if he were the Jolly Green Giant, "but I'm also warm. It's big and warm to you."

"Yes sir, Big and Warm. Is that your code name?"

"It is, and yours is Shorty."

We walked quietly for a minute, then Travis picked up the banter. "So, what is in store for our spies next? I think they're going to need another adventure after this."

His question could have been about the evening, or something much broader. Either way, I didn't know how to reply. For the first time since we sat on that bus, I felt unsure. My silence was a giveaway that didn't get missed.

"Hey, there's a cab. Are you ready to call it a night?" he asked.

"If you don't mind," I agreed.

He didn't hesitate, nor try to sway me; instead, his sharp whistle and waving hand set the cab in our direction. After a quick greeting, we hopped in and he gave the driver our destination. I stared silently out the window as we navigated through the bustling city streets. For the first time all night, we didn't touch.

Reality filled the gap as we drew nearer to the hotel. In no time, we arrived. Travis paid the driver and we walked the short distance to the entryway. We pushed through the circular door and crossed the lobby, finding our way to the elevators. A family stood beside us as we waited for the car to arrive. The overstimulated toddler in their keep bounced from foot to foot, smiling and giggling as he moved. The parents looked worn out and anything but pleased. I wondered if it made Travis think of his family.

The buzzer rang and the elevator doors opened. A young couple exited and we let the family enter first. The ride up was strange. I wanted to lean into Travis, but something stopped me. The doors opened on the fifteenth floor and the family took their leave. Finally, it was only us and the heavy air that was our gravity. My breathing shifted in anticipation of our arrival at the twenty-seventh floor. With a mild jerk, the buzzer heightened the experience and the doors slid open. I stepped out first, and we walked side by side down the hallway. Our footsteps against the carpet were the only sounds.

The inevitable moment arrived, and we were standing in front of our rooms. I pulled the access card from my purse. Travis stopped me and placed his hands on either side of my face until my head tilted back. Our eyes locked and I had no time to think before he swallowed me into a searing hot kiss. His tongue insisted and mine acquiesced. He tugged my hair and my back was against the door. His ski hat and my door card were casualties on the ground. My mind went numb, but my body came alive. My nipples hardened, and I could feel my spot swelling for him. He ran his hands down my back and stooped to cup my ass. It was now or never.

I don't know where I found the strength, because it wasn't what I wanted. I lifted my near-numb arms and placed both hands against his chest. That small gesture was all it took. Travis turned his back to me. He was out of breath and I watched him rake his hands through his hair. When he looked around, lust was in his eyes, and I knew we shared the same expression.

I broke the spell long enough to pick up the access card and hat, then squeaked, "Thank you for tonight. I won't forget it." Before he could reply, I turned to unlock the door and retreated into the safety of my room.

FALLING SLOWLY

The morning came and no alarm clock was needed. After a near-sleepless night, I awoke before 6 AM in need of coffee. Lane Fine and I were scheduled to have breakfast at eight, so I had time for a Starbuck's run. I pulled on a pair of sweats and my jacket then made my way downstairs. Though it was before dawn, the lobby was already abuzz with activity.

I walked toward the front door and approached the doorman. "Hi, could you tell me where the closest coffee shop is?"

"Good morning," his cheerful voice greeted. "It is very close, go left out the door and walk one block. You'll find it on the next corner."

"Thank you," I said, and exited through the revolving doors.

The morning was crisp, and I walked fast hoping to warm up a bit. Though it was early, the streets were already alive with people. Some appeared to be in route to the office, while others were just returning home after a long night on the town. The movement felt good, and I was grateful for the simple errand of finding coffee.

I crossed the street and entered Starbucks. After a few other guests, it was my turn at the counter. I ordered a Grande Latte and stepped aside to wait for the drink. I studied the streets outside and watched as the tiniest sliver of daylight began to highlight the world. Soon, my order was up and I had the motivation necessary to tackle the day.

Cup in hand, I walked back to the hotel and to the concierge. "Good morning, is there a market nearby?" I asked.

"Yes, we have one in the building. Let me show you." She opened a map and pointed, "We are here. If you walk down this corridor and take a right, you'll find it. It's a cute store with a deli and a few other gift items."

"Thank you," I said.

Following the diagram, I crossed the lobby and walked down the hall to the store. Apparently, they retained the original storefront as a part of the hotel renovation. As I entered through the side, it was like going back in time. An old-fashioned bell tinkled and an older man in a white apron greeted me. "Good morning, young lady." He practically sang the words.

"Good morning," I replied.

"What can I help you find?"

I surveyed the space. White walls and shelves were stacked high with goods. The man stood behind a deli case. "It's my friend's birthday, and he loves cheese. I was thinking of getting a wedge as a funny gift," I said.

"Well, you lucked out. We have quite the selection here. Come and take a look," he suggested.

I walked to the case and was amazed to find a wide variety of options. Most surprising, they had Humboldt Fog in stock. It seemed to be a sign. "May I have the Humboldt Fog, please?"

"Of course. I'll wrap it up."

"Thank you," I said, and perused the card section of the store while I waited. I was happy to find a packet of candles and decided to forego the card. I took them and a bottle of Nicholas Fueillatte back to the counter and waited as the man rang me up.

"Looks like a perfect birthday party to me," he commented.

I wasn't sure if it was my place, but I wanted to do something to acknowledge Travis' birthday the next day. I didn't know when, but I would find a way to surprise him before I left in the morning. "I have to agree," I replied. "Thanks for your help."

"Anytime," he said. I took my leave of the shop and rushed to the elevator. It was nearing show time and I still had to get ready.

⚜

THE ELEVATOR DOORS OPENED AND I GOT OUT, MAKING MY way across the lobby and to the restaurant. When I reached the podium, I was greeted by the host. "Good morning," he said, "table for one?"

"Good morning. I'm actually meeting someone."

"The name of your party, please?" he asked.

"His name is Lane Fine."

"Yes, this way. He's just arrived."

I followed him across the space until we stopped at a booth along the wall. "Here you are," he said, and left us.

"Good morning, Lane?" I said.

"Yes," he stood. "It's nice to meet you in person, Madeline." He took my hand to shake it.

"Thank you. I'm glad you were able to adjust your schedule to make this meeting," I said.

"Fortunately, I'm local. It wasn't too difficult to shift things around," he replied.

As I sat, a server arrived at our table. "Good morning. Would you like some coffee to start?" She held the carafe temptingly.

"Why not?" I agreed. "One more cup can't hurt anything."

She smiled and poured the steaming liquid into my mug. "Will you be having the breakfast buffet or do you want something from the menu?"

I looked over at Lane, who shrugged. "I think the buffet will do for us. Thank you," I said.

She walked away and I returned my attention to him. "Should we get something to eat while we discuss the agenda for today?"

"Yep, I'm starving," he said. We walked toward the buffet.

After filling our plates, we settled back into the booth. Lane opened the conversation between bites. "How do you feel about the company so far?"

I could have choked on my bacon, but held it together and replied diplomatically. "It's been interesting. I've learned a lot, but I know there is a lot more to figure out. You've worked here for a while, right?"

"Yes," he agreed, "twelve years next month."

"That's a long time. Do you have any advice for a new person starting out?"

His slick black hair unraveled as he moved, and his small brown eyes darted around the room. "I'd say, it's a changing environment and if you're going to stick, you'd better learn the landscape. There are some constants, even in this shit storm of an organization."

"Wow. That was both ominous and vague," I said boldly. "Can you shed any light on that statement?" I was nervous, but driven by annoyance. For the duration of my short employment, I'd been routinely strong-armed and for what? Here we sat, at the tip of a multi-million-dollar opportunity, and another person, whom I'd just met, is leading the day with a warning.

"Listen, I'm in no position to help, but I can imagine the predicament you're in. Here's the problem Lori is not well-liked by her peers. If you've spent any time with your counterparts, you know the sentiment is universally accepted. Your connection to her puts you in the spotlight, plain and simple.

"No matter what happens with this opportunity, you're going to have issues. If it goes well, there will be a promotion, and the team will hate you. If it goes poorly, you'll lose your job. John and Robert will say you went rogue. They'll blame you for missing their numbers and say it was because their new recruit was focused on the wrong thing, and listening to the wrong leader."

I was flabbergasted by his transparency and conclusion about my future, and also pissed. After a short deliberation, I took a sip of my coffee and responded. "I hadn't expected you to be so candid. If everyone is going to hate me anyway, I'll go for option one, the promotion. How do we make sure that happens?"

OUR LONG BUT PRODUCTIVE DAY WAS WINDING DOWN AROUND a card table in the makeshift break room. Workers wearing logoed hardhats moved around like ants behind us. Back and forth they marched, each with a task in mind, all of their efforts connected to the greater outcome—the finished project. The building's blueprints were strewn across the table, along with our abandoned cups of hot cocoa. The heat wasn't consistent yet, so frequent refills of the powdered drink kept us from trembling throughout the day.

The electrical foreman, Bradley, stood and said, "Madeline, Lane, it was a pleasure to spend the day with you both. Would you excuse me? I need to meet with my crew before I head out."

I stood as well and shook his work-hardened hand. "Bradley, we can't thank you enough for all of the information. With any luck, we look forward to working with you on this project."

He chuckled. "Well, good luck to you then."

Lane stood too. "Thank you, Bradley. I'll be in touch with any questions."

Bradley turned to shake Travis' hand. "Can I borrow you a second, boss?" he asked.

"Sure, I'll be right over," Travis replied.

Lane chimed, "I hate to do this, but I've got to take off as well. My son's hockey game is today. Travis," he continued while shaking his hand, "thank you for letting us look at the project. I have most of what I need to help Madeline with a solution. She'll take point, and I want you to know she's got the backing of the entire WVI team. We're here to help."

"Thanks, Lane. If you'll excuse me a moment, Madeline."

"Of course," I said. He took his leave and I turned my attention to Lane. "Well, what did you think about today?" I asked.

"Madeline, you did a great job here. I think we can

compete on price and we have the resources to get it done . . ."

I sensed a but, and confronted him. "What's your concern?"

"Honestly, I don't think our product is robust enough for their environment. They're not going to like some of the quirks that our system has when they try to scale it."

If what he was saying was true, why bother with the appointment at all? We knew what they needed going into it. Why not steer me away, instead of ask me to open the door? The look of defeat must have shown on my face.

Lane tried to cheer me up. "Don't worry. I'll give you everything you need to sell it. I'll even supply the white paper to prove the system will work for their application."

"What's the problem then?" I asked.

"We've never tested it to these limits before. In theory, it should work, but we have no case studies to support it. Do you think Swift is the best account to experiment with?"

The heat was coming at me from every direction lately, and I needed a break. I thought we'd rebounded nicely after our early morning sword fight, but here we were back in the mud. "Do you know what they say, Lane?"

"No," he replied blandly. "What do they say?"

"Sell it, and they'll figure it out," I said.

"Great theory," he huffed, "unless of course, you're *they*."

"Come on, tell me it'll be all right."

"I can't tell you it'll be all right, but I will tell you that you have my vote. I've got to run now or I'll be late. I'll send you the preliminary budget and design by the end of day, tomorrow."

"Okay, thanks," I said. "I'll be traveling so I won't get it until late. I appreciate your help on this one."

"Not a problem, Madeline. Safe travels," he said, and left the building.

While I waited for Travis, I made a few final notes and reflected on the meeting. I thought things went pretty well. Lane and Bradley seemed to speak the same language. Travis was professional and knowledgeable. We got our questions answered and took photographs to assist with the final proposal. In all, I couldn't have hoped for a better outcome. That was, until Lane's haunting, closing comments.

"Kind of a serious expression for someone who had a good day at work." Travis' voice came from across the table.

"Hey." I stood. "I didn't notice you there."

"You were deep in thought from the look of it," he said.

"Just thinking about a few of the details we learned today. Thank you, by the way. I'm sure you had a lot of other things to do. You being here helped so much."

"Not at all, it's a part of my job. I'm glad it worked out, and I really hope the best for you. I have to go take a look at something with Bradley and his team, so I can't leave yet."

"Oh, no problem," I said. "I'll catch up with you later."

"Listen, I planned something tonight," he said. "Can you be ready to leave the hotel by seven?"

There was no point denying myself, I wanted to spend the evening with him. "I can be ready by seven. I'll see you then." Our eyes locked a second longer than they should have and I took that as my cue to leave.

WAS IT MY DECISIVENESS, OR THE NEAR-EMPTY GLASS OF wine I sipped as I got ready to see him? Whatever caused it, I was strangely calm in light of my decision. I studied myself in the mirror. The velvet dress I wore cinched neatly at the waist and the skirt flared to above the knee, but the crushed flower overlay made it remarkable. Finished with a distressed pair of knee-high boots and my purple carpet jacket, I looked the part I hoped to portray—a sexy and daring woman.

There was a knock at the door, and I took one last look at myself. Smoky eyes, not entirely my own, glowed back at me. A fleeting thought of Nathan entered my mind. I hadn't been with anyone else in six years. If tonight went as expected, that was going to change. I looked defiantly at my reflection, picked up the tube of Carven from the counter and spritzed a bit more at my throat before going to the door. My hand on the knob reminded me of a photograph and I knew once I turned it, there would be no going back. I turned it anyway. In front of me stood a man who opened my mind and heart to something I'd never considered before.

Neither of us spoke; instead, he pulled me into a kiss that lifted me off my feet. When he let go, my legs nearly buckled from under me. I opened my eyes to find his soft lips suspended inches from mine, his nostrils flared, and his hand was firm around my waist. Without a word, he pulled himself to his full height and guided me down the hall. My blood pressure spiked in a good way, and I patted myself on the back for applying the 18-hour lip stain.

As we made turtle's time down the elevator, I snuck a peek at Travis. He'd just shaved. I recalled how his smooth face felt soft against mine, although his kiss was anything but. He wore a black dress shirt and coat atop his signature dark denim. This was the most dressed up I'd seen him and he looked good. We finally arrived at the lobby and crossed to exit the hotel.

The cool, damp air seemed to assist our vocal chords. He spoke first. "You look incredible, Madeline. Like a dream."

In an old-fashioned gesture, I hooked my arm around his

and saddled up close. Calling up the logic I'd grappled with earlier, I told myself to act like I was in a dream. Only in this dream, I could control things…or could I? If I were present, right here and now, I might convince myself that the rest of the world didn't exist.

Of course, I knew his family was real, but in the moment, facts were irrelevant. I likened it to knowing that he wet the bed until he was ten years old, not applicable to the present situation. It was easier than I thought to excuse us from reality. If we were a mystery of the night, like a dream and no one were the wiser, how could that hurt?

"It's for you," I replied to his compliment.

"I don't deserve it," he said, almost under his breath.

For the first time I could see he was struggling. "What's the matter Travis, or is that a stupid question?"

"Nothing is the matter, Madeline. That's kind of the problem. You're great, beautiful, smart, competent, and so damn sexy."

His words should have boosted me up, but his tone told me that a shoe was about to drop. "But?" I prompted.

He took a deep breath, and said, "We need to cross."

His not so subtle redirect told me to drop the subject. I followed him the last blocks in silence. No longer did I have the same confidence I'd channeled earlier this evening. Instead, the mood felt a little depressed. I wasn't going to let it rest like that between us.

"Travis," I said, clasping his wrist. He stopped to look at me. "I want you to know, I'm happy to be here with you."

He tried to smile, but didn't quite. "I'm happy to be here with you too." His eyes urged. "We need to hurry or we'll be late."

This time he did smile, and I knew something fun was in store. Our unspoken pact behind, we increased the pace until it was time to turn the corner. When we did, we were faced with a line of people. "This is us," he said.

The glowing sign above the theater entry said *Once*. I was shocked and looked over at him. His wide smile confirmed. "You're kidding. I didn't even know they made a play of it."

He faced me and rested his hands on my shoulders. "I knew how much you liked the music, and the movie. It's another thing we have in common." He smiled sweetly and said, "I hope you're happy about the surprise."

I was standing on line in New York City, waiting to see the musical, *Once*. Smiling down at me was this incredibly appealing man. From the time he walked me to the hotel that first night, to the scary Ferris wheel ride, the baseball game, seeing the sites of this tireless city, and the grand finale, a musical on Broadway, he'd gone out of his way to be good to me. I reached up, cupped my hand around his neck and pulled him close. Standing on my toes, I held him that way for a breath, then kissed him. I wanted to pour every bit of my gratitude into the action. A shuffling sound brought us to attention. It was time to go inside.

We arrived at the front and Travis showed our tickets to the attendant, then handed one to me. I slid it into my coat pocket, in case I'd need it later. His fingers linked with mine as we entered the theater.

He maneuvered past the shuffling patrons as if he knew where he was going. After a quiet left, we could see the stage. The theater was dim, sans the spotlights that brightened the platform and the wall sconces that cast shadows over the grand pews. Travis tugged my fingers, and we continued down the aisle toward the front. I watched in surprise as people climbed the narrow steps that led to the stage. I couldn't believe it when he guided me to do the same, pressing me to walk on first.

We saw a bar along the back. He asked, "Do you want a drink?"

I was a little taken aback by the setup, but tried to act nonchalant, a skill I was getting quite good at lately. "Yes," I agreed. "I'll have red wine, please."

I walked with him toward the stage bar and listened as he placed our order. Drinks in hand, we turned and walked a few paces to the side so others could place their orders.

"What do you think?" he asked, obviously excited for his coup.

I could no longer mask my awe, and why should I? "This is the coolest thing I've done in my entire life, Travis."

"Now we know what it looks like from their vantage point," he said. He surveyed the auditorium and asked, "Do you want to go and find our seats?"

"Sure. You lead the way," I said.

His hand never left mine as we retraced our steps across the creaky wooden stage. Moving toward the blinding lights, we exited the platform, walked back up the aisle and up a flight of stairs. We continued to the end of the walkway and found our seats at the bottom of the section.

"Here we are. The end two are ours. Go ahead," he said.

"Thank you," I replied as I took the second red velvet chair.

The seats were in the front row of a mezzanine that seemed to float over the stage. Above our heads were ornately painted domed ceilings, in hues of pea green and ivory. The subdued lighting and brightened stage blended with the architecture and I felt like I was sitting in a glass globe, the kind you give as a souvenir. All that was missing were the flecks of glitter. This was better. It was real, and it was my dream.

The lights flickered and ushers arrived to steer people to

their seats. The stage lights were cut. A few of the musicians took to the darkened stage, their attention trained on instruments and any last-minute tuning before the show. Their brief drills seemed to hasten the patrons to their chairs. I looked around the theater, and was surprised to find it was nearly full.

An overhead announcement instructed, "Ladies and gentlemen, the show is about to begin. Please take your seats." The lights flickered again, only this time rapidly.

"What a beautiful theater this is," I said as we waited.

"Isn't it?" he agreed, and put his arm around me.

The crowd fell silent as a single spotlight lit the stage, highlighting a man in worn clothes with a guitar in his hands. His fingers came to life, strumming gently, and the world fell away. Lost in his divine compilation, we were transported to those streets, and that fateful meeting when a captivating muse arrives to watch a curbside performance.

The subtle dance of the performers, as they blended in and out of focus, mirrored the peek-a-boo romance that was forming between the main characters. The old vacuum's wheels squeaked against the floor and we started to believe in magic as she followed him through the mock city streets, dragging it humorously behind. Their portrayal was so convincing, I wondered if they were together off stage as well.

The music elevated me to a hopeful place. Their depiction of a romance that teetered on the edge of wrong comforted me in some way. The inspiration the two characters gave one another was enviable. I longed to have that kind of love in my life.

I stole a glance at Travis, his eyes met mine, and I knew I was falling for him. That private admission weighed on me as the music reverberated, building to the powerful completion of the first act. My growing feelings for him supported my resolve. Tonight, there would be more than one final act.

The lights rose. "Ladies and gentlemen, please enjoy this fifteen-minute intermission while we prepare the stage for the grand finale."

Travis stirred, and asked, "Do you want another glass of wine?"

"Sure," I agreed.

With that, he stood and waited for me to continue up the aisle. Once we reached the common area, he looked over and asked, "What do you think so far?"

"It is so good. The singing, the music, the set, it's incredible." I looked at him and noticed a sweetness on his face.

"*You're* incredible, Shorty," he said, and steered me to a bar along the wall.

We stood in line to order and he held me from behind. I watched a cute older couple pass. The woman smiled at us. I was sure she'd look at us differently if she knew the real story. Still, I understood her fascination. If what I was feeling for him were tangible, the air around us would be raining with gold.

Travis noticed her attention and smiled back. She blushed and averted her eyes. He said to me, "Seems we have an admirer."

"Yes," I said, "I noticed that too." The words came before I had time to filter them and I said, "I wonder what we would really be like as a couple."

He paused, thoughtful for a time, then said with a sure smile, "People would hate us."

My thoughts went instantly to the guilty place. "Of course, you're right," I said.

He tilted my chin, forcing me to meet his eyes. "They would hate us because we'd be *that* couple. You know, the one everyone envies, because they're so in love." His eyes grew wide at the admission.

I got the impression he didn't mean to say that much, and I tried to lighten the mood. "Maybe we could get matching T-shirts," I joked. "Yours will say 'Big and Warm' and mine will say 'Bring on The Haters.' What do you think?"

He laughed and his belly moved with the action. "I'm in. We may want to see about getting them lined in Kevlar though."

THE HUSHED THEATER RESTED IN DARKNESS AS WE anticipated the next scene. Yellow beams like fingers pointing lit the platform, highlighting the lone piano. The stage splashed to life with melodies of passion so finely honed, it felt spontaneous. The actor's tragic voices teased and tortured us. Drawn into their haunting performance, we were returned to a story that shared a gut-wrenching similarity with our own. The tale was of unfinished love, and I foolishly wished that this time it would end differently.

The actor's tantalizing voices floated above the instruments, sometimes a cappella, making us believe and even root for the pair. Their harmony rose and I was eviscerated by destiny. Soul-baring notes of desperation and resignation mesmerized us as the crescendo unraveled at our feet. The glaring parallel to Travis and me was underlined by the final scene. Tears rolled unchecked down my face. Of course, I knew there was no other way for it to end.

THE BEEPING HORN AND RUSH OF WIND AS WE CROSSED THE threshold felt life-affirming. I was grateful to be outside, away from the leaded air that stagnated the theater after our fortune played out before our eyes. The chill felt honest against my skin. Like the whip of a belt across bare legs, the sting proved you were still alive. Funny how my thoughts ran to punishment.

In a low voice, Travis asked, "Are you hungry for dinner? We never found time for lunch today. I'm guessing you didn't eat?"

Such a benign question after the magnitude of emotions that were simmering inside of me. "I had some bacon at breakfast," I replied.

"You have to eat something. I hope this isn't too forward" he hesitated, and I waited for him to finish"but what if we get something to go and have a hotel room picnic?"

My answer would seal our already certain fate. "That's perfect."

❧

HE OPENED THE DOOR AND WE STEPPED INTO A TIME WARP. Worn rugs and faded booths blanketed the 80-year-old deli in hues of orange. Glass cases packed with oversized cakes and pies ran the length of the wall. The fragrance of grilled onions and grease permeated the air. I watched as a server carried two hefty plates from the kitchen, wondering how anyone found the room for dessert with servings like that. From what I could tell, little had changed in the place since it opened all those years ago.

"Here's a menu," Travis said.

I scanned it, but was undecided. "What do you feel like having?" I asked him.

He smiled and said, "There's only one thing I order when I come here."

"What's that?"

"The pastrami sandwich," he replied. "It's amazing. In fact, they even distribute the meat to other restaurants."

"That sounds good," I said. "I love pastrami."

"Why don't we get one and share it?"

"Will it be enough for you?"

He half chuckled and said, "Definitely."

We walked up to the register. A grey-haired man in white, with a black bow tie, greeted us. "Good evening," he said. "What can I get you tonight?"

Travis replied, "Hello, we'll take a pastrami sandwich with two pickles to go, please."

"Thank you." The kindly looking man asked, "Will there be anything else?"

Travis looked over at me and I shook my head. "Nope," he responded, "that'll do it."

I watched their exchange, knowing that once the food was ready, Travis and I would be alone for the first time. No woman goes to a man's hotel room with the childish thought that it will end innocently. My pulse quickened.

❧

THE LAST FEW STEPS DOWN THE CORRIDOR WERE DREAMLIKE, a fitting sentiment based on my resolve to treat the entire night as if it were one. It wasn't a stretch to convince myself, since the lead-up to this moment was straight out of a romance novel. A combination of nerves and something else bubbled at my chest.

As we stood at the door, Travis asked, "My place, or yours?"

I had no real preference and could barely speak. "You pick."

With that, he pulled the card from his jacket and slid it into the lock. Holding the door open, he said, "After you."

I crossed the threshold, and acknowledged the magnitude of the situation. It was a defining moment. From this point forward, there was no denying the truth. I was involved with a married man.

Travis came inside and closed the door. Crossing the room, he unfolded a pack of matches and lit a few candles that were situated on a table by the window. The room was cast with muted lighting, a result of the candlelight and the sparkling cityscape that shone through the floor-to-ceiling windows. I watched silently and tried to push the nagging questions out of my head. We were finally alone.

He gestured toward one of the chairs. "Come on," he said. "Let's sit."

I walked to the table and took the seat opposite him. Travis pulled the sandwich and a stack of napkins out of the bag. "I forgot something," he said.

"What?" I asked.

"We don't have anything to drink."

I remembered the bottle of champagne I'd picked up earlier. "I'll be right back." I stood and went toward the door.

Travis cleared his throat and I turned. "Why don't you take the spy door, Shorty?"

"Good idea," I agreed. "There's only one problem, I didn't leave it unlocked on my side."

"What kind of spy doesn't plan ahead? Someone may need to go back to basic training."

I responded in kind. "Spoken like a man who seems to have all the moves." I exited through the front door and quickly opened my own.

After I got inside, I took off my coat. Making my way toward the refrigerator, I pulled out the chilled bottle of bubbles but decided to leave the cheese for now. I took a deep breath and turned the lock on the adjoining door.

❦

When I returned to his room, there was soft music playing in the background. Travis had removed his coat and was sitting at the table. From across the room, I could see the tall sandwich making a shadow on the table. "Wow," I said. "You weren't kidding about the size of that sandwich."

He stood. "Told ya. What do you have there?"

I lifted the bottle a little higher as I approached him. "Bubbles," I said.

"I see that," he said. "Champagne and pastrami . . . there is no better combination."

"Have you tried it before?"

"Nope, but there's a first time for everything. I love pastrami and who doesn't like a glass of the bubbly. It will only enhance the experience."

His statement lingered in the air, but he busied himself by pulling glasses from the counter along the wall. I sat at the table and waited as he uncorked the bottle and filled two glasses. He handed one to me and sat. Drink in hand, he said, "Here's to spies and haters. Cheers."

"Cheers," I said, and I drained the contents of my cup.

Stifling a cough, I surveyed the view from his window. Since the scene was almost identical to mine, looking out was only a distraction from the tension I was feeling. With any luck, the champagne would kick in and I would once again become the daring woman I'd convinced myself to be earlier.

"Madeline," his voice pulled my attention back. I looked

at him squarely and noticed his eyes seemed darker under the glimmer of candlelight. His tone was fatherly as he asked, "Aren't you going to eat?"

"Of course," I said, and set my glass aside. "This is literally six inches high, Travis. I'm starting to detect a pattern here. Do you have the inside scoop on all of the mountainous beef sandwiches in America?"

He chuckled and picked up his side. "How do you think I got so big and warm?" Next, he opened his mouth as wide as he could, and still only made a small dent in the sandwich.

It smelled so good and I followed his lead. With two hands, I held the biggest sandwich—no, half sandwich—I had ever seen. The taste was all he claimed it would be. Salty peppered meat, layered with grilled onions and tart mustard, was held between fresh slices of rye bread.

"Mmm," I didn't even wait to swallow before saying, "this is outrageous."

"Isn't it?" he replied with a devilish glint in his eyes.

He attacked the meal with gusto and for a while we didn't say much. Instead we were lulled by the wine, the rich food, and the soft horns of the blues station he'd selected. The champagne bottle was draining as he refilled our glasses.

He ventured, "Do you want to talk about the work day?"

I replied without hesitation, "I don't. If Madeline Craig has any further questions for Travis Baker, she will email him tomorrow." There, I thought, my braver self was resurfacing.

"Yes, ma'am." He feigned submission. "Whatever you say."

I could feel my cheeks flush as the champagne worked through my bloodstream. "Don't misunderstand. I appreciate you offering, but I think it's best we keep things separate."

"Things?" He drawled the word, and pinned me with his silvery eyes.

I wasn't going to back down, or wilt at his suggestion. "Yes, things."

"What kind of things?" he continued suggestively, and sipped from his glass.

I caught a glimpse of the clock in the mirror and turned to confirm the time. It was 11:55 PM. "I'll tell you what . . . ," I said as I rose.

"What?" He grappled to stand.

I spoke over my shoulder as I walked toward the adjoining door. "I'll answer your question in about five minutes. If you'll excuse me?" I disappeared through the opening before he could say a word.

THERE WAS A STRANGER IN MY ROOM. SHE STARED AT ME from the mirror. I surveyed her from a distance, disassociating myself from the woman who wore only sheer black underthings and an open kimono. In all the years I'd been with Nathan, I couldn't remember a time when I was so brazen as to bare myself this way. I gulped and reasoned, if I finally became the kind of woman Nathan wanted, did all those things I'd neglected, maybe I could make it right. The clock struck midnight, and the stranger lit a candle that stood atop a slice of birthday cheese.

I OPENED THE DOOR AND SPOKE THROUGH A SMALL GAP, calling, "Travis?"

His response was immediate, "Yes?"

"Are you sitting?" I asked.

"Yes?" he said with a laugh.

"Close your eyes and keep them closed until I say," I ordered.

"Done."

Was it my atonement that drove me to stand before him this way? My hands shook, as did my voice. I tried not to tremble, and held the plate carefully so as not to blow out the flame. I sang seductively, but there was something silly about it, though I was barely dressed.

"Happy birthday to you,

Happy birthday to you,

Happy birthday dear Travis,

Happy birthday to you."

When the song was done, I set the plate in front of him and spoke softly. "Open your eyes and make a wish."

His eyes were wide as he looked at me, and I wondered if I'd made a mistake. I used a free hand to cinch the Kimono closed. The seconds felt like hours until he finally said, "What could I possibly wish for after this?" He looked down at the "cake" and quirked his neck. "Is that what I think it is?"

"Um, if you think it's cheese instead of cake, then yes," I said.

His grin was contagious. Like removing a plug from the bathtub and watching the water rush to be released, my anxiety dissipated. He closed his eyes and after a pause, took an audible breath. When he opened them again, he looked right at me, and with an easy puff, extinguished the little candle.

Then Travis said the very last thing I expected, "I can't believe you don't do that professionally."

It must have been my guilty heart, for I wasn't sure what to make of his statement and was close to jumping to the wrong conclusion. "What?" I asked.

"Sing," he said as he stood and walked to stand in front of me.

My shoulders were still tensed, only this time for a different reason. We were inches apart and I was close to naked. I had made the most aggressive sexual advance of my life, and now it was time to face my decision. My halted reply did nothing to diffuse the situation. "It's too much for me to sing in front of people. It makes me feel exposed."

We hovered in time, and I knew one press of his lips against mine, and I'd give him anything. My reaction to his scent was like something out of a biology class. Proof that my body yearned for him was evident by my taught nipples. It wasn't that he was some sort of God. He was a cacophony of oddities that somehow combined into the most handsome man I'd ever seen, and I wanted to be his.

He lowered his face to mine and with the brush of his lips, took my breath away. Ever so lightly, he suckled at my bottom lip. My nipples stretched even tighter. His tongue entered and retreated, and I basked in the blissful surrender of the moment.

When he came up for breath, his eyes told the truth of his longing, but his hands showed the restraint of an intuitive gentleman. With nimble fingers, he lowered his hands to the collar of my silken robe, and hooked his thumbs on either side. His fingers heated my skin. With the pace of a man with nothing but time, he shrugged my modesty over my shoulders. It landed in a pool at my feet. He stood back to look at me. I was wearing only a sheer black bra and thong, leaving the sliver of a barrier between us. After a second, he stepped closer and put his hand behind my back. With one snap of his fingers, my bra was released. Those deceptively lazy thumbs came back to life. One by one, he slipped the straps from my shoulders. His dilated pupils and slack jaw were proof that his reserve was starting to falter. I loved the polar nature of the two Travises colliding. The results were delightful, and somehow gave me confidence.

His fingers lingered on my shoulders and he asked, "Are you okay with this?"

My breasts heaved as I tried to find the words. He didn't wait for my answer. Those tender caresses continued down my arm and the side of my breast. He lowered himself, trailing his nose over my belly, until his thumbs reached my panties. From hands and knees, he looked up, as if to offer me one last chance to stop him. I didn't.

The sensation of the fabric slipping over my hips was so erotic, but nothing prepared me for the ecstasy I felt the second he buried his face in my spot. My head fell back and I steadied myself with the table. There was something about this man, how we connected, that emboldened me to accept a moment for what it was.

I was without shame as he held my hips and tasted the need that changed me. He possessed and I permitted, as his tongue explored my essence. He devoured me with tiny bites, then tentative flicks, and the softest tease of my center. My legs lost feeling, and I nearly came on his face. After weeks of talking, dates that would make any woman swoon, and tonight—the hottest and most romantic of my life—who could blame me? Under the glow of city lights, I let myself live.

The heat was rising and just before I exploded, his mouth relented. I tried to right myself as he got to his feet. The candles flared and dimmed against my naked body. The war on Travis' face was won, and the savage took over. In a lunging move, he plucked me from the ground and carried me to the bed, placing me gingerly in the center. His eyes never left mine as he adjusted my legs to part slightly. I was trans-fixed and pliant in his command.

Our wordless exchange, with him undressing, and me on display, was the most liberating experience of my life. I watched as he unbuttoned his shirt and tossed it to the floor. A few moves later, his pants and underwear joined the pile, and the world outside ceased to exist.

He eased onto the bed, and lay beside me. Bending his elbow, he rested his head in his hand and said roughly, "Madeline, I need to know you're ok with this. You have to say something."

It wasn't okay, and I wasn't okay with it, but I knew that didn't matter. I may have known it from the second our eyes first met, I wouldn't walk away from him. I rasped, "Kiss me, Travis."

With unexpected grace, the gentle giant moved himself to hover above me. When his mouth sank to meet mine, his kiss was accompanied by the smoothest entry, and in a single breath, we were one. There was no time to reconsider, my body wouldn't have it anyway. A moan escaped my lips, and was muffled by his insistent mouth.

When he raised his head to look at me, his breathing was ragged. Clear grey eyes scanned my face as he moved even deeper inside me. I met his motion until we were so snug that we were almost stuck. Enveloped in each other, we held eye contact as his fingers seared the flesh of my erect nipples, emblazoning my body with the permanent memory of our stolen night. He bent his head to tease my breasts. His gentle lips and tongue dismantled what little reserve I still held. He pinned me with desire, and I let him see my throat.

Hovering between a place of euphoria and bliss, I was met with the deepest sensation of my life. The image of Gustav

Klimt's *The Kiss* flashed into my thoughts and I accepted that golden embrace for all it meant. With every feather-soft caress, I willed him to know me, to feel me, to love me. My core tightened, and I gripped him. He cried out, but held himself back. We both did. His eyes bore into mine one last time, and I tightened the vice all the way. His mouth possessed mine in the sweetest assault of softness and demand. Our combined climax tore through my body. It felt like pieces of me were breaking off into a shatter of glitter. There was only us, and the glow of my dream.

❦

A HUSH FELL OVER THE ROOM, AS HE HELD ME FROM BEHIND. The blankets around us were messed, an aftereffect of our lovemaking. His gentle fingers teased my nipple as his breath warmed my neck. The glow of our bond filled the room, leaving space for little else.

He broke the quiet, "You okay, Maddie?"

How could I answer his question? Still, I tried. "I think so."

He released his hold and raised himself to his elbow. I turned to face him. His eyes made a lazy stroll down my body, and back up to my face. "I know I should be sorry," he said, "but this night is hard to regret. Every minute I've spent with you since we met has been like living in a dream."

I was grateful for the dark, as a lone tear rolled down my face, for I knew all dreams came to an end. I raised my hand to touch his cheek and he ever so lightly pressed his lips to mine.

When he raised his head, he said, "Love is love, Madeline. We're all just trying to find it. I'm not saying this—"

I raised my fingers to his lips and said, "I know."

Wordlessly, we sank back into our newly created world

where there was nothing but our honesty to sate us. For a little while longer, I languished in the dream of our nest. My greedy heart wanted permanence, but I knew it could never be more. Why must it become less? The image of that stage came to mind. I recalled the final scene, when the piano was delivered and the man who inspired her, the one whom she inspired, walked away from his love. I knew who I was in the story. I would be the one walking away. He'd changed my life, but he wouldn't be in my life.

My hands trembled as I wrote the note, and tears streamed mercilessly down my face. Setting the toboggan next to the letter, I read it one last time.

October 26th, 2019

Travis,

I'll never forget this night or you. In a short amount of time, you changed me. Go back to your life, knowing I'll remember you always. Happy Birthday!

-Shorty

Though my flight wasn't for another three hours, I gathered my suitcase and quietly left the hotel. There was no reason for me to say goodbye. Our entire relationship was one giant farewell.

I RESTED MY HEAD AGAINST THE WINDOW, OBLIVIOUS TO THE goings-on in the cabin. I could hear the overhead announcement, but the words didn't penetrate. I was lost in my own world. As the plane taxied down the runway, I accepted a new reality. I was ruined, not just by my actions, or the change in my morality, but by the tenderness with which he touched me. His glances were so lovingly administered, it was impossible to believe what we did was wrong. The plane lifted off, and I watched the foggy skyline fade, knowing the memories of our stolen night would stay with me forever.

CLOSING DOORS

The water was warm and calm, all bathed in white against the colorless sky. A drop landed in front of me, casting a circle in its wake. The water began to churn to join the ripple. It grew in size and speed. My feet were no longer stable, as the sand beneath my toes was sucked into the vortex. My legs quivered and I swirled, lonely, into the darkest sea.

I gasped for air and willed my eyes to open. Suddenly the four walls of my bedroom were in focus. My breathing was rapid, a result of the scary and telling subconscious cinema that was only a dream. A heaviness swept over me, and the tears started to flow. My heart was not broken. That phrase couldn't begin to express my hurt. No, my heart was untethered. My heart was untethered. My chest caved with the wracking sob of honesty. I let the pain in.

I don't know how long I lay there, but that morning I cried like I hadn't in years. I wouldn't cry again, or relive the memories Travis and I had stolen. Our time would be like last night's dream. After a while, the details would fade and eventually the entire experience would be forgotten. When I was finally spent, I wrote this to commemorate.

Anchor of Gold
"Wait," he said, the stranger I didn't know.
I kept walking, embarrassed by my tears.
He saw me, all of me, yet he didn't leave.
Gentle fingers soothed, gave hope.
His left hand weighted by an anchor of gold.
Wary, trying not, but needing him;
I rode the wheel.
Present in every way,
it was all and it was unstoppable.
We only exist, in the confinement of moment.
Held entranced by our eyes,
though his left hand wore an anchor of gold .
Did he feel the surge,
my feminine need to be owned by him?
Did he care?
An illusion some say,
but I stood taller by his side,
and the dust blew away from my soul.
My lips, my lungs, my heart drew in his essence,
greedy to soak up every particle he could spare,
crumbs that were left from his anchor of gold.
Still, I may have the best of it.
Once, pineapples and spies.
I will remember him softly.
Cheese, make a wish, say goodbye.
I hope he is blessed by his anchor of gold.

WHEN THE LAST SENTENCE WAS DOTTED, I GOT OUT OF BED
with the poem in hand and found my jacket that was thrown
over a chair in the corner. The burning memento, and only
proof that it wasn't a dream, called to me. I pulled the ticket

from the pocket and ran my thumb over his printed name, but only once. Taking both, I crossed the hall and went into the den. Facing the bookshelf, I pulled my favorite childhood story from the shelf.

I opened the book randomly and read the words written by Dr. Marcus Bach:

"It was light. I could not remember a lighter, brighter moment and amazingly I was creating the light by working my way out of a jade-green shroud, parting it with wings I never knew I had."

No better words could be found to ensconce my moment of change. I put the ticket and poem inside the book, and replaced it on the shelf. Our dream would reside in the world of innocence I'd lost so long ago. I knew it was time to wake up.

❧

The week sped by. It was impossible to comprehend that it had been seven days since New York. My nerves were frazzled as I worked day and night completing the response to Swift Communications. Though I knew Robert and John would take credit for a win, I'd done much of the heavy lifting with little support or input from them. Thankfully, it was behind me and now the only thing to do was wait for their decision.

It was 10 AM Pacific time and we'd expected to hear something by now. My hands were sweating as I tried to respond to another client's email. The sound of the phone ringing gave me a start. I flipped it over and saw it was Travis calling.

We hadn't spoken a word since I saw him last. Before I took off on Friday, I'd sent him a message asking him not to contact me for a while. He replied and agreed, saying he'd give me a little time. I knew I had to answer, but the fear almost stopped me.

On the fourth ring, I accepted. "Hello, Travis."

There was a brief pause, but I could hear his breath. "Good morning, Madeline," he replied. "How are you?"

I responded as if he were any other business associate. "I'm doing well, thank you. And you?"

"It's good to hear your voice," he replied.

I felt the same, but would not allow myself to go there. Fortunately, I didn't have to.

"Are you sitting down?" he continued.

His play on words worked, and I was instantly transported back in time, to that hotel doorway. I replied without a shred of acknowledgement, "I am."

"Your pricing and overall project approach outshined the other bidders. If your system can handle our environment once we put it through the paces, WVI will be awarded all three of the projects."

My ears were ringing. I realized I hadn't responded, and I found my voice to say, "Oh my god, Travis, thank you!"

"No thanks are needed, Madeline. Hands down, you led the pack. This is a board decision and it was unanimous, contingent upon the strength of the equipment. Congratulations on a job well done."

"Travis?" I wasn't sure what to say next, and he knew it.

"I'll email a confirmation of our intent to award, along with the testing details. Please have Lane and his team available next week to get things set up. We're testing in New York."

"Of course, I will, and Travis" what could I possibly say? I chose something safe and appropriate "have a wonderful weekend. Thank you again, for everything."

"You as well, Madeline."

The line went quiet, simultaneous to a ding in my inbox. As promised Travis sent the message that confirmed our near victory. There was now only one hurdle between WVI and a two-million-dollar, fourth-quarter win.

❧

THE WEEK PASSED WITH THE SAME STEADY LEVEL OF ANXIETY that was becoming a constant in my life. With the Swift opportunity in the hands of our technical team, I half-heartedly busied myself with setting meetings and responding to other customers. The pressure of the past weeks mounted and I was exhausted.

John, Robert, and I were at the end of our mandatory Friday "Pulse Call."

John announced as if he were divulging fresh information, "Well, the word from Lane is that they have everything set up at Swift. The test will take ten days and they'll publish the results within four days of the completion. Two weeks from now we'll have our answer."

Lane and I had spoken at least twice a day since our meeting in New York. I was well aware of the status of the testing. "That's right, John," I agreed.

"Well, it's out of our hands for now, best to focus on growing more opportunities. We're anxious to hear what new prospects you find in the next week. Until Friday."

God that guy was a prick, I thought, as I clicked the red

order button on the screen. I'd daydreamed about it all week. I would spend the weekend in bed, watching Netflix and eating takeout. Tonight's special was scab-picking pepperoni pizza. The pop-up screen confirmed my order would arrive within 45 minutes. A weekend of indulgence was about to begin.

My phone buzzed, indicating a text message. It was a picture, from Travis. In the frame was a pepperoni pizza and a wooden wall, on which my name had been freshly carved. He was at the pizza place where he took me. Underneath he wrote, "It doesn't taste as good without you."

I found a will power I'd never known, for every part of me wanted to reply, but no good could come of it. There would be no reckless abandon between us. The consequences were far too harsh. I locked the screen and waited for pizza with tears in my eyes.

❧

As I sat on the table with my bare legs dangling and a dampness across my back where the robe wasn't fully closed, I considered lying down for a nap. The thought kept me upright, since that was the reason for my visit to the doctor in the first place. A knock on the door got my attention.

"Hi, Madeline." Dr. Thomas entered the room. "How are you feeling today?" she asked.

"Pretty tired," I said.

"Yes, I understand that. Any other symptoms?"

"I've been a little extra thirsty."

She walked over and placed her stethoscope at my heart. "Breathe normally."

I sat oddly as she listened, coughing on command,

breathing and holding my breath. A knock at the door interrupted us and the doctor called, "Yes?"

The door opened slightly and a nurse handed over a file. "The results are complete, and I ran it twice."

Dr. Thomas took the file as the door closed. "Madeline, when was your last period?" she asked.

Wow, I hadn't thought of that in a while. I'd never been good about tracking it and I rarely paid attention since Nathan had a vasectomy. "Umm, I don't know exactly. Sometime in October I'm pretty sure. Why? Do you think I'm going through menopause?" I asked.

"Though not unheard of, forty is a little young for menopause. Madeline, we administered a pregnancy test and it's positive."

The blood rushed to my ears and the world went dark.

⁂

"MADELINE." THE VOICE WAS INSISTENT, AS WERE THE HANDS that moved my face back and forth. "Wake up."

My eyes fluttered open. I was met by blinding florescent light and Dr. Thomas' concerned expression. "You fainted," she announced.

I wrestled to sit, and the doctor examined my pupils. "I take it this news comes as a surprise?"

My reply was interrupted by a knock at the door.

"Come in," the doctor called. A nurse arrived, rolling a cart carrying some sort of equipment.

"Madeline, I have a basic ultrasound machine here and we are going to take a look at your uterus. Please lie back. It won't hurt at all."

On autopilot, I lay back. The nurse smoothed a blanket over my legs and raised the robe to expose my stomach.

"Sorry, this is a little cold," she said as she applied the clear gel. Next, she took a wand from the side and rolled it against my stomach. The pressure was strange as she moved it against me, and I had the sudden urge to pee. A rhythmic sound filled the room and Dr. Thomas finally said, "There it is."

I looked at the screen of shadows and tried to see what she was talking about. "There"—she pointed and I followed her finger—"that's your baby, and that little white dot is the heartbeat. I'd say you're six weeks along."

I stared, incredulous, at the screen.

৩৶৩

THE BRIGHT OUTDOORS DID LITTLE TO AWAKEN ME FROM THE trance I was in after hearing the reason for my recent tiredness. The phone rang inside my purse. I paused to find it. When I turned it over, Travis' name was flashing on the screen. Great.

I tapped accept as I got into the car. "Hello," I answered, but it wasn't me. I listened like a voyeur as some other person took over.

"How are you?" His deep voice soothed and instantly drove me to tears.

I inhaled quietly and willed my voice to be calm. "I'm well, Travis. How are you?"

"I miss talking to you," he said without hesitation.

Tears streamed down my face and I tried to stay quiet. The silence egged him on.

"I'm sorry." His voice sounded a bit more distant now. "I'm not calling with the best of news," he continued. "The testing didn't go well, Madeline, not at all."

I knew it should have mattered, that I should have been

devastated about the loss of a mammoth opportunity, and the bonus it would have brought. If Lane Fine's prophecy were true, this news would be my pink slip. Still, none of that concerned me. I had bigger things to worry about now.

I took a deep breath and did what was expected. "That is disappointing," I said, "but I understand your position. Can you give me any specific feedback?"

"I'll send you an email with our findings, but overall, it couldn't handle the capacity. The server crashes were the biggest obstacle for us. I know it was already tough for you at work. I hope this won't make things worse."

"Please don't worry, Travis. We knew from the beginning what the requirements were. I am grateful that you gave us the opportunity to compete."

"Maddie." His voice caressed my ear. I wished I could touch him, inhale the scent of his cologne, for one last comfort. "Please call me if you need anything."

I did the exact opposite of what I felt and said, "I won't. Take care, Travis." I didn't wait for his final words to hang up. When I did, I opened his contact and activated the block this caller option.

That saddening task behind, I collapsed at the steering wheel and sobbed like a crazy person until the five-minute alert buzzed on my phone. My weekly meeting with Robert and John was about to begin. Still ahead for today was the awful task of telling them we lost the Swift deal. I opened the glove compartment to get a pack of Kleenex and blew my nose before picking up my phone to dial in. I entered the information and was waiting on hold, when a text came from Robert.

No call today. We got the news from Lane and the email just hit our inbox. No need to dive into that before the weekend. Let's reconvene next week.

Finally, a break. I was in no shape for another ordeal today. I replied, *Thanks Robert. I'm sorry it didn't work out. I'll talk to you next week.*

❦

THE PHONE RANG AND I WAITED FOR HER TO PICK UP. A sudden feeling of nausea swept over me and I knew it was psychosomatic. On the third ring, Shawna's cheery voice answered. "Hey, Maddie. What's up?"

Her lighthearted question and tone didn't match my sentiments at all. "Hi," I said.

"What's wrong?" she asked.

The crushing foul of infidelity, once foreign to me, was now a constant companion. I steeled myself for what I was about to confess. "Shawna, I have something to tell you."

❦

I GASSED IT, SWERVED RIGHT, AND CUT OFF A SLOW-MOVING Prius, stopping at the curb by baggage claim. Shawna would walk out any second, and not a moment too soon. The aggressive driving matched my current mood, insane. I needed my friend to talk me down.

I looked up, and there she was strolling through the circular door, dressed like she was going to Alaska. I got out of the car to greet her. We met at the trunk and hugged like we hadn't seen each other in years. I finally said, "You look beautiful." I surveyed her designer boots and the cream-colored fluff of a coat she was wearing, though it was only forty-six degrees outside. "You do know we're not in the frozen tundra?" I tried for levity, but her expression was unwavering. I could tell she was worried and on the verge of tears.

"Are you ok?" She couldn't hold back, and began crying.

I shook my head and wondered what I was thinking by calling Shawna. I'd forgotten her tendency toward tears. "Let's get into the car before we get removed by security."

We settled in and I looked at the clock. It was 3:57 PM, time for my Friday "meeting" with John and Robert. "Listen, I have to call into a meeting right now. I'm sorry, but you can't talk, ok?"

She replied, "Sure. I'll be quiet, but after that call, you're done, right?"

"That's the plan," I said as I unlocked the phone and entered the meeting code. I pulled from the curb and we listened to the boingy elevator music.

A few minutes later, John and Robert joined the call, one after the other. The automated system announced their arrival and soon we were surrounded by the voices of my leaders.

"John here."

"Robert's on."

"I'm here too, guys." I looked nervously over at Shawna, and gestured with my index finger over my lips, making the whisper of a shh sound.

John, as usual, took command. "Madeline, can you hear me okay?"

"I can," I replied.

"Listen, there is no easy way to say this, so I'm just going to come out with it. The company is undergoing a reorganization and there have been cuts in every territory. Lori Haines has been replaced, and unfortunately, we are terminating your employment with WVI, effective today."

My mouth went dry and my pulse pounded in my ears as I tried to focus on his words while driving. I didn't dare look at

Shawna, that trifecta would be impossible to juggle. John continued without hesitation.

"On Monday morning at nine, a courier will come to your home to collect your computer and company equipment. He will bring your final check, with a projected bonus based on the performance you contributed to the team, and two weeks' severance. There will be some documents for you to sign. Can you confirm you understand this, Madeline?"

There was so much I wanted to say, so many words I could have spewed if only I had any amount of a hold over my rampant thoughts. Instead, I made the biggest statement possible, and ended the call.

৩৫৩

Shawna's knee touched mine as we sat on the couch, reliving the conference call that put me out of a paycheck. She took another sip of her rosé and said, "If you think about it, now all of your problems are gone."

"What?" I screeched, "Are you insane?"

"I'm not. Listen for a minute. You and Nathan were often at odds. He was so secretive and you are the complete opposite of that, Maddie. He and Peter were always at each other's throats and neither of them would ever back down. You no longer have to choose between your man and your son. That problem is gone."

"That's one way to look at it," I said.

"Hear me out," she scolded. "You haven't liked your job since you left the company in L.A. all those years ago. From everything you've told me, it is a toxic environment to keep working for companies that run like this."

"It's the industry, Shawna." My frustration was evident in my childish reply.

"It's the culture of a bunch of archaic old guys who don't have half of your talent and are intimidated you'll show them up."

Her strong statement surprised me. I had no idea she was paying attention to my confidences over the years. She was always a willing ear, but I never expected her to have such strong venom against my profession. Still, her pep talk wasn't working.

"Shawna, I'm pregnant and without a job. I'm not going to be able to find another one at this stage."

"Chris and I have talked about it, and we want to invest in you. I know your position on the subject, and that you don't want to mix business with our friendship, but that doesn't matter anymore. We are going to give you the seed money to start your own firm, in exchange for ten percent of the company. I believe in you and know this is going to be a good and lucrative venture for us. We aren't taking no for an answer."

"Even if I did take you up on that offer, which I'm not, I still have Peter to tell."

"I have thought about that, and I think it'll be fine," she said confidently.

I shook my head and replied, "Now I know you're insane. Do you think Peter is going to hug me or give me a high five? I can just hear him now, 'Well done Mom, not only are you a cheater, but you also managed to get knocked up after forty.' He's going to hate me and feel sorry for the baby. To him it'll be another fatherless child I brought into the world."

"Let me tell him." She said it so simply as if it were nothing at all.

"You tell him?" I demanded.

"Yeah," she said. "I have an idea."

"Shawna, I love you and I trust you, but that is too much. Just out of curiosity, what would you say to him?"

"I wouldn't say anything at all. Give me a minute." She stood, and ran toward the guest bedroom. A minute later she returned with a folder in her hand. She tossed the document on the table, and I read the title, *Anchor of Gold,* by Shawna Parr. There was a red "A" scribbled at the corner, and in the same ink, the comment was, "Keep going."

"What is that?" I asked, but I already suspected the answer.

"I needed a topic for my midterm writing class, and your story was too good to pass up. I titled it after your poem. Read it," she said nervously. "I only hope I did it justice."

Reluctantly, I reached for the manuscript, and settled in for a ride down memory lane that knew the essence of the bond I shared with Travis. When the last page was read, I looked up at Shawna through the cloud of tears. She leaned forward in her chair, and I said, "It's like you were there."

I watched a battle of emotions span Shawna's expressions. In one moment, there was pride, another empathy. The latter emotion was foremost and she asked, "Will you tell him, Maddie?"

I knew she was referring to Travis. I shook my head. "No, not now anyway."

"Do you love him?"

Her question wasn't a total surprise; in fact, I should have considered it already. I hadn't allowed myself because there was no point in knowing the answer. I answered in the best way I could. "Travis isn't mine to love."

Shawna huffed, and said, "Love doesn't follow the rules. I asked you a question. I need to have the right ending."

I inhaled, and shared my thoughts. "I loved the man I met, but I can't say I'd love him in the real world. I loved him in the moments we shared. I liked the people we were in those short scenes, the pieces we showed, our best angles and kindest touches. There was no anger, or demand, no expectation, or even hope. It wasn't about that between us. It was so much more, and almost nothing."

A tear slid down her face, and she said, "Trust me, Maddie, that isn't the ending."

SHAWNA SAT ACROSS THE BOOTH FROM PETER AND TOOK A SIP of her wine. "Peter," she started, "I'm so happy you could meet me before I take off in the morning."

"Ah, are you kidding, Shawna? You're my second mom. How could I miss out on seeing you?" He smiled.

"You may feel a little different after our conversation. Please hear me out on something."

His expression changed to serious. "Sure, what is it?"

"Your mom is amazing. I want you to know that she is one of the most special people in the world."

He looked at the glass of beer in front of him and said, "Yeah, I know."

"I'm serious, Peter. She has handled herself in situations that I could never imagine and she loves you with all her heart."

"Shawna, you're scaring me. What's going on?" he asked.

She took the letter Maddie wrote and slid it across the table. It said:

DEAR PETER,

The day you were born, my life was made. From the second I held you in my arms, I knew I'd do anything for you.

Your love has driven and empowered me to be a better person.

It is a strange day when a child learns of their parent's humanity. Today, I share with you a story that is so personal, I expected to take it to my grave, but circumstance won't have it. Read this knowing you played a big part in it. That may bother you, but the truth is, you are the person I care most about in this world. When I couldn't help you, I needed someone, and for one splendid crease in time, I found a comfort I'd never known.

Please forgive me. I love you, Mom

"WHAT'S THIS ALL ABOUT?" HE WAS FLUSTERED.

She pulled the manuscript from her bag, placed it in front of Peter and said, "Read this. I'll wait." She caught the eye of the bartender, and gestured for another round.

HARPER'S PATH

The high-pitched whine and vibration of the jet taking off got her squealing. "Wee!" She jumped on the chair and pointed excitedly through the glass. "Mommy! Plane!"

I looked at her and was torn to pieces by the dancing grey eyes that were her daddy's gift. It was hard to believe my baby was already two years old. "In a little while we'll get on too," I said.

She jumped from the chair unexpectedly, as toddlers do, and bolted. For her it was a game. I, on the other hand, was exhausted. Keeping her calm on the first flight was a chore, and this layover wasn't proving any easier.

She peeked over her shoulder to make sure I was still following. "I see you. Stop running."

Her giggle was joyous as she ran even faster until, suddenly, she stopped just shy of bumping into a man's leg. Her tiny body came to under his knee. I bent to scoop her up, and said over my shoulder, "Sorry. It's been a long day."

He cleared his throat which got my attention. I looked up and gasped, "Oh my god."

"Madeline." His voice resonated shock as did his expression. "Looks like you gained some weight," his eyes measured the baby on my hip directly.

Travis was standing in front of me in the middle of the San Jose airport and he was staring at his daughter. I stole a peek at his hand and noticed he wasn't wearing his wedding ring. I tried to be calm although my legs felt liquid. "It looks like you lost some," I replied.

"Who is this?" His voice sounded uncertain, but his eyes knew the truth.

There was no way around it, the same fate that brought us together had come full circle. The Universe wanted him to know his child. I looked at my sweetest girl, whose golden locks sprang from her head like a halo, and I finally introduced father and daughter. "This is Harper."

His eyes searched mine and he asked, "How old is she?"

"She turns two on Sunday. We're on our way to San Diego to celebrate her birthday. Big brother is already there." I made faces at her to distract myself from the intensity of the moment.

Tears brimmed in his eyes as he asked, "Is she"

I cut him off before he could finish. "Mine? Yes, she is. You're the dad."

"Why didn't you tell me? All those messages and you never replied once."

"You know why, Travis. I did what I thought was right."

"Maddie," his hand brushed a strand of hair from my cheek, "my divorce has been final for over a year. After what happened between us, I knew it couldn't go on."

"I'm sorry," I said, and meant it. I only ever wanted him to be happy.

Travis' eyes and voice implored, "Can I hug you?" He didn't wait for my answer, instead, he wrapped his arms around the two of us. There amid the throngs of travelers, the brightest part of our love brought us together again.

Harper's tiny voice chimed, "Smells pitty, Mommy."

The scent that kept me warm on the long nights when I was missing him, was once again near. Only this time, it didn't emanate from the hidden bottle I bought to wean myself off of him. This time it was real.

"Yes, baby. Daddy smells pretty. That's one of the reasons you're here." His mouth swallowed mine in the sweetest homecoming.

"Come on, don't be shy." I pulled his arm.

"Shy? I'm not shy, but this is kind of a lot."

Travis dragged his feet, but it didn't belabor the inevitable because Shawna heard us pull up and was already bounding out the front door. In close carriage were Chris, Kaylee, Jordan, and Peter. To round out the mix, Harvey's excited barks rang over us all.

The baby was plucked from my arms by Peter as Shawna peppered Travis with introductions. He shook everyone's hand and finally there was only Peter left. I stepped in.

"Son, I'd like you to meet Travis. Travis, this is Peter."

They shook hands, while Peter clutched his little sister protectively. He was sizing Travis up. Shawna noticed his scrutiny and in her bubbly way, tried to cut through the tension. "Who's ready for a cocktail? I am!" she exclaimed.

Amid the positive responses, the men unlinked hands. I walked past them and into the house, leaving they and Harper behind. Shawna and I whispered in the kitchen as she poured margaritas for everyone. "Oh my god, Maddie. I can't believe this is happening. How are you doing?"

"I can't even begin to answer that question. Travis must be a wreck, and did you see Peter's mean mug?"

"How could I miss it?" She chuckled. "He's a big boy, he can handle it."

☙❦❧

HIS HEART WAS POUNDING, AND THE BABY SQUIRMED IN HIS arms. She wanted to get down and play, but Peter needed a minute with this guy, Travis. He wanted to see some glimmer of what his mom saw in him to make sense of it.

Travis spoke first. "I'm not sure what you know about how your mom and I met."

Peter fired, "I know the whole story, everyone does. It's about to be published."

His eyebrows shot up and he asked, "What?"

"My mom told everything to Shawna, and she's a writer. That's how they told me when she was pregnant. Mom was afraid I'd disown her or something, so they told me in a story, like I was a little fucking kid."

Travis flinched at his language, but he understood the bravado. "Your mom talked a lot about you. She really loves you. I'm sure she didn't want to disappoint you. I'm sorry I was the cause of any problems between you."

"I'm glad you know. I wanted her to tell you, but she wouldn't. It bothered me, even though I understood her reasons."

"Brober, go," Harper squirmed and demanded.

"Go," she repeated, only this time both of her hands were on his cheeks, demanding his attention.

"Okay, I will." His animated expression made her smile. "Do you want to hold her?" Peter reluctantly offered.

"Can I?" he asked.

He gingerly handed his baby sister over, and watched as father and child made eye contact for the first time. "She looks a lot like you," Peter said.

Travis looked in awe of his daughter. "Please don't say that. She's a miracle, like your mom."

Harper wasn't placated for long, and her little voice ordered, "Down, go," cutting the tension and causing them to laugh.

Peter agreed, "The princess has spoken. We'd better go inside."

☙❧

WHEN THEY WALKED THROUGH THE DOOR, I WAS OVERTAKEN by a joy I'd never known. It was an unbelievable moment, seeing my son and daughter standing beside the man who changed my world.

Acknowledgments

Everything begins with family as do my thanks. Without you, I wouldn't be the person I am today. I love you all.

To my friend, Dorothy; Thank you for reading my crappy first drafts with enthusiasm. I'm astounded by your wisdom and courage, and happy just to rub shoulders with you.

To Sarah Benelli, my friend, fellow gem hound, teacher, former roommate(ish) and editor; Thank you for your patience and direct approach to everything you do. Your contribution improved my work and I know the end result is better after teaming with you.

To Kimberly Bogaski (kimberlynicolephoto.com); the friend I get into trouble with and who knows all of my secrets. Thank you for the fun stories and for your treasured photograph.

To my test readers & the people who were there when it all began; Thank you Myrna Oakley, at PCC, Paige Lehmann and Tom McConnell from the Tuesday night writing group, Cindy Rawlings and Jo Rittersbacher, for your invaluable feedback and support.

To Author Ashley McLeo; Thank you for your guidance with the final steps in readying the book for market.

Finally, I'd like to recognize the outstanding career experiences of my past and the people who helped me along the way. I have not been without fortune and I did nothing alone. I can't wait to see what's next...

In gratitude,

H

•LOVE TEST•
A ROMANCE NOVEL
ONLINE DATING
WEDDING PLANNING
BACHELOR WEEKEND TWIST
WWW.HOLLYMANNO.COM

Times Two

Book II
LOVE TEST Matchmaking Destiny series
Times Two
HOLLY MANNO

My Diary of Disaster